Will crossed the shop and was reaching for the row of switches on the wall over the main workbench when he happened to glance over at the new car they had towed home that afternoon. Something caught his eye and he was forced to do a double take.

There, sitting in the driver's seat, was Rocket Rob Wilder.

What on earth was the kid doing there? As Will walked over to the car, he could see the kid's hands on a steering wheel he had fitted on the column, and that he was sitting in a makeshift seat he had apparently installed. He was staring straight out the windshield, his eyes hooded, his expression looked for all the world as if he was taking determined aim on some brazen competitor who ran just ahead of him, that he was sizing up the so-and-so for an inside pass.

Will kneeled down next to the car and looked sideways in the window at Rob.

"How long you been in there?"

"I don't know. Hour, maybe. I was just checking her out, getting familiar with her. I figure me and this old gal are going to be spending a lot of time together and I just wanted us to get to know each other better."

"So what kind of car is she going to be?"

Rob smiled. "Fast."

Follow all the action . . .
from the qualifying lap
to the checkered flag!

Rolling Thunder!

Rolling Thunder

STOCK CAR RACING

INSIDE PASS

Kent Wright & Don Keith

TOR®

A TOM DOHERTY ASSOCIATES BOOK
NEW YORK

This is a work of fiction. All the characters and events portrayed in this book are either products of the author's imagination or are used fictitiously.

ROLLING THUNDER #7: INSIDE PASS

A Tor Book
Published by Tom Doherty Associates, LLC
175 Fifth Avenue
New York, NY 10010

www.tor.com

Tor® is a registered trademark of Tom Doherty Associates, LLC.

ISBN: 0-812-54508-7

First edition: October 2000

Printed in the United States of America

0   9   8   7   6   5   4   3   2   1

Rolling Thunder

STOCK CAR RACING

INSIDE PASS

Part 1

THE BEGINNING

Finis origne pendet
(The end depends on the beginning)

—from a plaque on the wall of
the Billy Winton Racing shop
in Chandler Cove, Tennessee

1

THE NEW CAR

"Come on, cowboy. Let's take a ride."

The pair of legs sticking out from beneath the red race car didn't indicate whether their owner had heard the command from the taller dark-haired man standing next to the vehicle. The slender body they were attached to stayed under there, deliberately finishing up applying torque to a stubborn bolt. Finally, slowly, the heels dug in, and the creeper rolled out. The unnatural brightness from the overhead fluorescent lights fell on the young man's face, revealing tanned features and longish hair so blond it looked sun-bleached—though sunlight certainly never found its way beneath the race car.

"Will, you know I want to finish up with this today," the young man said. His eyes squinted and his white teeth flashed as he grimaced. Even with the grime and sweat on his face, he was clearly movie-star handsome. And, at the moment, just a tad bit irritated. "I got my eye on a first-place trophy this weekend, even if nobody else on this team seems to."

"That old rear end'll still be here when we get back if one of the other boys doesn't get to it first," was all the tall dark-haired man offered in reply.

"Aw, all right then," the kid answered peevishly, pointedly dropping his wrenches with a clatter on the shop's cement floor as he climbed to his feet.

Technically, he supposed, Will Hughes was his boss, and he was bound to do his bidding. Will could order him to stand on his head and stack bowling balls if he so desired.

Will was crew chief on the 06 Ford race car, and Rob Wilder, the tall blond kid, was only its driver. No denying the pecking order on that rather well defined organizational chart. And if Will Hughes ordered him out from beneath the car and proceeded to drag him off on some time-wasting joyride, Rob figured he had no choice but to obey the man.

But if the rear end of the car came ratcheting right out from under him smack-dab in the middle of next Saturday's race, well, that was no fault of Mr. Rob Wilder. No, sir!

Wilder stood, dusted himself off, slipped out of the coveralls, hung them on a nail near the door, and then followed Hughes outside, muttering under his breath the whole while.

Will could tell the kid was irritated, but he simply ignored him.

Once outside the shop, the bright sun and warm temperature surprised Rob. The first few days of October had been unseasonably cool so far, even for the foothills of the Smoky Mountains in eastern Tennessee. It had been downright cold that morning before daylight when he had shown up at the shop. He had been unable to sleep and eager to get something done, so instead of wearing out a spot spinning idly in his bed, he'd climbed out of the sack, came on to the shop, and gone to work before any of the others had even thought about showing up. The first thing he had done, though, had been to turn up the thermostat on the big electric heaters.

But this day had turned out nice, as if Nature was having a last gasp at hanging on to summer, despite the Technicolor leaves and frosty nights that already heralded an early winter.

Now, despite his annoyance, Rob couldn't help but notice what a glorious day it had turned out to be, and he was glad to be out in the midst of it. He admired the golden sunshine and bright blue sky as they eased along in Will's big pickup down the long gravel drive that led to the highway. An empty trailer on the hitch bounced noisily behind them. The kid even felt a twinge of guilt that he had been wasting one of the last beautiful days of the year underneath a race car in a stuffy, noisy old shop. Lately, more than one important person in his life had been urging him to slow down, enjoy the beautiful things in life, and not to allow his only view of the world to be through the windshield of a bright red Ford race car as it zoomed around an asphalt oval somewhere. But he was driven toward a goal, reaching for a prize that was near at hand, and he didn't want to lose sight of it when it was so tantalizingly close.

He cranked down the truck's window and breathed in the clean, warm mountain air. Beside him, Will Hughes hummed tunelessly. Rob wished the man would turn on the radio and dial around for someone who could actually carry a melody. But he decided not to let that aggravating racket bother him either. Still, he couldn't figure why, for the life of him, Will had insisted that he ride along with him just go pick up some parts. His boss had been vague when he asked him. But now, when Rob glanced over at him and thought about asking again, he decided simply

to let it ride. Will was gazing straight ahead, his eyes
half-shut behind his mirrored sunglasses, likely thinking
about something seriously technical about the car while
he made all that irritating noise.

Will's World—that's what the rest of the crew called
it when the boss would go stone-faced for chunks of time,
then suddenly emerge from his trance having solved a
particularly knotty problem with the racecar's setup. Or
having worked out a whole new way to do something
that had baffled them all so far. It would do no good to
ask him what he was thinking about when he drifted off
to Will's World. Will Hughes was a graduate mechanical
engineer, and sometimes the language he spoke might
just as well have been Swahili to Rob Wilder and the
rest of the team. Or he would simply ignore the ques-
tioner until he was ready to provide the solution.

Even now—his dark hair carefully combed, his golf
shirt and khaki slacks unwrinkled, his shoes carefully
shined—Will Hughes looked more like a banker on the
way to a golf outing or an architect off to survey a project
than he did the crew chief of one of the hottest teams
on the Busch Grand National stock car racing circuit.
He was ten years older than Rob, about the same height,
with darker hair and eyes, but considerably stockier than
his almost-skinny young driver. Still, they sometimes
seemed more like brothers. Donnie Kline, the crew's jack
man and chief mechanic, had dubbed them Dumb and
Dumber, Yin and Yang, Tweedledee and Tweedledum,
as well as a long list of other colorful and often profane
names that he used interchangeably. Billy Winton, the
man who had put the team together in the first place, in
keeping with the family theme, simply referred to the two
of them as "the sons I never had."

But all the kidding didn't belie the fact that both young
men were happily living their dream. Will Hughes was
the subject of much speculation in the racing press and

the garages around the circuit. Many swore to know for a fact that the North Carolinian would soon announce a jump to this team or that one over in the Winton Cup garage. That he would certainly confirm any day now that he would catapult to the sport's big league and leave Billy Winton's relatively new Busch Grand National team behind.

The same loose tongues wagged endlessly about Rob Wilder, too. They had heard from someone in the know that the hot-driving twenty-year-old sensation from down near Huntsville, Alabama (Rocket Rob they had named him), would soon make a move himself, jumping to a new ride and joining the superstars and new young guns over there in Winston Cup racing. That old Billy Winton would just have to go fishing for another hotshot to pilot his bright red Ford. After all, the kid had won the pole position for the Daytona Grand National race in February, the first race of his first full year. And he had won the race in Nashville outright. He might have been driving Grand National for a little over a year, might still be inexperienced and might sometimes show it, but he was already one of the most popular drivers out there. And definitely one of the most promising. Surely he would soon leave Billy and Will and the 06 Ford behind and make that seductive leap for the stars.

There was little truth to any of the garage gossip. Sure, Will had been approached by some of the well-funded multi-car teams. And a couple of teams-in-the-making had pulled Rob Wilder aside and made overtures. But Billy Winton and Will Hughes had built this team from the ground up. They had their hot young driver already, as good a crew as there was in racing, a sponsor that was solidly behind them, and they were more than ready to make their own jump all together in one big red package. And to make the jump directly from their little launching pad tucked among the hills and hollows of far eastern Tennessee.

As flattered as Rob was with the offers, he knew he had a good thing going in the Winton garage and that the opportunity to run with the big boys would come when the time was right. The folks he had cast his lot with were the ones he wanted to be in his pits when that time finally came. He knew he owed everything to Billy and Will, and he was confident he could best reward them by staying right where he was.

"Where'd you say we were going?" Rob finally asked Will, a puzzled look on his face. They had turned west on the highway, not east toward town.

"Get some parts," Will answered cryptically.

"Yeah, but where? Next parts store this direction is halfway to Charlotte."

"Jodell's."

Okay, that made sense. Chandler Cove was so small it didn't even make most road maps, but its environs were home to two very successful racing teams: Billy Winton's and that of racing legend Jodell Bob Lee. And Winton's operation often bought engines and borrowed parts from Jodell's first cousin and chief engine builder, Joe Banker.

The proximity of the two shops wasn't mere coincidence. Jodell Lee had grown up there in Chandler Cove, had gotten his start driving when he delivered his granddaddy's moonshine liquor to thirsty customers up and down that whole end of the state and into far western North Carolina. And he had run his first race back in the mid-fifties in a pasture just up the way. Then, in the late sixties, Billy Winton had joined the Lee team as a mechanic—more by accident than anything else—and he had been, for the better part of two decades, a member of one of the winningest teams in the game. Billy had eventually retired to his farm to ride herd over a few head of hobby cattle and some well-placed investments. But the lure of the sport had been too strong to resist. He was back now. Back with Will and Rob and the 06 team. Back with a vengeance.

"All right," Rob said, confirming his understanding. "To Jodell's."

Will turned then and grinned at the youngster. Sometimes the kid could get himself coiled up just a little bit too tight. But that intensity was one of the things that made him such a natural race car pilot, too.

"Glad it meets with your approval, cowboy."

"I just wanted to finish with that rear end, that's all."

"Look, Donnie or one of 'em will get that done. Haven't you figured out that Billy pays you to steer that thing, not to do surgery on it."

Rob sighed. They had plowed this same ground many times before.

"I just think I have a better feel for the car if I know how she's been put together."

"Thank the Lord you don't have the same notion about airplanes!"

This time Rob Wilder grinned back, but he still had that familiar intense look in his deep blue eyes.

Just then, Will slowed to make the turn into the narrow drive that suddenly popped up at the side of the highway. As they made their way between the rows of big chestnut trees that lined the driveway, they could see the old house ahead where Jodell Lee had been born, where his grandparents had raised him. There, too, was the old unpainted barn they had once used for a race shop, and where they had kept Grandpa Lee's whiskey car running before that. Several large modern outbuildings were scattered along the hill behind the barn. They housed the paint, fabrication, and engine shops. The barn itself had recently been converted into a small museum filled with mementos and trophies and photos the Jodell Lee team had collected through the years. The team's offices were now inside Grandma Lee's old house. It had been restored years earlier for that purpose. Jodell's daughter, Glynn, occupied the family home on the other side of the drive from the offices. Named for the legendary driver Glenn "Fireball" Roberts, she now operated the museum and helped manage the team's business affairs. Out of sight, around the next bend in the driveway, was where Jodell's stately brick home hid from curious fans who came calling sometimes.

Lee Racing was better than forty years old and had been carefully built up to be one of the most daunting operations in the sport. Lately, though, the coming of multi-car teams had put a crimp in their success. As one of the last competitive single-car contingents left in Winston Cup racing, they still managed to win a race or two each year, but even that had become a struggle. The days of claiming a half dozen or more victories each year were long gone.

Will Hughes pulled up next to the huge shop building and then backed the trailer up toward a large overhead door that was now closed tightly. The door was used for the team's big race hauler and the tractor that towed it to pull in and out of the shop. Both men hopped out of the truck and walked in the direction of a nearby entrance.

Will ignored a renewed look of puzzlement on the kid's face.

"Why didn't we just pull up to the loading dock around back?" Rob asked. He didn't relish having to carry boxes of heavy parts all the way from the parts room on the other side of the shop, halfway across the building, and then out the side door to the truck.

Will couldn't suppress a sly grin. "This is where Waylon told me to park. He said what we're picking up is waiting for us over by this door."

"So what are we picking up that's so dad-blamed mysterious?" Rob asked, clearly perplexed. He had assumed they were to bring back some suspension parts or maybe a couple of sets of headers that had been tuned for some of the tracks they would be racing on over the next few weeks. But Will was acting like it was some kind of military secret.

Why the trailer when that stuff would fit in the bed of the pickup? And why park at the big door instead of at the loading dock?

"Aw, it's just some stuff we need to go racin'," Will answered as he disappeared into the shop door.

The inside of the building was brightly lit and race cars in various states of repair or preparation were resting everywhere. The striking thing most visitors noticed, though, was how clean and organized the place was. It could almost have been a surgical suite in a hospital, littered with exotic equipment and implements.

"Well, if it ain't Mutt and Jeff!" Waylon Baxter called from across the shop. He often tried to outdo Donnie Kline when it came to nicknames for Will and Rob, but so far that had been the best he had come up with. Will met the big man halfway across the wide shop and shook his massive hand. Rob lingered behind, peering longingly into the cockpit of one of the Lee Racing Fords that had caught his attention. "Your little skinny buddy excited?"

"I haven't told him yet."

Waylon winked, then tiptoed over to where the kid was sprawled in the driver's side window of the race car, examining its dash. He suddenly goosed Rob hard in the ribs under both his arms. The kid jerked spasmodically, bumped his head hard on the car's roof, and then squirmed backward out of the window. The big man guffawed and slapped his thighs in merriment while Rob massaged the crown of his head and pretended to be stunned and staggering about.

"Way', don't you know it's dangerous to slip up on an Alabama boy like that? We've been known to be totin' a possum-guttin' knife, you know. And, sometimes we cut first and take excuses later."

"Shoot, I could give up a slice or two off this belly and not miss it a'tall," Baxter said, patting his ample gut and still laughing. Waylon was the son of Bubba Baxter, another longtime member of Jodell's team. Bubba had been with Lee since the very beginning and now his son was the crew chief.

"This is one fine-looking race car," Rob offered, laying a loving hand on the vehicle he had been examining.

"We're taking that one down to Homestead. If we get lucky and some time to test, we might can even get her on the pole."

"How about this one over here?" Will called to them from across the building, over near the big door. "This one any good?"

Waylon and Rob wandered that way.

"Yessir, that's one fine car," Baxter intoned. "That's the one Rex drove to second place in the 600 in Charlotte back in May."

Rex Lawford was the driver for Jodell Lee's Winston Cup team.

"She's beautiful," Rob said lovingly as he stroked a fender. Lovely maybe, but only to someone who could see beyond the car's ugly coat of gray primer and lack of a driver's seat or even a steering wheel. "As pretty as any girl I've ever seen."

"Really?" Will asked, cocking his head sideways with a funny look on his face.

"Well . . . uh . . . almost, anyway."

"Hmmm. Waylon, can I borrow your phone long enough to call a certain Miss Christy Fagan out there in California?"

"Will!" Rob whined.

Christy Fagan was the sister of one of the principals in the company that sponsored the Billy Winton 06 Ford. And Rob had proceeded to fall head over heels in love with her the first time he had seen her. He tended to be protective of her and overly defensive in the face of the barrage of jabs he had to endure from his crew over the relationship. The kid took the romance as seriously as he did his racing, and that made him an even more attractive target for the barbs from Donnie Kline and the rest of them. But he simply chalked it all up to jealousy. Christy Fagan was actually one of the most beautiful, most wonderful women he had ever met. Even more beautiful and wonderful than the primered-up seatless Ford race car he was caressing at the moment. Unfortunately, Christy was in school in Los Angeles, twenty-five hundred miles away, and the gorgeous race car was close at hand.

"Well, Rob, what do you really think of her?" Waylon asked.

"I'd give an arm and a leg to drive her in a Cup race," he answered without hesitation.

Waylon had hit the button, activating the motor that lifted the heavy door and allowed the warm air and sunlight to spill inside. The race car looked even better in the bright light. Rob couldn't keep his hands off her. He walked all the way around, studying the sleek lines of her body, fondling her. He always loved the feel of a race car, any well-put-together race car.

"Well, you better get to choppin'," Waylon said. "She's yours now."

Rob's eyes grew wide, and he stopped romancing the racer. "What do you mean? Will?"

"That's right. Billy bought this old jalopy off Jodell. Jodell's been adding some new cars they've built for the quad-ovals like Charlotte and Atlanta, and he needed to get rid of—"

But a sharp happy whoop from the kid interrupted

Will's explanation. Rob proceeded to dance his way all around the car.

"I guess that means you don't like her. . . ." Will started, but Rob gathered him up and began to dance him around the car, too. Waylon, and several of the other Lee crew members who had wandered over to get a glimpse of daylight, hooted at the sight.

"If you'll quit acting like a fool and help us push the thing out to the trailer, we might get to take her home before Jodell changes his mind," Will panted, freeing himself from the kid's grip.

But Rob suddenly stopped dancing and looked almost serious. "You lied to me, Will," he said, nearly sorrowfully.

"What do you mean?"

"You said we were coming over here to get some parts."

"Well, we did. I never said they wouldn't be all attached to one another, now did I?"

Rob grinned sheepishly and then seemed to have another quick thought. "When can we run her? In Winston Cup, I mean?"

"Well, sir, if we ever quit jawing and get her on the trailer, we intend to try to qualify her for Atlanta the last race of the season. But at this rate, we won't even be back to the garage by then!"

It was no secret in the Winton shop that they would make the move to the Winston Cup circuit the next year, even though they had carefully avoided the subject with the media so far. They had been setting that plate all year in relative secrecy. But with the tight battle for position they were fighting in the Grand National points race, Rob had assumed Billy and Will would not do anything to detract from that effort this year.

But suddenly, it all made sense. The Atlanta Cup race in mid-November was to be held a couple of weeks after the last Grand National event was run at Homestead, south of Miami. The move to the next level was, in reality, going to be a giant leap for the team, like a player going from a good college football team to the NFL in a single bound. The Atlanta race would give them a running start at spanning the chasm.

They pushed the car out into full sunlight, the racer rolling easily since it was still missing its engine and transmission. A couple of the other boys in the shop came over to help them push it up onto the trailer. Once the job was done, and while Will and Waylon chained the car in place, Rob stood back and stared at the Ford's sleek lines. It was hard to believe this was going to be his car, his chariot that would deliver him right into the midst of the greatest automobile racing on the planet.

Will was still standing there, jawing with Waylon and some of the others.

"Don't we have stuff to do back at the shop?" Rob asked impatiently.

"Now you're in a hurry?" Will replied.

Waylon chimed in: "We're just talkin' racin'. Talkin' and takin' a break. Shoot, me and the boys have been going like a house afire since seven o'clock this morning. It's nice to stop and get a breath of fresh air and some sunshine."

That much was likely true. Teams this time of year often worked twelve- and fourteen-hour days in the shop. But soon they were on the way back, the kid constantly twisting around in the seat to make sure the car and its trailer were still obediently tailing them.

Back at the shop, Rob continued to dance around the new car as Donnie and several of the crew rolled it off the trailer. They shoved it through the big doorway and over to one of the prep areas inside the shop. Donnie looked over the car for a few minutes, sizing it up like a sculptor perusing a chunk of marble he was about to begin chiseling away on. Then he spit some of his wad of chewing tobacco into his cup, tapped the car's fender with a fist, and then ambled on back to work. They had another car they had to make faster and prettier much sooner than they did the new one.

Soon the others had drifted off as well, pressed by the work that needed to be done to load the truck and get everything else ready to go. They would have to pull out before daylight Thursday morning and it was getting to be Thursday quicker than they needed it to.

They all left Rob Wilder standing there, still admiring the new car.

While the others worked, Will Hughes spent the early evening in his office going through the volumes of notes the team took at every single race. He was reviewing Billy's scribbling and his own precise writing so he could decide what final setup they would put under the car for Saturday's race. It was tedious work, crunching in a staggering number of factors, including the age and type of the racetrack's surface, what setups had worked before, the steering geometry, and, lastly, the weather, which was likely just as important as any of the other things. Spread before him on his desk was a blizzard of papers including the long-range forecast, still more notes he had borrowed from Jodell Lee's team, as well as complicated charts and computer spreadsheets detailing various spring-and-shock combinations.

Will had actually begun writing some computer code in Visual Basic, trying to rough out a program that he hoped might do some of this work for him, but the constant burden of the season had prevented him from nursing that project along very far. He had even toyed with the idea of seeing if their sponsor, Ensoft, might take over the project if he turned over his code and specs to them. They were a major software company, after all. But he had not even had the time yet to do that much.

After a couple of hours of the tedious matching and cross-tabbing, his head was pounding from the strain, his eyes crossing from studying all the charts and figuring in all the engineering math he was doing in his head. Finally, he looked up at the clock. It was nine-thirty already, the day practically spent.

Reminded of the late hour, his stomach growled ominously, insistently. He had missed both lunch and dinner again. Good thing his wife, Clara, was a saint and knew full well that she shared her husband with a far more demanding mistress. She had understood the particulars of Will's chosen profession when they spoke their vows in front of an altar draped with checkered flags in the Baptist Church in Statesboro, North Carolina. Luckily, they still loved each other too much to let such hindrances get in the way of their marriage.

Will pulled off his reading glasses and massaged his pounding temples. Where had the time gone?

There had been nothing but silence from the shop for at least the last hour or so. Donnie Kline had stuck his head in the office door as he left. "Rear end's in. We can finish up everything else tomorrow. We might actually get that buggy ready to race after all," he had reported.

"Good job, DK. Go tuck your young'uns in for the night."

"Young'uns? I got young'uns? Ain't been home in so long I forgot! They already callin' me Uncle Daddy."

"See you bright and early."

" 'Night, bossman."

Will settled back in, trying to bring the work before him to a stopping point. After a few minutes he gave up and shoved aside all the spreadsheets and charts. He would need a new day and a clear head if he was going to make any sense of all that data. Right now, his circuits were fried.

He rolled the chair back from the desk, stretched his

long legs, stood, unhooked his jacket off the back of the
doorknob, and flipped off the light switch in the office.
But then he saw that the shop was still brightly awash
with the garish light from the overhead fluorescent tubes.

"Dang it, Kline!" he muttered out loud. Donnie knew
to cut off the high-powered lights when he was the last
of the crew to leave.

He crossed the shop and was reaching for the row of
switches on the wall over the main workbench when he
happened to glance over at the new car they had towed
home that afternoon. Something caught his eye, and he
was forced to do a double take.

There, sitting in the driver's seat, was Rocket Rob Wilder.

What on earth was the kid doing in there? As Will
walked over to the car, he could see the kid's hands on
a steering wheel he had fitted on the column, and that he
was sitting in a makeshift seat he had apparently installed. The youngster was staring straight out the windshield at the wall, his eyes hooded, a fierce look on his
smooth boyish face. But his expression looked for all the
world as if he were taking determined aim on some brazen competitor who ran just ahead of him, that he was
sizing up the so-and-so for an inside pass before another
swift lap was done.

Will could only shake his head and smile. What had
he and Billy Winton done to deserve such a committed
driver, one who would rather win a race than eat when
he was hungry?

"Kid, you gonna pass him or punt?"

Wilder almost jumped out of the race car's wobbly
interim seat. "Lord a'mercy, Will. You scared me out of
ten years' growth."

Hughes kneeled down next to the car and looked sideways in the window at Rob.

"How long you been in there?"

"I don't know. Hour, maybe." He couldn't tell his crew chief about the voice. The voice that urged him to climb inside the car and become one with the machine. It was the same voice that sometimes rode with him when he raced. The one that always seemed to have the right suggestion for where to place the nose of the car in a particularly tight point in a race. "I was just checking her out, getting familiar with her, that's all."

"An hour? You been sitting there an hour?"

"Maybe a little bit longer. You know me, Will. Ain't never met a race car I didn't like. I figure me and this old gal are going to be spending a lot of time together, and I just wanted us to get to know each other better." Rob Wilder grinned crookedly. He knew how goofy that must sound to Will. And how much crazier it would sound if he told him about the voice.

"Aw, I guess that's not a bad idea," Will finally agreed. He doubted he would ever fully comprehend the almost mystical connection the skinny blond-headed kid seemed to have with a piece of machinery like this one. But he knew for a fact that it was a good thing for them all that he did. A good thing indeed. "So what kind of car is she going to be."

"Fast," Rob answered without a second's hesitation.

"Well, she's not going anywhere at any speed tonight. Let's get out of here. I've already missed dinner for the second time this week, and Clara's likely got me a bed made out in the doghouse with Shep." He stood and stretched out the kinks in his legs. "Wanna grab a bite of supper with me on the way home? I believe I could eat an anvil if somebody fried it for me and I had some ketchup."

"Sounds good."

Rob had suddenly realized how ravenous he was, too, but he sat there behind the wheel of the new car a mo-

ment longer anyway while Will switched off the lights
and checked the locks on all the doors.

The two men finally headed out the door toward their
trucks, the crew chief leading the way and the kid driver
following along behind him. They talked for a moment,
decided which one of Chandler Cove's two fast-food
places would most likely still be open, then climbed into
their respective vehicles and pulled away. Will led in his
shiny sport truck with the red and orange running lights
atop the cab, followed closely by the kid, rattling along
in his own battered old pickup with the single headlight
blinking and the Crimson Tide-Alabama license plate on
the front bumper hanging by one bolt and a piece of wire.
As they pulled out of the gravel lot and onto the driveway, Rob already had some hip-hop song thumping away
on the ancient truck's new and completely out-of-place
stereo system—the system Donnie Kline insisted had
cost more than the truck itself was worth. He claimed,
too, that the loud volume the kid usually maintained
would soon disintegrate the old truck right down into a
pile of rust.

Across the yard and up a gently rising hill, an older
man with reddish-gray hair and the beginnings of a
paunch sat there in the dark at his kitchen table, idly
sipping steaming black coffee from a big mug. Through
the curtains that billowed gently in the soft night breeze,
he had watched the pair leave the shop building, talk
quietly together for a moment, then climb into their
trucks and pull away.

Once they had left, once distance and the chirping of
the crickets had wiped out the trucks' engines and the
kid's pumping music, it was again a still, quiet evening
there on the hip of the mountain. So quiet the older man
could hear the faraway mournful call of a whippoorwill.
The stars were especially brilliant this night, the moon-
less autumn sky clear and black and impenetrably deep.

Anyone else might have felt lonesome there in that big house all by himself, in the quiet stillness of the night. But not Billy Winton. He knew he was surrounded by more friends than anyone deserved to have in one life. That he was fortunate enough to spend most of his days in the company of folks who shared with him his most abiding love, his passion for stock car racing and for winning.

And even then, if someone wanted to press the point, some of his oldest and dearest friends—Jodell Lee, Bubba and Waylon Baxter, and Joe Banker—were only about the length of a Talladega Superspeedway lap over the mountain that rose up from his own back porch steps.

No, he didn't feel lonesome at all. Instead, he felt especially blessed this dark stardusted night. Blessed to have the crew chief he had on board. Blessed to have had the amazing young driver dropped into his lap. Blessed to have been able to assemble such a talented and devoted race team and have them loyal to him and to his dreams of excellence.

As he stood and walked over to the old-fashioned percolator still bubbling away on the stove eye, he thought once again how fortunate it had been that the chemistry between the kid and the crew chief had been so perfect from the very beginning. Talent and skill were hard to find. Talent and skill and chemistry all in one team package were downright rare. One never knew in this game. Egos and mad-ons had likely destroyed more race teams than crashes or sour cars ever had.

As he poured himself another mug of the strong chicory coffee, Billy Winton smiled contentedly. He could not have forged a stronger bond between a driver and a crew chief if he had blacksmithed it that way. It was by far the most solid he had seen in his thirty years of racing, and he was delighted it was happening right there in his own garage, on his team.

But then, as he stepped through the front door and out onto the wide porch, and as he eased down into one of the cane-bottomed rocking chairs that waited there, Billy Winton had a sudden revelation.

He actually *had* seen such a bond before.

That magical pairing had been between a wildly determined up-and-coming young driver and a wiry, red-headed kid fresh out of the Army and coming off a couple of tours in Vietnam. A steely-eyed racer with natural ability and supernatural grit. A red-haired kid with a fiery ponytail, a tattoo, and a special touch with a wrench. And an even more exceptional knack for knowing how to handle people.

That was the bond that had been formed between Billy Winton and Jodell Lee once upon a time.

It had been pure serendipity when Bubba Baxter had picked up Billy that night long ago as he hitchhiked in the rain, bound for no place in particular. Pure dumb luck that Bubba had been driving the Lee racing rig and that the chance encounter had led to all those wonderful years. And eventually to all that was spread out down there below where he sat, too.

As he gazed up toward the Milky Way, Billy Winton decided that what he had percolating in the shop just down the hill from the house was nothing more than a still-brewing reincarnation of himself and Jodell Lee. It was yet another bond developing between strangers, men whose only connection had been a race car and the intense desire to get all they could out of it so they might, together, win the prize they had been eyeing individually.

First prize.

Billy smiled, took another sip of the sky-black coffee, and listened contentedly as the echo of the whippoorwill's call ricocheted off the mountains.

Part 2

GETTING READY

Most people have the will to win. Few have the will to prepare to win.

—Indiana University basketball coach Bobby Knight

2

PREPARING TO WIN

I t was a brisk November day, and there was a championship on the line. Tense faces were as numerous as the brittle leaves that skittered along the pavement at the behest of the chill wind. Race teams were looking at the upcoming event as their last chance to turn a bad season around, to salvage some pride. Hungry young drivers were there, too, looking for that first win. Eager clear-eyed rookies had shown up with intentions of using this venue to make a run at the big show.

They were all there, their desire burning so hot they hardly noticed the nip in the air. Winning would warm everything up in a hurry.

Rob Wilder shuffled nervously from one foot to the other, tugging absentmindedly at his driving suit as he watched Will, Donnie, and the rest of the crew as they prepped the car. His car. The new one they had prepared for this track and this race.

The youngster had noticed already that there was a

different atmosphere in the Winston Cup pits compared
to the more relaxed mood he was accustomed to in Grand
National. There was not nearly as much of the joking and
horseplay among Billy Winton's team members. To a
man, they seemed more serious, more determined to keep
their minds on the task at hand.

They had already convinced each other that simply
making this race would be almost like winning. More
than fifty teams had shown up at this track south of Atlanta, all of them trying to qualify for the race. And most
of them were convinced that they had what it took to
actually win it. But with only forty-three starting spots
available, some relatively good race teams would be going home early. For a rookie team like Billy Winton's,
it would likely take a Herculean effort just to get the car
fast enough to make the race. They would think about
actually winning the thing later, after they had secured a
starting spot.

An attractive blond woman ambled up and punched
Rob in the arm. He was so engrossed in watching the
crew work on the car that he hardly acknowledged her
presence. Michelle Fagan was the director of marketing
for the Ensoft Corporation, the giant software company
that was the primary sponsor for the team. Fagan's company had ponied up a tremendous amount of money to
allow the team to take a shot at making this, its first
Winston Cup race. And Michelle had been one of the
people who had urged Billy to go ahead and challenge
the Jarretts, Earnhardts, Gordons, and Martins of the racing world. Now, as she studied the grim faces of the men
she had watched work all year, she couldn't help but
wonder if she had done the smart thing.

"You ready?" she asked the young driver.

"Naw. I reckon we ought to just put her back on the
trailer and go home," he answered in mock seriousness.

She gave him a sharp glance, realized he was putting

her on, and then punched him again, harder this time. It seemed she had spent most of the last two months jetting back and forth between the West Coast and the mountains of east Tennessee, trying to make sure all the details were taken care of, that all the contracts were finished and properly signed. She was in no mood for such a joke.

"Hey!" He rubbed his shoulder. "I know Ensoft is paying plenty of money to sponsor us but does that give you the right to pummel the driver?"

"Yes. With a hammer if I want to!"

She gave him her best mean look but it quickly dissolved into a smile. She couldn't stay mad at Rob Wilder for long. He had such an innocent look on his handsome young face that it was hard to imagine him being so aggressive out there on the racetrack. But Michelle certainly understood how her baby sister could have fallen so hopelessly in love with him. If she, herself, were only a couple of years younger . . .

"Gee, I better check the fine print in my contract then."

"What are you talking about? You'd pay us to let you drive that car on Sunday if you had to."

It was true, and Rob Wilder knew it. He grinned that crooked smile of his, the one that was already drawing fan mail and love letters from women all over the world. He reached over with one arm and gave Michelle a sincere hug.

Rob could only imagine how hard Michelle had worked to pull this all together, how much she had riding on his entry into Winston Cup racing. It wasn't so much about Ensoft and its commitment of money. Granted, it was a staggering sum from Billy's and Rob's point of reference. But Ensoft likely spent more money each year on computer diskettes or on their annual commercials in the Super Bowl than they did on their race sponsorship. No, the pressure was on Michelle to see that they got the most from that investment. And that everything associ-

ated with the move to the Cup circuit was wrapped up
and ready in plenty of time to give them a running go at
the next season. To have any hope of success, they had
needed to get everything under way by Labor Day. Contracts had to be finalized, new race cars had to be ordered,
and additional crewmen needed to be hired. And while
all that was going on, they were running races virtually
every weekend as the team fought to hold on to a top-
ten spot in the Grand National points competition.

Will placed the order for the new cars right after the
Darlington race over Labor Day weekend. The first of
them couldn't be delivered before the end of October,
though. That wouldn't allow them nearly enough time to
prepare a car for this race. That's why they had bought
the completed, race-proven car from Lee Racing. That's
the one Will Hughes and the crew were scrambling all
over now.

It looked beautiful, resting there in their garage slot,
freshly painted and, hopefully, race-ready. In another
hour they would know how close to ready they were to
make the quantum leap up to Winston Cup after only one
full season in Grand National.

Some in the sport questioned their wisdom in even
trying. Rob and Will and Billy didn't have time to think
about it.

"You nervous?" Michelle asked. She had noticed how
he was having trouble standing still.

"Uh-uh. I get impatient waiting. I wish I could drive
the car off the truck and right out there and get to practicing."

"I'll talk to the powers-that-be and see if we can ar-
range that next year."

"I'd be much obliged."

She punched him one more time. Among her many
other duties at the track, Michelle saw it as her task to
help keep the young driver relaxed, and not to allow the

downtime to bother him. She had come to enjoy that role, too, just as she had enjoyed about everything else about this crazy, fast-paced sport.

Will Hughes ordered the car pushed to the inspection line, that being the first order of business. The new car would have to clear inspection before it ever had a chance to taste the track. Rob joined a small group of drivers for the rookie meeting that was to be led by one of the sport's superstars. The order of business consisted of the usual cautions and warnings, but the main admonition was for the youngsters to be certain to move over and let the veterans drive on by. Rob listened intently, adding what he was hearing to all the things Jodell Lee had told him about the track already. Then, as he walked back to the garage, he glanced out at the racing surface itself. He felt a rush of adrenaline and his gear-shifting hand twitched. He was more eager than ever to steer the new car out there and see what they could accomplish together.

As Rob approached the stall where the Ford rested on a set of jack stands, he could see Donnie, Will, and Paul Phillips, one of the new mechanics they had added to the team. They were all standing inside the front fender wells working on the engine compartment. Rob's stomach fell. Were they changing the engine?

"What's up?" Rob asked, leaning over a fender. "Something wrong with the motor?"

"Relax, cowboy," Will said. "We're just making a few last-minute adjustments before we send you out there."

The look of relief was obvious on the driver's face. Will knew the kid was getting skittish as the time for their debut grew closer. They all were. This was a giant step up, a move rife with potential pitfalls. With all the cars they would be competing against likely running within a couple of tenths of a second or so of each other, it was going to be a tough, tense two days as they worked to try to make the field.

"I was just afraid something was wrong."

"Motor's fine. In fact, Joe Banker came by while you were at the rookie meeting, and he pronounced her ready to go. He said there was no need for you to worry about being short on horsepower. You'll have plenty."

"Good. I just wish they'd hurry up and get this practice started."

"We still got to get the tires bolted back on this baby. You'll have a hard time driving any laps without the wheels."

"Aw, I could drive it with or without wheels," Rob stated matter-of-factly.

Will smiled and turned to finish overseeing what the others were doing.

Rob shuffled over to the water cooler and poured himself a cup of water. He leaned an elbow up on the upright handle to the jack and watched the crew finish with the last-minute details. Michelle finished up another of her seemingly continuous cell phone calls about then, and she walked over to where he stood.

"Doesn't look like the waiting is bothering those guys," she said. She nodded over to where Dale Jarrett, Ricky Rudd, and Mark Martin stood talking and laughing. "I guess they've been doing this long enough."

"Yeah, but trust me, the pressures are the same on them as they are on us. Still, part of the pressure I'm feeling is wondering how they'll accept me when I step into their arena. I'm just anxious to get out there and earn their respect along with everybody else's."

"Don't you suppose the easiest way to earn their respect is to get out there and beat them. You do that and you do it cleanly and they'll all know who you are and what you can do. That is, if they don't already."

"Well, I know one thing. I wouldn't be here if I didn't think I could beat these guys."

"Hey, we wouldn't be spending all this money sponsoring you if we didn't think you could beat them," Michelle said with a smile.

"I'm going to get you so many trophies you folks are going to have to build a new building just to have a place to put them all."

"I don't care about the trophies. But I'll tell you one thing."

"What's that?"

"You really want to impress Toby Warren, you beat all the others to the checkered flag at the Daytona 500."

Toby Warren was the head man at Ensoft, a self-made millionaire before he had even turned thirty years old, and a recently converted stock car racing fan. And he was not easily impressed. He had insisted that anything with the Ensoft name attached to it had to be first-class, had to be a winner.

"Well, let me go on record right now. I'm planning on winning me about eight or nine Daytona 500s, starting with the 2001 race. Reckon that would make Mr. Warren a happy man?"

They carried on for a few more minutes until, finally, Will Hughes pronounced the car ready. Donnie, Paul, and the others pushed the car out to the line as Rob walked along beside it. They wanted to be toward the front of the line so they could get the car on the track as soon as it opened and not have to wait for others to come back in before the officials would let them out. They usually allowed only twenty to twenty-five cars out at a time during practice. With the limited amount of time before qualifying, they needed all the track time they could get to help them make this race.

Rob walked along with his shoulders hunched against the chilly breeze. Michelle walked alongside him, talking on her cell phone once again. Rob would have preferred continuing their conversation, using it to keep him from dwelling too much on the car and the track. It seemed she was constantly on the phone back to the coast, trying to run the marketing department of the huge company and handle the racing commitment at the same time. He swallowed his irritation. Most companies hired folks to do what Michelle was doing. She insisted on doing it herself for the time being. She said it was because she had quickly fallen in love with the sport and because she wanted to personally oversee the move to Cup racing. And she usually added, "I like the people, too. Especially the people."

As they approached the end of the line of cars, Donnie stood there next to the driver's-side window, waiting patiently for his driver. Rob could see Michelle was nowhere close to wrapping up her chatter on the phone, so he stepped over to Donnie. The big man's shaved head glistened in the dim sunlight as he motioned for Rob to climb in.

"You don't get in and drive this thing, I'll have to," he growled.

"There's got to be rules about somebody being too ugly to drive a race car," the kid shot back.

Kline never lost his scowl as he helped Rob climb into the car and the kid settled into his routine of buckling himself in, just as he had been doing in his Grand National car. So far, everything felt the same, but there would be key differences once he got out onto the track. Even now, he could see Will Hughes talking with Bubba Baxter, making sure they had not missed anything with the car's setup. Baxter had his own car to worry about, one the Winton team would eventually be trying to beat, but he still took the time to offer his advice. The higher horsepower of the Cup car's engine meant it took an entirely different handling package than the ones they were used to running in the Grand National car. That's what they had to check on these first laps. That and how their driver reacted to it.

Bubba Baxter gave Will a thumbs-up, signaling that he thought they had a good baseline setup under the car, one that gave them plenty of room to work with. Rob knew they had doubtless talked about what role the weather might play on the baseline. The pressure was on all of the teams to have the cars close to right coming off the truck, but it was especially crucial for the Ensoft team and its young driver. If they were off by too much at the beginning, if they started practice too far behind, they might well be making the long drive back to Chandler Cove a day early. That's why they had worked so hard on the car back at the shop and why they had been working on it constantly since they'd arrived in Atlanta.

Now, they were minutes away from seeing if they had missed the mark, if their first Cup effort was doomed from the start by poor preparation. Everybody here wanted desperately to win. One of those who had best prepared eventually would.

Rob cinched up the safety belts. Donnie talked back and forth with Will, who was still back in the garage, making sure they all knew what the plan would be for these first few laps of practice. Then he leaned in the window to update Rob, who knew his crew chief well enough to know that the plan would change anyway as soon as he took a couple of hot laps out on the track.

The official ordered the cars sitting lined up on the pit road to start their engines. Donnie slapped the Ford's roof with his hand, signaling his driver to crank it up. Rob reached over and hit the starter switch, waiting for the engine to roar to life out there in front of him. The starter ground a time or two before kicking over with a healthy growl. Now, with the engine vibrating loudly under his feet, Rob finally was able to smile inside the full-faced helmet he wore.

It was time to punch the clock and go to work. This was what he came here to do, what he was hired to do. All the waiting around was over, and it was time for him to drive his race car.

Donnie reached over and grabbed the window net, then stretched it tight to pull it into place so it would slide into its slot in the doorpost. Then he snapped the fastener, locking the safety netting into place. A quick tug confirmed it was secure. Paul came around from the other side of the car, and the two men stood there, surveying the car as if they could eyeball something wrong under the hood just by staring at her. Then they backed away, giving the car one last once-over before heading across the pit wall to watch all the action once the practice started. They would also have to start getting tools and equipment ready for the first time they pulled in for changes.

The car idled impatiently, the rumbling motor gently shaking the car, ready to roll. Rob goosed the engine, listening closely to the increase in its pitch as he revved it up. He contemplated the steep bank of the first turn that loomed out there directly in front of him. He thought of how he would attack the turn, how the car would react to it, which line he would take when he got the opportunity.

But as he sat there waiting for the roll-out signal, he couldn't block out the thoughts of the first time he had been offered the opportunity to see a race in this place. He had been a kid, and a friend's dad had offered to take him and his buddy to the race in Atlanta. Even then, Rob Wilder had a deep fascination with racing. It would have been a dream come true to actually attend a real live one. He begged his mother to let him go.

"You don't need to be wastin' no time at an old racetrack," she had said vehemently. "You'll be as sorry as your daddy was, spendin' money we don't have on such foolishness."

The painful memories of her refusal still burned deeply in his soul. It was only after discovering the scrapbook full of his father's racing clippings years later that he got some idea of why she so adamantly denied him that trip to Atlanta.

Painful as that episode had been, he could still remember his first sight of the half-mile turns and short quarter-mile straightaways of Atlanta. It had come several years later with the same friend and after he no longer needed his mother's permission to do anything. The sight of the famed blue-and-red Pontiac of Richard Petty running in the high groove right up against the wall had proved to be one of those defining moments in a young man's life. It had been there, that day, that he decided he wanted to be a race car driver. From that point on, nothing else ever mattered as much to him as racing and winning. Nothing.

Along the way, he raced bicycles, go-carts, riding lawn mowers—anything that had wheels and would roll. All the while, though, he dreamed he was Petty, Earnhardt, Elliott, or one of the others taking the checkered flag here at Atlanta. It amazed him to think that here he was, ten or twelve years later, sitting in his own race car, only a few feet away from one of the famous blue machines owned by the Pettys. And he was about to take his car out onto the track for the first time and actually rub fenders with them, challenge them, pretend he had what it took to beat them.

He shook his head as if to clear the thoughts, but he was still grinning when the official at the head of the line gave them the sign to pull away. Just being here was proof that dreams could come true. That is, if the dreamer was willing to work hard, to seize the opportunities when they came.

This was not going to be like his only other Cup experience, the day he had filled in for an injured Rex Lawford the previous year at Charlotte. That had all come
about so quickly and unexpectedly that it been mostly a
blur, an amusement-park ride in a strange roller coaster.
This time he would be piloting a car that had been readied just for him, set up the way he wanted it. It was time
to see if he deserved such a custom ride, if he had what
it took to step up to the next level. Rob was certain that
he belonged here, but that didn't count for much. He
knew he still had to prove it to everyone else.

The black Chevy in front of Rob finally rolled off the
line with a slight puff of smoke. Here he was, a mere
rookie, not even old enough to have finished college, racing with a seven-time champion, several one-, two-, and
three-time champions, and a whole slew of would-be fu-
ture champions. And also here, but for the very last time,
one of the sport's all-time greats, old Darrel Waltrip himself, preparing for what would likely be his final race.

Jodell Lee had pulled Rob aside the previous week
before the Grand National race in Homestead, Florida,
and reminded him of the similarities between this race
and another one not that long ago. Richard Petty had
been the legend who was retiring then. And a youngster
named Jeff Gordon was running his very first Winston
Cup race.

That had been a very obvious changing of the guard.
Everyone there that day had known it.

"I ain't saying you'll go out and win three championships like Gordon has done so far," the old driver had
said. "But if you're the race car driver I think you'll be,
this could be another changing of the guard folks'll be
talking about someday."

"Aw, Jodell, I don't . . ." Rob had modestly interrupted.

"Naw, listen. It's time for a change again. Gordon's

team has been struggling. Chrysler's coming back into it next year. Looks like D. W. is giving up his ride, and some of the others are gettin' ready to step aside. It's time, son. And I got a feeling you're in the right place to help the transition to the next generation take place."

Rob had been flattered by the thought at the time, but he had since put it out of his mind. Out of his mind, that is, until this very moment when he pulled away and guided the Ford's nose toward the Atlanta track's first turn.

Would Rob have what it took to seize the baton and run with it? Could he really hope to someday win all those championships? The time had come to find out. Rob guided his bright red Ford out onto the track and gunned the engine as if sounding a challenge to the old guard.

Soon he'd be challenging the status quo in racing, attempting to make an inside pass on the old guard and leave them behind, bobbing in his wake.

The kid couldn't wait for the opportunity.

3

MAKING THE SHOW

Rob Wilder eased into the gas as he steered the car toward the towering bank that comprised turn one of the D-shaped speedway. He accelerated off in that direction as he ran easily through second gear.

"How you feel, cowboy?" came Will's reassuring voice crackling in the radio earpieces.

"I was ready to let this thing gallop two hours ago."

"Like Grandma Hughes used to say, 'Patience is a virtue.' Let's just do what we always do. Take it easy for a few laps so we can make sure everything is good and tight. Then we'll let her go and see what we got to work with."

"Will, you sure know how to take away a man's fun. Just once I wish you'd let me gun it hard right from the get-go."

"I don't do that because I like you too much. For some reason, I've got this thing about not wanting to see you smashed hard into the fence."

Will appreciated his driver's eagerness, his aggressiveness. And he also knew Rob understood the need for taking it easy out there. Still, they had this same conversation on the first lap of practically every practice session they ever ran.

"Just once?" Rob asked again hopefully as he worked through third gear.

"Not today. Way too much on the line. We don't have time to play around here. These cats will eat us for lunch if we are even off half a tick."

"I know, boss. But that don't mean I can't ask." Rob lifted his thumb from the steering wheel mike switch to make his final shift. Then he hit the button one more time. "Well, I'd love to carry on all this chitchat with you, but I got work to do and time is a'wastin'."

Will smiled and looked over at Billy Winton as they stood there together in their stall in the garage. Billy grinned back, shaking his head. It was a mixed blessing, having a young driver who was so eager to run flat-out, who was often frustrated when he wasn't allowed to stomp and go. They had to work at keeping him throttled back, much like a racehorse that sometimes needs a slight tug on the reins to keep him from doing what he felt he was born and bred to do. Otherwise, they suspected, he would go full tilt all the time, never slowing down. Luckily, he was bright enough to know his owner and crew chief were right and usually obeyed their admonitions.

Just not always silently.

Even Michelle Fagan did her part to help Billy and Will keep Rob Wilder reined in. She had quickly become both his friend and his confidante. That meant she did far more than handle all the marketing chores for the team and its sponsor. She also rode herd over their driver whenever he needed a strong hand. It often fell to her to keep the youngster from overfocusing on the car, the race, the track. If he had a fault, it was that he sometimes got too wrapped up in the sport, in winning.

Maybe just as bad, many of the drivers tended to let their outside activities distract them from their jobs at the track. Not Rob Wilder. Everyone was certain he would sleep in the race car if they would let him, and he was always eager to do whatever he needed to do in order to help the team win. Win on and off the track.

Meeting Michelle's sister, Christy, had helped, too. She had a knack for detaching Rob's attention from the track or racing whenever she could come to wherever the week's event was. However, his busy schedule and the fact that she was a junior in prelaw at UCLA all the way out on the West Coast limited their opportunities to see each other. That left mostly hurried telephone calls between his practices or trips to races or appearances or all-night work sessions or even her class schedule. Christy Fagan could certainly calm his nerves when he was frustrated with the car or with his own driving.

For all its challenges, theirs had become a heavy romance. But even she knew that racing was his first love. She told him more than once that she knew if he ever had to choose between her and a race car, the race car would get the checkered flag. He had only weakly challenged her opinion.

Of course, Billy Winton liked for her to come to the track as often as possible, not only because he liked her personality, but for business reasons, too. For a handsome young race car driver, there could be far more lethal distractions. Her effect on him had been especially evident in Nashville back in the spring. Rob had overdriven the car during qualifying and that had cost them what would certainly have been a top-five starting spot and probably even the pole. Christy had been the calming influence that seemed to help him overcome his frustration, to keep him focused on driving a smart race after the mess-up. Several members of the team gave her full credit for helping Rob overcome the poor qualifying run and bring home the victory.

Unfortunately, she had been able to make few of his races. Even now, Billy was hoping she would be able to hitch a ride on the Ensoft corporate jet to Atlanta for this race, for this important first step they were taking. The Ensoft people had wisely decided to wait and see how the first round of qualifying went before they confirmed the trip all the way across the country. It was clear to everyone their driver was wound tighter than a coiled spring all week. Michelle was doing what she could. Christy Fagan's presence would be their ace in the hole.

Rob gunned the car down the backstretch, loving how smoothly the car was running, how powerful she felt at his touch. He pointed the Ford through the center of the turn, leaving the inside line open for the cars behind him who were pushing their rides already. He used the banking to build speed as he accelerated down past the mostly empty grandstands lining the front straight. Then he flashed under the flagstand, setting his sights on the banking in turn one again.

Rob set his line entering the corner and felt the car bite down into the asphalt of the turn. There was no doubt about it. The racer carried a noticeably different feel than the Grand National car he was used to driving. He pinched the left-side wheels right down on the white line running around the bottom of the track. The car drifted up through the center of the corner and then pushed slightly as Rob brought her off turn two. Together, he and the car quickly crossed the short backstretch before heading into turn three. Rob checked his mirror then glanced furtively down at his gauges as he came up out of turn four to pass in front of the long row of grandstands that framed the quad-oval of the frontstretch.

"Okay, cowboy, how is she running?"

"A-okay. All the gauges are straight up."

"Good. Let's see what kind of vehicle we brought down here, then."

"Roger," Rob answered, and immediately hammered the throttle to the floor.

Those first laps had let him get acquainted with the Atlanta track while also giving him an opportunity to get used to the different feel of the car. Now he was ready to learn more and do it at speed.

Donnie stood next to the pit wall watching their car circling the track. He heard Will's call on the radio turning Rob loose and now he anxiously fingered the stopwatch in his hand as he got ready to time the car. He could tell that the Ford looked okay on those first couple of laps, but he knew it was no indication of what the car could really do until Rob actually shoved her right out there on the ragged edge.

The next five laps told them what they were up against. The motor had plenty of power but the car had a bad push coming off the corners, the front end tending to want to head for the outside of the track. Rob was having trouble getting back into the gas as he came off the corners, as the car tried to take its own line up to the high side of the track. He had to ease back on the throttle and lost serious momentum in the process.

Finally, Will called him back to the garage. The waiting crew, already briefed on what would likely need to be done, immediately went to work.

Donnie slapped the jack under the right-side of the car, hoisting it up with two quick pumps. Paul and one of the other crew members slid jack stands under the front and rear of the car. Will and Billy both disappeared under the front end to make a few changes under there. Will had Donnie adjust on the track bar while he and Billy checked the front camber on the right front tire.

Someone handed Rob the clipboard that held the tire temperature readings. He studied them carefully, especially noting the ones on the right-side tires. The outside temperatures on the tires were much higher than the readings across the middle and the inside. That explained why Will and Billy were so interested in the camber on the right front. Rob handed the small clipboard back out to Michelle and accepted the cup of brightly colored sports drink she offered him. He finished it off in a couple of swallows, then wadded up the paper cup and tossed it back at her. It missed her but bounced off the car in the stall next to them. She threw him a mean, squint-eyed look as she bent down and retrieved it. Then she zinged it right back at him, laughing out loud as it bounced off the window netting onto the garage floor.

As soon as the work was completed, the jack stands were removed, and then Donnie lowered the car back down onto the concrete. Paul buttoned up the hood and snapped the hood pins back into place.

"Let's give it another go, kid," Will said over the radio, even though he was only a few feet away. Rob would never have heard him over the racket in the garage as all the teams made noisy corrections to their own racers. "Let's see if that helps to free her up in the corners some."

"Roger. How many laps we need to do?" Rob asked as he reached to hit the starter switch. The roar of his own engine joined the cacophony ringing through the garage area.

"A couple to start with. I'll call you in once we see what these changes look like. I want to see if we're going in the right direction. Even if we're on the right track, I want to try a few more things early on."

"Gotcha!" Rob said as the boys pushed the idling car out of the stall. He steered her through the opening in the pit wall then accelerated as he hit pit road.

Rob charged off toward turn one, already running quickly up through the gears. He hit his stride down the

short backstretch before diving low through turn three.
He kept the car down to the inside as he sped through
the sweeping turn and then hustled off down the front
straight. This time the car felt noticeably better as he
swept through turn one. The push was still there coming
off the corner but it was not nearly as bad as before. He
reeled off a couple of more laps before Will called him
back in.

The same procedure was repeated many times more
through the rest of the practice session. In and out, back
and forth, run and stop, nothing exciting, merely grunt
work as they tweaked on the setup in the car, working as
quickly and orderly as they could. As the session played
out, they realized that they were not going to light any fires
at the front of the field come qualifying time. But they definitely were posting middle-of-the-pack times. A good run
during qualifying could likely get them into the field.
And the cool weather conditions should give them a shot
in both days' sessions if they needed them. In the warmer
months, trying to make the race in the second round was
close to impossible. The late afternoon first-round session
usually had an advantage over the second-round session,
which was held in the heat of the day.

When the practice ended, Will gave Donnie and Paul
and the rest of the crew a list of things he wanted done
before they took their quick break for lunch. Will took
the notes he had scribbled down during the round over
to where Bubba Baxter was knee-deep in the preparations
for his own team. He found Bubba talking with Jodell
Lee in the back of their hauler. They waved him on inside. Both men were clearly in a good mood.

The Lee car was flying. Rex Lawford had run consistently among the top ten in practice speeds throughout
the session. There were smiles everywhere among the
Lee crew, and those had become more and more rare

recently. Bubba and Jodell wanted the pole and they wanted it badly. It would help them end on a good note what had otherwise been a generally disappointing season. The continued rise of the multi-car teams was fast putting single-car teams like theirs in danger of becoming extinct.

"The kid looked pretty good out there from the times I got off the watch," Jodell said. He always took special interest in how Rob was doing anytime they found themselves at the same track for a weekend. After all, Jodell had first spotted Rob Wilder at a small out-of-the-way track and had recommended him to Billy Winton. Now, he followed his discovery almost as closely as he did his own driver. He actually enjoyed being the kid's mentor, a position he had never been able to fully occupy with his own son, Bob Jr.

"Yeah, the car's not too bad. We're in no danger of winning the pole, but we should be able to place her somewhere in the middle of the field."

"You just need to get the kid in the race, Will," Jodell said. "That's your battle this weekend. He'll have plenty of time to worry about picking up some poles in the years to come. Right now, making the show, learning all he can learn out there, y'all gettin' a feel for the competition at this level, that's all that matters this trip."

"I know, Jodell. But you know Robbie. If he's in the race car, then he's going to try and win the pole, the race, or something. Woe be unto anything or anybody that gets in his way."

All three men nodded. They knew Will spoke the truth. That was also the reason the kid made such a perfect fit with the car. Rob Wilder might drive smoothly and with intelligence, but he also had a tendency to drive nothing less than flat-out.

"It's a different game up here. Driving hard and aggressive can hurt you as much as it can help you," Jodell

said. "That's what I told the kid over lunch last week.
He has to remember you can't win the race if you don't
make the show. There are just too many good cars trying
to make their way into the field every week."

It had been Rob's natural, smooth driving style that
had first caught Jodell's eye at the little track the summer
of the year before. Unlike most of the other young drivers, he didn't tend to drive overly aggressively, to bull
his way to the front. The kid had shown talent on that
ragged old bull ring that night that few drivers would
ever hope to learn, no matter how long they steered race
cars.

"Well, let's see what we can do to get him into this
race. What do y'all think of his speed charts? On fresh
tires, we were looking at speeds in the twenty-eight-
point-nine-second range."

Bubba took the clipboard and looked over the meticulous notes Will had taken on the setup and the speeds
for each lap they'd run in practice. Most of their changes
had come in an effort to fix the push in the car coming
off the corners. Will was fishing for suggestions from
Bubba and Jodell after they took a look at the direction
they'd gone with the changes. After all, they were more
familiar with the design of the car than Will was, and he
hoped they might help him get a better handle on what
they might do to make the car faster.

"I think it will take a minimum of a twenty-nine-flat
to make the show. Might need something a tad better,"
Bubba said, never looking up from the clipboard. "What
did the tuner say about the motor?"

"No complaints there. The kid said she had plenty of
power. Joe himself came over and double-checked the
tune. He said the plug checks looked good, that we had
a nice, clean, even burn across the top of them."

"Will, I'd say all you need to do is keep that young
broncobuster nice and calm. Like Jodell said, keep him

thinking while he's driving instead of trying to make the car do what she don't want to do, and he'll be fine. Looks to me like y'all got a pretty good handle on things. I don't think I would do anything real drastic other than to keep chasing her in the direction you're going already. You might try dropping the pressures on the right side another pound, but no more."

"I was thinking about that," Will said, rubbing his chin as he contemplated what another pound less of pressure in the tires would do to the handling coming off the corner. That was where they were losing most of their time.

"For one lap, he'll be fine. That thing is going to drive like it's on skates anyway."

"I know. But he likes a slick track, thank goodness."

"You get a good clean lap in qualifying, and the kid should make the race," Bubba proclaimed as he flipped through the rest of the time sheets.

"Thanks, Bubba. I felt like we were going right, but I haven't got forty years of experience like you do. Nobody in this garage knows chassis setups better than you do. I just don't want to overlook anything."

"Will, ain't none of these young cats in the garage any better at figuring a car out than you are," Bubba said as he passed the clipboard and the compliment right back to Hughes.

"The kid'll be fine. Just keep Michelle talking to him and keeping him distracted right up until he qualifies. You can bet his pulse is gonna be runnin' faster than the motor. Keep him calmed down, and he'll be fine."

"Don't worry, Jodell. We've figured that out already. Seems like that's quickly turning into a full-time job for her," Will said with a laugh. "I just wish her sister was here. We might get the pole and win the race if she was."

"Those two gals keep him from hooking up with some of these racer-chasers, too. You know some of those ladies would love to latch onto old Robbie. That'd be nothing but trouble for a young'un like him."

"Why do you think we like this long-distance relationship so much. Michelle can keep a pretty good watch over him in the meantime. All I want is to get the boy qualified. We can worry about his love life later."

"Getting qualified will be tough," Jodell said, suddenly turning serious. "Some good cars are gonna go home, I expect. The kid's got what it takes, rest assured of that. He'll stay focused and get the job done. Don't worry."

Rex Lawford joined them then with some questions for Jodell about some things he wanted done on his own car. That gave Will a chance to exit and head back to the Ensoft Ford's garage slot. As he walked, Jodell's words circled inside his head. He knew he had to make the correct changes on the car. And he also knew to make sure Rob Wilder was in the right frame of mind come time for qualifying. Sometimes he figured he was as much a psychologist as he was a grease monkey.

It dawned on him then that he needed not to worry so much about Rob, but instead make sure he, himself, was ready for qualifying. If the car was off, it wouldn't matter how focused his driver was on the qualifying run. That was considerable weight to carry. And he knew it was on his own shoulders. But that was precisely where he wanted it.

It had been a longtime dream of Will Hughes to be crew chief for a competitive Winston Cup team. And now, here he was. It was his chance to prove some things, too. Some things he had been planning and building on since he was a kid, watching his own father drive race cars.

Yes, Will Hughes had some things to prove, too. He stepped a little faster as he made his way down the length of the garage.

The activity was frantic around the car as they readied

it for the trip out to pit road. The qualifying line was already forming, and there were only a few minutes left before they would need to push the car out to take their spot in line. The pressure was almost visible now, the tension hanging in the air like tire smoke.

Donnie carefully taped the openings in the front end of the Ford, closing off most of the air flow entering the engine compartment. The tape would help to cut down on the car's drag through the air as it made the one-lap qualifying run. It would help push the nose of the car downward, sending more air over the hood of the car to the spoiler in the back. These days, down-force was the name of the game. Although to the unpracticed eye the amount and positioning of the tape seemed haphazard, it had actually been carefully calculated. If it cut off too much of the airflow, the fragile qualifying engine could be blown to pieces, even in one short lap. Not enough and they might just as well be running uphill.

Paul Phillips checked the adjustment of the rear spoiler, making sure they had the correct angle on it. The rest of the crew carefully put away everything leftover from where they had changed to the qualifying motor from the one they had been running in practice. If they qualified for the race in this first round, they would be changing the engine again later in the afternoon.

Rob sat impatiently on the steps to the truck watching all the activity. He refused Michelle's repeated suggestions that they go into the lounge inside the hauler where it would be warm. She sat beside him, shivering in the cool breeze as they watched the crew work. Rob now brushed aside her attempts at small talk as he tapped his foot nervously.

"Stop that!" Michelle finally said, motioning toward his foot.

"What?" he snapped back.

"That!" she said, stepping on the bouncing foot with her shoe.

"Watch it! That's my gas foot."

"You're gonna have to drive left-footed if you don't stop that annoying tapping up and down like that."

She made another stab at his driving boot.

"Sorry," he apologized. While he professed to not be nervous, he wasn't doing a very good job showing it. "I guess I'm just thinking about what I have to prove out there in a minute."

Michelle stood, grabbed his hand, and dragged him into the crew lounge inside the truck.

"We all do, Rob. I pushed Billy until he went ahead and made the move to Winston Cup. He doesn't want egg on his face. Will's out there with a strange race car trying to get it qualified against the best drivers and race teams in the world. We all got a thing or two to prove down here."

He took the soda Michelle offered and eased down onto the couch.

"I guess so. Sometimes I forget that we're a team, that it's not all on me."

"Right! And a good team, too. All you have to do is go out there and drive the way you know how, and everything will be fine."

"And I will. Once I get in the car, I will. It's this waiting that makes me goofy."

Just then, they heard the grumble of a race car taking to the track, it's deep-throated roar seeping through the thin walls of the trailer. Billy stepped inside the lounge and poured himself a cup of steaming coffee.

"Ready, kid?"

"Been waiting all my life for this day."

"Good. Will and the boys just pushed the car off toward the line. We need to head that way. You coming, Michelle?"

"No way I'm going to miss this." She motioned in the general direction of west, toward California and Silicon Valley and Ensoft headquarters. "I'll have to give Toby a blow-by-blow account of the entire lap."

"Well, let's go qualify us a car then," Billy said, and ushered them out of the hauler toward the track.

They headed across the garage toward the pit road where a dozen or so cars were lined up waiting to take their turn at qualifying. The bright red Ensoft Ford was being pushed into its place at the back of the line. Out on the track there was the deep whine of a car being pushed to the limit as it tried to find all the speed it could muster in the space of a single lap.

"I can't wait to get her out there, Billy," Rob said as he surveyed the big fast speedway. "We got a good car. I want to see what I can do with her."

"Just remember what we always tell you. Don't go out there and try to win it all on this lap. Be smooth."

"Don't worry. I will. Oh, and Will and I have already had this talk. Besides, I learned my lesson at Nashville. I won't make that mistake again."

"I know, kid. I'm just giving you the benefit of this old man's years of experience. If you're not smooth, that bump down in turn one will get you pushed all out of shape, and you'll have to crack the gas. And you know we can't afford that."

"I told Will to unhook the brakes," Rob laughed. "That way we'd make the race for sure. I don't think he much liked my idea."

Billy winced. The kid had likely done just as he said. He could imagine the look on his crew chief's face. But he was glad to have the kid on his team. When it came to cars and speed, this unassuming young man was a bona fide natural. And he had no lack of confidence in his own abilities. He couldn't imagine what in Rob Wilder's past had happened to make him so driven to win, but he was glad he was now driven to win in the Billy Winton Ford.

There was something else about the kid, too. Sometimes, Billy, Jodell, and the other old-timers could swear someone else was helping Rob drive the car. Whether it was the spirit of Curtis Turner, Little Joe Weatherly, or even Fireball Roberts helping him make some of the moves he made out there, it seemed like someone else might be riding with the kid, guiding him, nudging him to the spot where he needed to be.

The idea had begun as a joke, but now it was being taken a bit more seriously. Racers are a superstitious lot by nature. When the young driver made some sort of amazing move out there on the track, why couldn't it be Fireball or Davey Allison or Alan Kulwicki whispering in the kid's ear? Bubba Baxter had long ago decreed that if it helped the kid win races, it didn't matter what the phenomenon was. Bubba was likely the most superstitious one of the bunch. He had already declared that there would be no more making light of the possibility that ghosts rode with the kid. Otherwise they might break the spell the racing gods had cast on the young driver.

Today, though, Bubba was concerned with his own car and their attempt to turn their good practice speeds into an inside-front-row starting spot.

Rob was a little surprised that the reporters seemed to be leaving him alone at this track. At this level, he was simply another hot young kid trying to break into the big leagues. The numerous reporters milling around on the pit lane didn't seem to notice him at all as he walked along beside Billy toward his car. They were much more interested in Jeff Gordon, Tony Stewart, Jeff Burton and the other stars. Rob accepted their indifference. He had to prove to them, too, that he belonged in such elite company, that he was worthy of their attention. Once he had done that, the reporters would come flocking.

Billy was glad the reporters were leaving them alone for now. Today, the kid needed to be single-mindedly focused on the run he was about to make. If they made the field, they would reap plenty of exposure. Today, the run for the Cup championship was the prime story the press was chasing, not that of some green kid taking a spin in a Cup race.

Rob strolled up to his bright red Ford sitting there in line. She was sandwiched between two other racers about a dozen cars from the front. He caught his breath. Behind his Ford sat the black number 3. And just behind it was the familiar silver-colored Pontiac of Stacy Locklear. Then, ahead of him was the rainbow-colored Chevrolet.

He smiled tightly as he looked over the line of race cars, ignoring the howl of the car that was making its run out on the track.

I belong here, he thought as he surveyed the row of familiar brightly colored cars that were all lined up together. This, right here, was his destiny. But it was up to him to show them all that he had as much right to be here as anyone else, as the 3 or the 24 or Locklear's Pontiac or any of the rest of them.

When Rob Wilder was nervous, it showed in his driving. He tended to push the car too hard, leaving him open to mistakes like the blown qualifying lap at Nashville. On the other hand, when he handled the car with his usual quiet confidence, anything was possible. He had shown that earlier in the year when he had won the Grand National pole at Daytona to start the season. Whenever he drove confidently, those invisible, ghostly voices would always show up to guide him straight and true. Maybe they knew he was more likely to have the good sense to listen to them then.

Today Rob was coolly confident as he stood looking over the polished machine while Will and the others finished their last-minute work. He looked around him, sizing up the competition. Many other Grand National drivers might have been intimidated by the heady company. Not Rob Wilder. Even at his young age, he was certain he had what it took to mix it up with the very best. If he didn't, he wouldn't be here. He'd be home, getting ready for the next Grand National season.

Rob was ready to get into the car and see if he could better the practice speeds he'd been running. With the times these early qualifiers were posting, something around a flat twenty-nine seconds or a couple of tenths better should be good enough to make the field. Their practice speeds had been in that range. With a brand-new set of Goodyears bolted on the car and the primed qualifying engine under the hood, they should be able to get it done.

That is, if the driver was able.

"We all set, Will?" Rob asked as he stood beside Billy, watching them finish up with the car.

"Fast as all get-out," Will responded, running his hand along the smooth surface of the front fender.

"Good."

"Ten minutes and we'll know what we got. We made all the changes. Dropped a pound of air pressure on the right side and jacked a half round of wedge out of her. With the soft springs and Joe's superspecial qualifying motor, you should be ready to go."

"Superspecial qualifying motor?" Rob said, looking suspiciously at Billy. Superspecial qualifying motor? Were they trying to pull another one of their pranks on him?

"That's what Joe called it. He said he built this motor just for you. Did it all himself. You know there's gonna be a ton of torque in that engine."

"If Joe built it, it'll be plenty powerful. I'll make her sing!"

It was no joke. This was a special engine. Joe Banker

spent dozens of hours personally handcrafting the motor. He wanted Rob to have the best he could build for his first race. Like Jodell, Banker saw a lot of himself in the kid. The eagerness, the drive to win reminded him of the way they all had been back in 1958 and 1959 when racing was still mostly for fun and not such a big business.

The boys pushed the Ford up another spot as the racers in front of them rolled out to take their one-lap· shot at the pole. Rob pitched in and helped push the car, leaning into the driver's compartment and steering. He glanced over at Michelle, who stood over to the side, talking on her phone again, solving software marketing problems long-distance. It was time for him to climb into the car, but he wanted to tell her something beforehand.

Get off the phone! he thought. But then he caught himself. No reason to get irritated now. He'd tell her when he got back. He had work to do.

With four cars left in front of him, he swung his long, lanky legs through the open window. Just then, Michelle punched the button on the phone to hang up and jogged over to give him a good-luck hug. The feel of her reminded him of her sister. Her voice even sounded like Christy's as she whispered encouragement in his ear.

"I'm glad you're here, Michelle. I do appreciate it."

And he meant it. She had become much more than a sponsor's rep. Her job was so demanding, even before the racing thing had started, and she could easily delegate the track PR duty to someone else. But she had not missed a race yet. And it was clear that this was more than simply another part of her job. She had become a racing fan. And even more important, she was clearly a Rob Wilder fan. Win or lose, she was there. He was glad he had had the chance to tell her how much he appreciated her before he pulled away for his biggest lap yet. And that she had acknowledged his words with that lovely Fagan smile.

Will Hughes took her spot when she pulled out of the window, offering Rob some final instructions as he helped him finish buckling himself in.

Will avoided his usual admonitions, the pleas for patience. Instead, this time the crew chief brought words of encouragement. The normally dour Will Hughes was smiling as he tried to pump his driver up.

"Remember, we got the motor combination perfect. You got four fresh sticker tires. The chassis is adjusted just the way you like it. I don't see how you can miss."

"Good. I'm ready to see if I can dust these guys," Rob replied as he fitted the radio plugs in his ears.

"Get the rpms up coming off of four as you come down to take the green. We only have the one shot here, and you need to be riding high when you take the start."

"I'll make the best of it. Whatever happens, they'll know that we've been here by the time we finish that lap."

"Cowboy, I have no doubt about that."

Will was actually smiling. He didn't have to worry about Rob doing anything but all the car would do. The kid's enthusiasm was contagious. Will felt his own confidence growing. Besides, as Billy had reminded all of them over and over, the pressure should actually be off them. No one expected them to come roaring into Cup racing, duplicating their almost instant success in Grand National.

Rob pulled the full-faced helmet down over his head, signaling an end to the mutual cheerleading session. It was time to hush and drive for a change. Rob hardly paid any attention as the crew pushed the car slowly up the line. He busied himself instead with the restraining belts and getting situated and comfortable in the seat. He pulled on his racing gloves, retrieved the steering wheel from where it rested on the dash, and set it on the steering column. Carefully, he lined up the piece of tape that marked the top of the wheel, making sure it was in the twelve-o'clock position. Then he clicked the pin into place, securing it onto its shaft. He gave it a tug in each direction to make sure it was solid.

Then all he could do was sit there and study the back end of the multicolored car in front of him. For some reason the sponsor logos looked as if they were going to jump right off the rear deck and start doing a dance. After all the years of watching that very familiar car race, on television and in person, Rob now found it odd to be lined up directly behind it on pit road, ready to follow it out onto the track and try to run a faster lap than its veteran and very famous driver was about to.

Rob smiled. He had certainly chased the other young racing star enough in his dreams. Now, he was about to do it while wide awake.

Finally, that was the only car left in front of him. Rob focused all his energy onto the track, all his concentration on how he would attack every foot of it. He ran the lap mentally, focusing on the precise spots where he would tap the brakes, giving them the slightest caress in order to set the car for the corners. He visualized the points on the track where he would ease up on the throttle and those where he would climb back on again.

Then, there was the shadow of someone standing next to the car. Rob glanced up. It was Stacy Locklear. The driver had had limited success on the circuit in his five years, had actually bulled his way to a couple of victories and had used his aggressive if not sometimes downright shady driving style and rough-edged personality to earn a decent following of fans.

"You think 'cause old Billy Winton bought you a pretty new car you belong up here with the big boys?" There was nothing good-natured about the tone of Locklear's question.

"I'm just here to see what I can do," Rob answered,

his voice muffled by the helmet. "Same as you."

"Naw, you're wrong, slick. I'm here to win this race, and if you or anybody else gets between me and the finish line, I plan to drive right up your tailpipe." With that, he turned on his heels and strode back to where his own car waited.

Rob snorted. If Locklear was trying to intimidate him, he was wasting his time. He had had some of the others try, and he simply shrugged them off each time. Most of the drivers had welcomed him to the circuit, let him know that if he belonged there, everyone would soon know it and would acknowledge his presence. He doubted Locklear would do anything stupid out there during a race. It was too easy to retaliate, and rough drivers quickly learned they didn't have enough eyes or rearview mirrors to watch for the payback when it came.

The rumble of the engine of the car in front of him interrupted his thoughts.

Will leaned in the window then to check the belts as he always did back in Grand National prior to qualifying. Then he fastened up the window net, tugging on it, stretching it tight so he could secure it. That simple routine was enough to remind both men that this was, after all, only racing. And they were as ready for this run as they had been for any of the previous ones they had so far made together.

"What did Locklear want?" he asked.

"Aw, he was just wishing me luck," Wilder said with a grin.

Will doubted that. But he was sure the kid could shrug off whatever the guy had been preaching about. He watched the car pull off pit road then threw a glance over to where Billy Winton stood with Michelle Fagan at his side. Donnie and Paul stood there, too, not far away, with a knot of crewmen from the black number 3 and some of the Stacy Locklear crew behind them, giving them a hard time, mostly in a good-natured way. There had been the usual joking and bantering going on all morning, everyone in the garage trying to calm his own nerves with foolishness. Even Locklear's guys had more tact than their driver showed.

"Look at them," Billy told Michelle, nodding over toward where Donnie and Paul were pretending to jaw with the 3 crew and to appear to be ignoring their own driver and car as it pulled away. But anyone who knew Donnie Kline could see how he really felt. "This is about as nervous as I've ever seen Donnie. Looks like he's wound tighter than an eight-day clock."

"If Donnie's on edge that much, what about Rob?" Michelle asked as she watched the shiny new Ford pull into turn one and begin to gain momentum.

"I'm not worried about him. There is something about that kid when he's under pressure. He seems to have a real knack for using the tension to his advantage and making the car do things that nobody seems to be able to explain. Even him."

"Lord, please don't start on those ghost stories again!" Michelle said with a laugh. Try as she might, she still couldn't buy all those racing superstitions and phantoms that kept popping up everywhere they went, or the straight-faced haunting stories these big, burly men told from days gone by as if they were the actual truth.

"Don't underestimate how much luck has to do with racing, young lady," Billy said with a smile. "The racing gods are either on your side or they're throwing darts at you. You don't want to be doubting or testing the issue if you know what's good for you."

Will's heart was thumping hard as he watched their bright red Ford gain speed down the backstretch. He watched his driver drift high into turns three and four. Rob was taking the car high up into the outer groove, trying to build speed and impetus while keeping the en-

gine's rpms up. Will found himself unconsciously
crossing his fingers as the car growled down to take the
green flag that was being waved at it by the flagman high
above the start/finish line. Will, like his driver and team
owner, like Michelle Fagan and the rest of the crew, was
completely aware that they were watching the passing of
a crucial milestone in the team's development, in Rob
Wilder's driving career.

They were all attempting to qualify for the first time
in a Winston Cup race. And they were doing so in a
machine they had all worked to perfect. The next phase
in their lives symbolically began with that flagman's
bright green banner being waved at the nose of the Ford.

Of course, there were questions. What about the setup?
The handling? Would the car be fast enough or embar-
rassingly sluggish? Was there anything else they should
have or could have done that, left undone, would show
up now in a clumsy run or a lethargic time?

Will pondered those questions as he stood to one side
and waited for his driver to take their car and make the
one-lap kamikaze run.

Billy felt yet another twinge of excitement course
through his body. It was only then that the magnitude of
what they were attempting hit him full force: it was his
car out there, sandwiched between a couple of household
names, men famous enough that even non–racing fans
would recognize them, making an attempt at qualifying
in the premier division on the circuit, and in what was
arguably the most competitive racing in the world.

Funny, he thought, how things seem to come full circle
in life.

Somehow it reminded him of that first race he attended
with Jodell Lee over thirty years before. Watching Jodell
come around to take the checkered flag that day in a car
that he had helped build was a thrill like no other he had
ever experienced. Today, watching Rob take to the track

in this new racer, the same jolts of electricity were snapping through his body.

Everything seemed to run in slow motion now as Billy and the rest watched the warm-up lap. The flags around the track at the top of the towering grandstands snapped in the stiff breeze. The multicolored tractor trailer rigs were lined up neatly in rows in the infield. Even the air seemed charged with electricity. Everything seemed to suddenly be visible in sharp contrast, the colors more brilliant, the sounds more intense, the smells magnified, the senses heightened.

Rob charged across the start/finish line at full bore and swept off toward turns one and two. Will clenched and unclenched his fists. He had full confidence in the abilities of his young driver. Sometimes, even he sensed there was more to the kid's driving ability than raw talent alone. There was just something intangible about the way Wilder handled a car that left the old-timers shaking their heads and looking at each other squint-eyed. Was he a reincarnation of some of the greats? Or was he merely the latest in the new generation of hotshot young drivers who were trying to make their own marks on the circuit, trying to make the old-timers forget the legends long enough for them to make a pass to the lead?

Rob had sat there impatiently, itching as he awaited his turn to go. He was glad, at least, for the silence on the radio net as he psyched himself up for what was, to him, too, the most important run of his racing career so far. He saw nothing but the black stretch of asphalt that was to be his and his alone in a few moments. He had paid no attention to Will as he fastened up the window net, gave him the usual thumbs-up, and wished him luck.

Rob may have nodded back an acknowledgement. He may not. He frankly couldn't remember.

The wave of the official motioning him out on the track had snapped him back to the here and now. Rob had hit the starter switch, felt Joe Banker's carefully constructed engine cough to life. As soon as it fired and settled into an idle, he let out on the clutch, sensed the gears engaging, and felt the race car start to roll off the line. For a moment, he watched the black number 3 disappear in his rearview mirror before he focused on what was in front of him: the patch of track he would have to follow to his destiny.

This wasn't the end-all. If worst came to worst, they would fail to qualify, go back home, and then get serious about preparing the other new cars, bringing in the new personnel and equipment and making the Cup move in February in Daytona.

But that wasn't the way Rob Wilder was wired together. This was the next challenge, the next race. Whether it was on a tiny bullring in front of a hundred folks back home in Alabama or qualifying for his first real Cup race in Atlanta, he wanted desperately to get the most out of the car, out of the run, out of himself.

He gritted his teeth, grinned, checked his eyes behind the helmet mask in the mirror, and gripped the wheel so hard he could feel his fingers tingle inside the driver's gloves.

The car was in turn one already before he shifted to the highest gear. She bounced over the slight bump right before she hit the center of the corner, then continued to pick up speed as Rob guided her expertly around the course. She felt good beneath him, as he sped down the back straight, as he steered high, doing all he physically could to try to continue to build his velocity through the high line into turns three and four.

The throttle was stomped down hard while the car was still in the middle of turn four. Rob never eased off as the car zoomed toward the green flag, already being waved down there in front of him.

"Let's get it, girl," he whispered, and the Ford seemed

to hear, to actually respond to his entreaty as much as to his foot jammed hard on her throttle.

Together, Rob and the new Ford rocketed over the painted stripe that marked the start/finish line, the left side of the car only a foot or so away from the autumn-browned grass that lined the inside edge of the pavement. He never hesitated, keeping the gas pedal shoved rudely to the floor as he cut across the short chute. The car hurled toward the steep banking of the first turn, her tires already beginning to squall in protest as they strained to keep a grip on the track's surface.

Now, car and driver were one, a single machine made of steel and rubber and plastic and flesh and bone. Their minds were one, too, their parts meshed into a well-honed contrivance built to accomplish a common task—reaching that stripe once again that they had just passed over and doing it as quickly as possible.

Right on cue, a slight, quick tap on the brake as the car approached the banking set her up perfectly for the run through the corner. Wilder yanked the wheel, aiming to hold the heavy race car tight and down toward the inside line. She bounced over the bump in turn one and Rob sawed back and forth on the steering wheel, concentrating on trying to keep the car headed in a straight line, bucking all logic and basic laws of physics. The high-pitched growl of the motor reverberated around the speedway as the car dug its way up and off the corner.

Then, together, car and driver hurtled out toward the concrete retaining wall that separated the racing surface from the long low set of grandstands that ran the length of the backstretch. It was in this very set of grandstands that Rob as a boy had watched his first race. It seemed so very many years ago. These stands had originally lined the front stretch when the track had been a true oval, before the start/finish line and pit road were flip-flopped to where they were now. The change in configuration had accomplished what the track owners had hoped, boosting the speeds of what had already been one of the fastest of the unrestricted racetracks. And that, accordingly, had increased the tension and nervousness of everyone who had to compete at this place.

Rob wasn't thinking about any of that, though, as he pushed the car out to within inches of the retaining wall coming off turn two. It seemed to everyone watching that the car would inevitably graze the wall, that there was no way it could come so close without at least scraping before zipping down the short back straightaway. But Rob knew precisely where he was, within inches, and he kept the gas hard to the floor, trying to milk every ounce of speed he could get out of the powerful qualifying motor that sat out there in front of him, responding obediently to his every command.

Once the close pass by the wall was behind him, he lined the car up going into turn three, again tapping the brakes gently, expertly, perfectly. Then, renewing the clench of his jaw, he took aim on the turn itself. The car shook and shuddered and bucked, but she stayed where he knew she needed to stay.

"Easy! Easy now!"

At first, he thought the voice was his own. But he still had his teeth clenched. And there was no crackle of static that would have accompanied a radio transmission. No time to wonder who was riding along with him, advising him. He simply accepted the words and watched the track unspool in front of the nose of the car.

He mechanically followed the instructions though, avoiding the natural urge to overdrive the car into the corner in an attempt to find that last extra hundredth of a second that might possibly be wrung from the car. And there it was. That familiar feeling that someone else was actually steering the car, that Rob Wilder was little more than a passenger, along for the wild and woolly ride. But whoever was in charge, the car stuck to its line, never bobbling one iota as she came charging through the corner, running flat-out to take the checkered flag.

Will stood, stopwatch in hand, anxiously watching the car and not the hand on the clock's face. They had to have a smooth lap if they had a prayer of making the race. The car had sailed hard off into turn one without even the slightest of bobbles over the bump there that sometimes gave raw drivers enough of a start to cause them to ease slightly.

Not his boy.

Then the car stayed low, right down next to the white line before pushing out against the wall as she roared down what Will still thought of as the "old front stretch."

As the car nosed off into turn three, it appeared that the kid was doing precisely what was needed. Will stole a quick glance at the stopwatch, more out of habit than any hope of actually being able to decipher what kind of speeds they were accomplishing out there. He realized then that he was, at that moment, more nervous than he had ever been at a racetrack. And so far, Will Hughes had been in plenty of pressure-cooker situations in his young racing career. But now, his stomach tied itself into a knot as he stood there his fingers crossed, the numbers spinning across the face of the stopwatch. His eyes were locked on the car for which he was responsible as it charged low through turns three and four on its first Winston Cup qualifying attempt.

"Come on, cowboy! Come on," he urged in a hoarse whisper that was drowned out by the jetlike noise of the Ford. "Smooth as silk. Don't overdrive it, young'un," he implored as the car seemed to stay where his young driver wanted to keep it, pegged right down on the inside line as it swept through the corners.

A slight smile crossed Will's face as the car raced back

to the checkers. It may not have been the fastest run of the day. May not even have been in the top thirty or forty. But the kid had actually finished a solid, clean lap. He had run without mishap from green to checkered.

As Rob flashed past, throttle wide open and engine singing as he took the flag, Will clicked the stopwatch and quickly took note of the numbers. The time was a tick under twenty-nine seconds according to his watch. That wasn't the source whose opinion counted, though.

It seemed like forever before the official time finally flashed up on the giant scoreboard mounted to the back of the tractor trailer in the infield.

Twenty-eight-ninety-two. And they were now, unofficially, a Cup team.

Will shrugged his shoulders and looked over at Billy Winton. It was a solid time to be sure. Not as fast as they had hoped but certainly as good as they could have expected. Now, would it be fast enough to hold up and keep them in the field for the race? With better than twenty cars left to qualify, including a bunch of good fast veterans, there was still a better than reasonable chance that they could get themselves bumped.

Still, Will thought, it was a superb effort on the part of the team, considering all the work they had done over the last month getting this car ready to race. And considering all the preparation they had been doing at the same time on the Grand National cars, keeping them competitive during the last few races of the season. The look on Billy's face told Will he agreed.

Back inside the Ford, Rob had urged the car across the stripe and then looked back at the still-fluttering checkered flag before he finally allowed himself the luxury of a breath of fresh air. Only then did he realize that he had apparently not breathed during the entire thirty seconds of the last lap. He concentrated on sucking in and letting out air as he steered through the cool-down lap and on back into the pits.

Normally he could have recited each detail of a completed qualifying lap, every single bump or bounce on the track. This time, though, his mind was surprisingly blank as he tried to recall where and how he had put the car during the lap. He shut the Ford's engine off as he coasted down the entrance to pit road so it could start cooling.

A strange feeling settled over him as he steered the now-silent car back toward the garage. Typically, he would have been eager to get his time, maybe begging Will to tell him what his watch showed even before he could see the results on the scoring kiosk. But this time, Rob was surprisingly relaxed, almost unconcerned about how he had done on the run. He waited patiently for the call from Will with the results. He knew it wasn't a pole-winning run but he had been realistic going in. Merely making the starting grid had been his goal, the team's goal. They had never planned on pacing the field down to the line to take the green flag to begin the race on Sunday. He had done what he had set out to do: he got a good, clean lap in, no slipups trying to overdrive the car.

Billy and Michelle hurried back to the garage to meet the car at their stall. Michelle assumed from Billy's and Will's faces that they were not displeased with the run. As they trotted along together, she finally asked.

"Are we okay?"

"He had a good, smooth lap. Not as fast as we hoped but right in the range we expected. That was a heck of lap the kid ran. One heck of a lap."

She noticed Billy wasn't even breathing hard, even though they were actually jogging now. She was in good shape but she had to pick up the pace to keep up with him.

"Where will we start?"

"Don't know yet. Still some good cars to make their runs. At this level, they're all good, though. Won't be but a tick's difference between the pole and the back marker."

She understood what Billy wasn't saying. That many factors would tell who started where, who finished where. And that included conditions totally out of everyone's control, like tomorrow's weather.

Donnie was already pulling at the Ford's window net, trying to drop it down, when Michelle and Billy showed up. They paused to allow the black number 3 to coast past from its own run, heading to its own garage stall. The entire garage area now bustled with activity, cars coming and going, teams scurrying to get their racers out to qualify or already going under the hoods to make changes, already getting set for the race itself.

As soon as the window was down, Rob reached up to the roof railing and pulled himself out of the car. He was surprised to feel sweat on his forehead and face when the chilly wind hit him. He fished a rag out of his pocket and wiped his brow.

"Where's Will?" he asked.

"Still out there watching the rest of the cars take their runs," Billy answered. "He's one nervous cat right now."

The reason for Will's apprehension was obvious to everyone. That is, everyone but Rob Wilder.

"If we are good enough, we're good enough," he said matter-of-factly. "If not, we'll adjust a little more and I'll take her back out there tomorrow and put her in the field. No big deal."

Billy could only chuckle. Confidence was one thing the kid didn't lack. Someone with less of that precious commodity could easily worry himself right out of the race. Nope, Billy would take Rob Wilder, maybe a tad naïve, maybe a bit cocksure. He much preferred a driver who assumed he was going to win every time he took the car out on the track. And that's one of the reasons he had chosen a young, unknown, inexperienced pilot for his car. What he lacked in seasoning he more than made up for in confidence and talent.

They drifted over to the computer monitor and stood there watching as the latest qualifiers and their run times were flashed on the screen. It also listed out where each driver would start based on the times so far.

They all groaned in unison each time the results flashed up and their slot fell farther downward.

With about ten cars to go, it became evident that their time would not be fast enough to keep them in the top twenty-five. The question quickly became whether the speed would be good enough to keep them from having to make a second qualifying attempt the next day.

Will paced nervously back and forth in his spot on pit road, fidgeting as each new car pulled out onto the line to make its run. If they were still in the top thirty at the end of the day, it would be a tough decision as to whether or not they should try to improve their time the next day with a second run. If they ended up the day any worse than that, the decision would have been made for them.

This was the toughest part of racing for Will Hughes. If you showed up with a good fast car, if you posted a top ten or fifteen speed, it was not only exhilarating and a huge confidence builder, but it also allowed the team to concentrate on setting the car up for the race itself. Otherwise, precious time and effort would have to be used to get a decent qualifying spot during the second day's round. Will supposed that was something he would have to get used to for a while at the Cup level. At least until they got their program realigned for the almost unbelievable level of competition they would be facing every single weekend from now on. And the decision they would likely be looking at come the end of first-day qualifying was a prime example of how it likely would be for the next little while.

Will watched the last car finish its qualifying run then checked the final posting of the lineup.

They were thirtieth on the grid.

He shook his head. It would be a long night back at the hotel. Will headed back to the garage to pick up the notebooks he would need at the hotel, already running the lists and options through his head.

To requalify or to stand on their time—a wrong decision could abort their first Cup attempt in a rather ignoble way.

Part **3**

PREPARING FOR BATTLE

The winner is determined before the battle begins.

—Chinese general Sun-Tzu in *The Art of War,*
a volume on Billy Winton's bookshelf

4

LONG NIGHT

Rob sniffed the air around himself pointedly, then quickly disappeared into the truck to change out of his sweaty driving suit. He and Michelle had plans for a dinner with a couple of Ensoft's key customers from Atlanta. He usually didn't mind doing whatever his primary sponsor asked him to do. This evening, though, he had his mind on other things and actually wished he could wiggle out of the date. He would have preferred grabbing a pizza with extra sausage or a burger-all-the-way, corral Will Hughes, and go on back to the hotel and spend the evening going over their notebooks. He figured his time would be far better spent trying to unlock the secrets of their new race car so they could figure a way to coax a tad more speed from her.

Rob noticed his arms and neck were still stiff from all the day's tension and his firm grip on the wheel during practice and qualifying. When he stripped off the sleeves and top of the suit, his sweat-soaked T-shirt clung to his body. He shivered in the cool air. He had not noticed at all how hot he must have gotten in the car, even over the course of such a short run on the track. Then he realized he had likely been perspiring more from the anxiety of trying to run a perfect lap than from the hot air inside the car.

He stuck his head out the door of the lounge. "We have time to go back to the hotel first, Michelle?"

She looked at him sideways, hands on her hips. "No. No way. With the way traffic is in this town, we'll be lucky to get there on time now. Not that I wouldn't love a chance to change out of these clothes and into something that's not dirty and wrinkled and smells like gasoline."

Michelle usually preferred dressing well, but lately she had adopted the standard racetrack casual uniform of slacks or jeans and a golf shirt, then added a racing jacket once cool weather moved in.

"So, where we going?" Rob asked through the crack in the door as he slid off his driving shoes.

"A little bistro in Buckhead," she answered distract-edly as she punched away on her palmtop computer, al-ready reviewing her schedule for the next day. "It's supposed to be really good. I think you'll like it."

"I doubt that I would like anything they could serve up at any place called a 'beestrow,' " Rob mumbled to himself as he peeled off the rest of the driving suit. The nearest fried chicken buffet would have been far more to his liking. He had to admit, though, that all the traveling and dining in different styles of restaurants were working on changing his palate. "Sounds good to me," he an-swered cheerfully, but this time loud enough so she could actually hear what he was saying.

It wasn't Michelle's fault they had to go all the way across town to this dinner tonight after a full day at the track. She would be working just as he was. And they were still down South so there was always the slightest possibility that they might have something on the menu that he would recognize.

"You take longer to get ready to go than a woman," she called.

"Let me rinse off in the shower here real fast, and then we can head out."

He lingered awhile in the warm water in the cramped shower, letting the soap wash away the tension, then he dried off and pulled on the bright red Ensoft logo golf shirt and a pair of black designer slacks. They were a recent addition to his wardrobe, compliments of Ensoft and Michelle Fagan. She had given them to him and pointedly told him to wear them to casual dinner meetings instead of his preferred worn and faded jeans.

Whatever his reservations about going out tonight, he knew he would simply take a deep breath, go on and enjoy himself, just as he usually did. It was for a good cause, after all, and these dinners always seemed to come back to help the team get better some way, however indirectly. He could do this part of the job as surely as he could the driving part. Even when the salads showed up with rose petals on them and the fish was surrounded by odd steamed vegetables instead of hush puppies and french fries.

Rob was still combing his wet hair when he emerged from the hauler's changing area.

"Give me just one more second," Michelle said as she scribbled a few more notes on the green screen of the electronic planner.

He took advantage of the opportunity to stick his head back into the changing room, giving a last look at the way long blond locks were arranged. He tucked his shirttail in, straightened the crease of his new slacks, and decided he looked as presentable as he possibly could.

"Whew, look at how pretty he is, boys!" It was one of

the crew members, more than ready to give him a hard time as usual.

"I'll say," another one of them chimed in. "Ain't a girl safe in Atlanta tonight."

The kidding continued as several other members of the crew shuffled into the lounge to warm up after they had finished securing the race car for the night. Rob turned a color not more than a few shades off the hue of the Ford. He hated it when they picked on him in front of Michelle or Christy, and they, of course, knew it. That only caused them to do it as often as they could manage.

He took Michelle's arm and guided her out of the hauler.

"Slow down! We have plenty of time," she said, scooping up her purse off the seat as he dragged her toward the door.

"I've had enough of these silly jackasses for one day."

"They're just having a little fun at your expense."

"They're always having fun at my expense."

He was leading her quickly through the garage area toward the rental car parked in the infield. It was just outside the fence from where all the tractor trailers sat lined up in a row.

"Lighten up," Michelle advised with a laugh. "If you didn't make yourself such an easy target, they'd find somebody else to pick on."

"They treat me like I'm a little kid. I want them to show me the kind of respect the other drivers get."

Michelle stopped cold and looked up into his face. "You are a little kid to them, Rob. You remind them of their own children or at least their kid brothers. Everybody except Will, that is. I think he sees you as the little brother he never had."

"Okay, I guess you're right," Rob said, chastened. "As usual, I might add. I know if I'd just act like it didn't get to me then they'd leave me alone."

"Yes. And remember, if they didn't like you so much, they wouldn't be picking on you."

They hurried along through the infield then, crossing through the gate leading to where the car waited. The brisk breeze caused them to rush along even though they had plenty of time to reach the restaurant. Plenty of time provided the notorious Atlanta traffic didn't get in the way, of course.

Rob drove, since Michelle had more telephone calls to make. Business was still being done three time zones away on the West Coast. They were already well past the busy airport and headed north in the bustling rush-hour traffic downtown before she could pause long enough to take a breath.

Rob sang along quietly to the song on the radio, ignoring all she was saying into the tiny phone as he wound around and through the traffic, past the gold-domed state capitol building. It was only a midsize rental car on a jammed freeway, but he enjoyed driving it anyway.

Rob didn't get back to the hotel until well after eleven o'clock. He waltzed right on past his own room and tapped gently on Will's door. When he opened the door, Rob could see Will was still in his stocking feet, still wearing his work clothes from the track. There was a half-eaten box of room-service pizza lying on the bed and notebooks and papers strewn all over the room. Will's ever-present laptop computer sat unhinged on the small desk, its screen glowing warmly.

"I figured you might still be up," Rob said as he brushed past Will and invited himself into the room.

"Yeah, I'm not all that sleepy, I don't guess. I've been going over everything one more time, trying to see if we've missed anything in the setup. Something . . . anything . . . that might give us a boost."

"Find anything yet?" Rob asked, settling down lengthwise on the bed within arm's reach of the pizza.

Will nodded toward the open box. Dinner engagement or not, he figured the kid was still hungry. Rob didn't hesitate. He grabbed a slice and attacked it. It sure was a far cry more tasty than his so-called dinner, a dry slab of duck breast covered in bland pear sauce with a few whole, crunchy half-cooked green beans on the side.

"I've spent all night, and I gotta admit that I can't find anything so far," Will said, picking up one of the notebooks and idly thumbing through it. "There are some sodas in the cooler over there. How 'bout tossing me one, too."

"So, reckon can I help?" he asked as he tossed a soda can over to Will.

"I could use all the help I can get. I sure as heck wish I had a better book of notes, though."

"Well, why don't we take it from the top?" Rob nodded toward the remaining slices of pizza. "You mind?"

"Eat all of it if you want. We just haven't quite hit the right shock-and-spring combination under her yet. I don't know if playing with the weight ratios front to back will help or not. But we need something."

"Let's go through it step-by-step. I've got all night if you do," Rob said, reaching across the bed with the hand that didn't hold the loaded slab of pizza pie and picking up one of the notebooks.

"I guess we can give it one more run-through before calling it a night."

Will punctuated his sentence with the pop of the top on his can of soda. Rob absentmindedly wiped the sauce off his hand on his new slacks as he began sizing up the rows of figures and scrawled notes on the notebook's pages.

Before long they were lost in all the data, speaking a language foreign to most, desperately but deliberately looking for the elusive haystack needle that would mean a far more successful second day in Cup racing than today. Billy Winton had once told Rob that more than a few races were won in hotel rooms the night before they were to be run.

He hadn't doubted him then and he certainly didn't now.

5

STAND OR RUN?

The next morning dawned hazy and cool, a fog obscuring the streets around the hotel and a brisk wind hinting at approaching winter. It had been well after one o'clock in the morning before Rob and Will finally settled on the changes they wanted to try to make on the car before practice the next morning. They would also need to watch some of the other cars during these sessions to see if those teams' late-night skull sessions might have led them to some positive changes, too. Unless some of the other teams found ways to coax a lot more speed out of their cars and showed it in the first session, then Will pretty much decided that they would stand on their time from the previous day. But he was a long way from sure that that would be their strategy.

Rob walked along groggily, hands in his jacket pocket and bent over against the early morning chill, as he followed the others to the van for the trip over to the track. The boys in the crew were surprisingly quiet this morning, their banter and mocking as scarce as the rays of a warming sun. That signaled that they must have spent a late night out, prowling around the various night spots in and around Atlanta. As he considered the tight, gray faces on Donnie, Paul, and the rest of them, Rob was once again thankful that he still wasn't old enough even to get into any of those places, much less foolish enough to do it. Unlike many of his counterparts, he was more than happy to focus on racing and winning and leaving the other cats to do the prowling if they so desired.

He had never had a hangover in his young life but he suspected such a malady would be quite a distraction when he climbed into a race car and fired up the ear-splitting engine. Rob couldn't, for the life of him, understand the attraction of bouncing from club to club, getting loaded, and then suffering the consequences the next day. But then, he was not one to judge those who did.

The team arrived at the garage area just as it opened for the day. Will spread out the list of changes on the hood then began assigning each crewman a set of tasks to perform. Rob stepped up inside the hauler with him to choose the new set of shocks they had decided the night before to put under the car. Will placed the pairs they picked in the Shock Dyno, checking to make sure they actually carried the correct pressure. A slight variation could make a big difference in how this day went. Rob watched as Will meticulously tested each one. Precisely picking the right shock absorbers had become one of the trickiest parts of setting up a race car in the last few years. Gone were the days of taking a set out of the box, bolting them on the car, and then forgetting about them.

"Here are the ones for the right side. Front, rear," Will said, noting where each one went as he adjusted the safety glasses he wore. "How about taking them out to Paul so they can start bolting them on?"

"Okay, I'll be right back."

Rob grabbed the two shocks and headed back to where the car sat in the garage. When he got within sight of the Ford, he stopped cold, his mouth open in amazement.

The car looked nothing like it had only a few minutes before when he and Will had left to check the shocks. Now she sat up on jack stands, the pairs of Goodyear tires removed and stacked on either side. Both the hood and trunk were popped open, exposing the innards of the car. Parts and pieces were scattered everywhere, as if there might have been some kind of explosion. Tools lay on the concrete, on the roof, along the top of the radiator, and even on the ground underneath the machine.

It was hard to imagine that this was the same car he had driven at close to a hundred and ninety miles an hour only the afternoon before. Or that had looked like a perfectly trackworthy race car mere minutes ago. Or that was expected to run like the wind again in a short while.

But even in the middle of the apparent chaos, it was clear that there was some kind of regimented organization. Each member of the crew worked on a specific project that Will detailed before the group started working. The team labored together, meshing like well-greased gears. The racket of metal banging on metal, of tools clanging on the concrete of the garage floor, seemed to have its own syncopated rhythm.

Rob looked around for Paul Phillips, but he was nowhere to be seen. But then, as he walked around to the other side of the car, he finally spied a familiar pair of legs protruding from under the right rear of the racer.

"Hey, old man! I've got your shocks for the right side," he called as he nudged the booted foot.

"Pass 'em on down," Paul answered, sticking out a hand. "I been waitin' all morning for them."

Phillips was careful to match the shocks to the right spots on the car. He pushed the one for the right front up toward the front fender well so there could be no mistake where it went, then he began to bolt the right rear one in place on the car. Rob bent down to watch.

"Want to help me with the front one?" Paul asked.

Rob grinned. He still loved to have a wrench in his hand. Not as much as a steering wheel or the gearshift, but he enjoyed helping with the car.

"Yeah, I'll get it from the top side," Rob said, sliding along on his knees in that direction.

Rob was still working on the car when Will showed up with the other two shocks. Donnie and the engine tuner from Lee Racing were both kneeling inside the fender wells as they jetted the carburetors, adjusting them for the day's weather conditions.

Will grinned as he watched Rob work for a moment. The kid was whistling tunelessly, his face all screwed up with concentration, obviously enjoying the work. He finally touched Rob on the shoulder.

"Better change into that driving suit, cowboy. Practice starts in half an hour. We can finish with the car."

"I guess time got away from me," Rob replied as he slid from underneath the car. They'd finished the shocks and had been working on adjusting the rear sway bar. "Michelle here yet?"

"Yeah, she's over at the truck talking to Billy. She was wondering where you disappeared to. She brought your drinks."

"Did she mention anything about Christy?"

Rob felt guilty for not calling Christy when he got back from the restaurant the night before. Then, when he and Will had become engulfed in their long night's work, he had forgotten all about it.

"Maybe you ought to ask her yourself when you get over there to change clothes. I'm in charge of the car.

You're on your own when it comes to your love life."
Will pointedly picked up a clipboard that had been lying
on the roof of the car. The crew members had been
checking off each task as it had been completed and there
were apparently quite a few items with no check mark
next to them. "We still have a ton of work to do on this
car in the next thirty minutes unless you think you can
practice it without tires on it."

"Will, you know . . ." Rob started to reply. But then
he realized that Will was merely stating a fact, not picking on him like the others did. He winked. "I do need to
go and get changed. I'll be back in a few minutes."

Rob crossed over to the truck, looking at his watch,
deducting the hours in his head to see if it might be too
early on the West Coast for him to call Christy now, or
if he even had time to call and still get ready before the
practice started. He concluded yes, it was too early, and
no, he didn't have time to do a decent call. He hoped she
would understand when he explained that he and Will
had been so involved in getting ready for the day, for the
next biggest race in his career, that he had not been able
to call her. Hoped that she would not be mad that he had
not even tried to find out if she was coming all the way
across the country to see him, to watch him run.

But he could only hope.

A blast of cold wind hit him in the face. He looked at
his watch again, checking to see if maybe it would tell a
different story this time.

Billy Winton and Michelle Fagan were inside the
truck, magazine slicks and publicity photos littering the
workbench top. They looked up when he came in and
offered their good mornings and a cup of coffee. He acknowledged with his patented movie-star smile, declined
the brew, and, when their heads immediately dipped back
to the work they were doing, he disappeared into the tiny
changing area.

He'd ask Michelle later if Christy was coming. Maybe after practice.

His mind was awhirl as he stripped out of his jeans and T-shirt and pulled on the driver's suit. There was a lot to learn in a short period of time during the practice, and he would be a key part of that effort. Had they gained anything with the morning's work so far? Would they try to requalify the car or decide to stand on yesterday's time? Would they ultimately get bumped by the others who did a better job of preparation last night and this morning than they had? Would they be headed back north before the day was over, devoid of anything to show for their first run at Winston Cup? And would he finally get to see Christy for the first time since Labor Day in Darlington, now better than two months past?

Rob zipped up the bright red driving suit and quickly hung his clothes in one of the lockers along the wall. He laced up the driving shoes and emerged from the changing room, then headed straight for the refrigerator in the lounge and fished out a plastic bottle of water.

Billy looked up again from the advertising materials he and Michelle were studying.

"You ready, kid?"

It was Billy Winton's standard question. He always knew the answer he would get from his confident young driver.

"I was ready when I crawled out of the rack this morning. Will and I stayed up half the night working on the setup. He thinks he's figured out what we were missing. I just want to get this baby out on the track and crank out some more laps. I think we'll be fast this morning. Real fast."

He showed his white teeth again and gave them the "okay" sign.

"If I know Will, he'll figure this car out or wear the tops off the bolts changing it till he does."

"We got it figured out. The boys are putting the setup under her now."

Billy stood up and headed for the door.

"Well, come on then. Let's get on over there and see what the two of you cooked up last night while the rest of the crew was out painting the town Ensoft red."

They passed Stacy Locklear's garage stall on the way. The driver was leaned back against a wall, holding court with a few fans who had finagled garage passes. He looked up when Rob, Billy, and Michelle walked past.

"I see you had a tough time yesterday, rookie," he called to Rob. "Looks like your first chance to get in my way's gonna be when I put that first lap on you."

The fans giggled. Rob kept walking. "Good luck to you, too, Stacy," he said.

"Provided you don't get your butt bumped right out of the race today. Maybe you oughta go on back to Grand National and see if you can make a living there first."

The assembled group of fans sniggered again, but nervously this time. It didn't sound as if Locklear was kidding at all. His tone was much more serious.

"And a Merry Christmas, too," Rob replied with a broad smile, still walking on.

Billy Winton slapped him on the back. "Don't pay any mind to the likes of someone like that. There's only one way to handle somebody like Stacy Locklear. Ignore him and let him eat your exhaust smoke out on the track. Those that can do it don't have to talk about it!"

Billy had noticed all week that his driver didn't seem intimidated in the least by the other racers in the garage, regardless of how big the names. Most of them had simply been ignoring Rob as if he wasn't really a factor in their lives at all. To many of the veteran drivers, rookies like Rob Wilder either were no threat to worry about or were accidents-in-the-making, sent by the racing gods to deny them their shot at winning the race. Sometimes seeming to be invisible was more of a slam to a driver's ego than harsh words, like those of Stacy Locklear. Of course, some drivers would go out of their way to give young drivers a welcome and perhaps throw some pointers their way, but they were generally few and far between.

Regardless of what kind of reception he had gotten, though, Rob Wilder seemed to be taking it all in stride. He had come all the way from Chandler Cove, Tennessee, to give the Ford the best run he could, and that's exactly what he intended to do. He really didn't care about what anybody else thought.

Most of the drivers and teams were simply too busy with their own preparations for this season-ending race to pay much attention to young Rob Wilder or anybody else. This would be their last shot at capping off a successful season, or the final place where they might have a chance to turn around an abysmal campaign. There was too much at stake for most of them to take more than a passing interest in newcomers. That was another reason that Will, Billy, and even Jodell Lee had preached to him that whatever else he did this weekend, he had to keep out of everyone else's way. Go out there and do something silly, end up wrecking one of the contenders, and he would spend years trying to rebuild the ill will he had created in a split second out there on the racetrack.

Billy would now admit that he, too, was excited about the prospects of getting the car out on the track. If the speeds picked up like he hoped they would, they should be in good shape for the 500 on Sunday. But he also tempered that excitement with the realization that this was just a taste of what was hopefully to come next year. The real test would come in February in Daytona. But every time he had even a fleeting thought of Daytona in February, Billy Winton was dragged right back to the reality of all the work yet to be done. It was an almost overwhelming sensation.

The car had miraculously been pieced back together by the time Rob and the rest of them walked up. It actually looked like a race car once again and not some horrible roadside accident. Donnie was busy with one of the air guns, bolting on the last of the tires. The shrill screech of the gun filled the garage as the last of the lug nuts were tightened. Once finished, the car was gently lowered down off the set of jack stands onto the concrete floor.

Will Hughes was sitting there on a toolbox, feverishly updating his notes, documenting the morning's changes. The rest of the boys were putting the tools and extra parts back into their proper places so they could locate them in a hurry if need be.

Billy surveyed everything before nodding his satisfaction with the preparations on the car. As far as anybody could tell, she was ready for the track. Will hopped off the toolbox and stepped around the car to where Billy, Michelle, and Rob waited. He studied his driver's face, trying to read his intensity, his frame of mind. He seemed relaxed enough as he bantered with Michelle, telling some tale about their dinner the night before at the "bee-strow" in Buckhead.

Yes, the car was as ready as they could make it. Their driver seemed relaxed and ready, too. Soon, they would know. And soon, they would have all the input they needed to decide which way to go on the day's qualifying session.

Once in the car and on the track, Rob gave the gauges one last look as he guided her down the back straight-away. It was time for the first hard lap. He allowed her to drift high through turns three and four then hammered the gas pedal with his right foot, jamming it down to where the metal of the floorboard would let it go no farther. Joe Banker's perfectly tuned motor jumped to new life under his feet, singing contentedly as it sent him and the car off briskly.

Rob steered through the quad-oval portion of the raceway and felt as if he were strapped to a missile as the car shot past the start/finish line. He could feel every ripple in the track transmitted up through the car's suspension as vibrations resonated up through the steel of the steering column and into the padded wheel, which throbbed in his gloved hands. Rob didn't seem to notice, though, as he reveled in the awesome feel of raw power that he alone controlled. There was no other sensation in racing or in life quite like the sheer stimulation from the speeds at places like Daytona, Talladega, Charlotte, or Atlanta. The bigger and faster the track the more Rob rejoiced in the primal thrill of it all.

He heard the tires begin to screech in protest as he held the car down as low in the corner as he dared. The Ford bounced over the turn-one bump, causing Rob to grip the wheel even tighter in an effort to keep the pressure from jerking it away from him. The G-forces propelled him down deeper into the seat, even as the centrifugal forces through the turn shoved him hard up against the seat's right-side padding. His helmet rested tightly against the side of the headrest, too, as he worked the pedals expertly, urging the car emphatically up and off the second corner then out onto the backstretch.

He continued to push things, trying to get a feel for the new setup. As he sensed the car's response through the corner, he could tell that it was considerably more comfortable to drive than it had been the day before. The severe push off the corner was gone. She felt better in the center of the corner as well. Rob forgot about the sluggishness from the previous day and concentrated on getting the car around the track as fast as he could push it so Will and the crew could get a good feel for how far they had come with the recent preparations.

Rob was only getting warmed up when Will called him back in for the first time. The kid would have been content to continue circling until he ran out of gas, but Will wanted to get a tire check to see how the temperatures were building up across the rubber, to get a reading on what the air pressure had risen to.

Will liked what he saw in those early laps. The times were not all that much better than before, but he could tell the car was handling better through the corners, that his driver was not having to fight to get that impetus. Will trotted back to meet the car as it came down onto pit road then made the hard left-hand turn into the garage area.

Rob coasted up to their stall, where Donnie and the others waited patiently, armed with the proper tools. Will was already barking orders for checks and changes over the radio so not a minute of precious practice time would be wasted. The tire temperatures were taken, the sheets handed in the window to Rob for him to study. Michelle offered Rob a bottle of water, but there had not been enough track time to get him thirsty yet, so he declined. He did accept the offered towel and wiped away the sweat that already streaked his face.

"How'd we look?" he finally asked no one in particular.

"Real good. The last lap you ran was a twenty-eight eighty-five. Will looked real pleased." It had been Michelle Fagan who had answered his question. Everyone else was busy.

"I think if I could have run a couple of more laps I could have picked up another tenth. Those new shocks sure did help in the corners."

The right side of the car was being jacked up as he spoke. Donnie and Paul were banging ferociously on something in the right rear fender well.

"From what I hear, you're going to get plenty of laps in the next hour. He wants to make one or two more small adjustments, then he wants you to do fifteen to twenty laps to see how the car changes on a longer run."

"Good. I hate all these little one- and two-lap runs to test a change, then you come in and sit stock-still for five or ten minutes. I'd rather be out there where the action is, cranking off the laps and flying."

Rob took the water bottle the second time she offered it, unscrewed the cap, tilted it up, and drank as if he was parched.

"Don't give me that. As long as you're sitting in a race car you're happy as a clam," Michelle said as she leaned back against the car next to the driver's window.

"Okay, you got me figured out," he said, yelling to be heard over the banging.

"I gotta watch out for my little sister, make sure she knows what she's letting herself in for."

He saw the opening and he drove through. "Speaking of which, is she coming in tonight or not?"

"I don't know. Didn't you talk to her last night?"

"Well . . . uh . . . no. Will and I . . . we got so wrapped up . . . then it was so late. . . ."

"You should've called," Michelle chided sternly. "But I figured you wouldn't, so *I did*. Toby's going to stop and pick her up at the airport in Pasadena later this afternoon if they get the word that we made the race."

"Call 'em now! We're going to make the race."

Rob tossed her the water bottle just as he saw Will tap the hood, signaling they were finished, that he could return to the track. Rob cranked up and screeched away with renewed vigor.

Christy was coming!

Bubba Baxter stepped up into the back of Billy's hauler minutes after the practice session ended. Their driver was in the field, set to go from near the front. Now, he was happy to join Billy, Will, and Rob around the table in the lounge. The notes from the morning practice were spread all over the table along with a list of the practice speeds posted by most of the cars that that qualified behind them. It was crunch time. They had to decide right then whether or not they needed to make a second qualifying effort or whether it would be smarter to sit on what they had already.

Six cars would have to beat their time from the previous day to send them packing. Normally, that would mean the decision to keep what they had would be the wiser one. But the times some of the laggards from the day before had posted this morning during practice suggested they might be able to move up. Could six cars beat them? That was the question they needed to answer.

Bubba and Billy relied on all their years of experience and that certain intuition that comes from having done this very thing so many times before. They looked carefully through the notes and speed charts laid out before them.

Will was nervous and admitted that he would prefer making another qualifying run. He argued that it made even more sense because they had managed to pick up another couple of tenths during their own morning practice.

Rob was confident, too, and voted with Will. He knew he could pick up his qualifying time. If they agreed that he should make another run then he was game. He would put them solidly in the field.

"Well? What do you gurus think?" Will finally asked when Bubba leaned back from the table and took a big swig of his cola.

The big man didn't answer at once. He got up slowly and walked over to the counter where a pile of sandwiches waited on a platter. He seemed to be thinking as he picked up a ham sandwich and finished it in four bites.

"That's some fine ham there," he said, and reached for another of the sandwiches. The other three men held their breath, waiting for his pronouncement. He finished the second sandwich and chased it with the rest of his soda before he spoke. "I think y'all better sit tight. Way too much can go wrong if you try to requalify, and a bunch of them old boys are going to have to find some blistering speed somewhere if they intend to bump you out of the field. All you need to do is have a slight bobble during your qualifying run or have that motor hiccup on you, and you'll be taking this rig home tonight."

"I agree," Billy chimed in, still scanning the time sheets over the top of his reading glasses. "Let the others take the risk."

"I can pick it up out there, fellas. Don't you worry," Rob said, still brimming with confidence.

"I know you can, kid, but now is not the time to take chances. We need to make this race for the sponsor, for your experience, and for my peace of mind. We just can't take the chance."

Billy leaned back, set his reading glasses down on the table, and turned to face his crew chief to see what he thought of the decision. Will was chewing on a knuckle, his eyes closed. When he looked up, he had his jaws tensed.

"I guess you guys are right." He picked up the list of the other cars' practice speeds, the ones who qualified behind them and would have to improve their own qualifying times to get ahead of them. "I just hate to settle when I know we're faster today." He knew Billy and Bubba had faced this decision plenty of times before. He also knew he should trust their judgment.

Bubba Baxter took several more of the sandwiches and piled on several whole dill pickles on top of the stack.

"I got to run. Y'all will be okay, boys. You're in. Thanks for the snack."

"Yeah, thanks for the help, Bubba. We'll catch up with you later this afternoon," Billy replied. He stood to shake the big man's hand, but realized he was loaded down with food, so he waved instead.

Sixteen cars lined up for the start of second round qualifying. It was one of the largest group of cars to attempt to better their times anyone had seen in a while. With fifty-one cars trying to make the field and with the next race almost three months away, the stakes were higher for everyone. It promised to be a tense hour or so while everyone waited to see who would be in the race and who would be jettisoned and on their way home.

Subdued crews pushed their revamped machines into their places in line. Tension was palpable all along the pit lane. This was the end of the season for some of the teams that were about to go out and make their last run. Or possibly for some of those who had decided to stand on their effort from the previous day. Their off-seasons would begin shortly. A stern look of determination marked the face of every driver who was about to make the attempt. Those who stood a chance to get eliminated looked equally focused.

The considerable crowd in the stands seemed to feel the tension, too. They were on their feet, quietly awaiting the first car to roll off the line.

A steady stream of folks climbed the ladder up to the top of the Winton Racing truck. They, too, wore grim, anxious expressions. But the decision had been made. They would soon know if it had been the proper one.

Billy led Rob and Michelle up the ladder to join Will and Bubba Baxter. Jodell Lee and Joe Banker showed up soon, too. Joe was making one of his rare visits to a racetrack. Unlike Bubba and Jodell, he had grown tired long before of the weekly grind of the circuit. He preferred staying back in Chandler Cove, nursing his new engines and playing with his grandbabies.

Joe took great delight in needling Billy Winton, giving him grief about sacrificing his comfortable retirement so he could travel all over the country and watch cars go fast. He couldn't understand why a man would deliberately accept all that punishment at Billy's age. And especially the pressures that went with the proposed move to Winston Cup so quickly after putting the team together.

Billy gave it right back to Joe, though. Banker had cut back to only fifteen or so events a year as opposed to the regular thirty-five weekends' worth of racing. He had once been one of the most serious all-night partiers on the circuit, always at the center of any soiree that might break out. People often mentioned his name in the same breath as Curtis Turner, Little Joe Weatherly, and Tiny Lund, all legendary good-timers. Now, Billy liked to point out how sedate he had become in his old age, how sad it was that he was out to pasture, swigging Geritol instead of moonshine.

There was no teasing today. They all stood quietly together, leaning slightly into the stiff breeze atop the truck.

Jodell knew what his old friend was going through. There were no provisional starting spots to fall back on. They had to make the race on speed or go home.

Bubba Baxter propped against the railing, watching the first car that had elected to make its second attempt. He chewed absently on a fried meat skin he had pulled from a big bag he held, still assuring anyone who would listen that they were fine, that they were in the race.

Will Hughes stood nearby, listening to everything the big man said. Bubba treated Will much as if he were a second son. Will, at the same time, viewed Bubba as almost a surrogate father. Without all the help and support from Bubba Baxter over the last five or six years, Will was certain he would still be working on dirt cars in somebody's backyard back home in North Carolina. The two of them talked quietly of setups and tire wear as they waited for the first car to go off the line.

Jodell Lee and Rob Wilder were disarmingly calm and relaxed. Both men knew there was nothing they could do now, that the decision not to attempt to requalify had been made and it was final. Jodell was well aware of the tension coursing through the rest of the operation, but as a driver himself, he knew that it would take more than luck for them to be bumped out of the field. The weather was a tad warmer and the wind blowing in from the southwest was much stiffer. The wind had actually picked up significantly since the morning practice. That was something the drivers would have to reckon with out there.

The group looked on in silence as the first car roared away. It built up speed, circling the track for the warm-up lap. Will clicked his stopwatch as the car flashed under the flag stand to take the green flag for the start of the timed lap. Every eye on top of the truck followed the car all the way around. Will clicked the watch again as the car crossed the line and the second car in began a slow roll off pit road. The four older men knew without checking Will's watch or the official scoring board that the first car's speed was not good enough to hurt them.

The second car was a different story, a rocket ship right off the pad. The veteran driver had made a slight bobble in one of the turns on his first attempt the day before and that had left him mired way back in the field at the end of the first round. Today, he drove like a man on a mission, to prove that it was only a fluke, that he had not lost the edge at getting around a racetrack quickly.

The car hugged the white line running around the inside of the track and was lightning fast off the corner. As it flashed across the stripe, Jodell glanced over at Billy and nodded.

That was one. Were there five more? The sign flashed the numbers up in big letters, confirming Jodell's estimate. Twenty-seventh fastest.

Five more cars took to the track and one more beat the Ensoft team's time. Will nervously studied the remaining eight cars. Billy and Jodell relaxed even more. Joe Banker had disappeared after the fifth car took to the speedway. Michelle stood off to the side, resisting the urge to chew on her fingernails, anxious to report to her boss that they had made their first Winston Cup race, to tell him he could come on out and watch them run in the big time race on Sunday.

The next car up bumped another car out of the field, but its speed was five hundredths of a second slower than Rob's time. They were still okay.

Will spent an uncomfortable few seconds after looking at his own watch. It had showed the car had been dangerously close to his own car's time. He let out a deep sigh of relief when he saw the official time flash up on the board.

Finally, there were four cars to go, and all four of the racers would have to best Rob's time in order for them to be shoved out of the field. The last two cars in line had each run times in practice that were better than Rob's qualifying speed. The other two had been close by the end of the session. That meant all four could conceivably do the trick.

The first of the four was from an underfunded team that had struggled to make races all year long. Normally none of the people on top of Billy Winton's hauler would have pulled against an underdog trying to make a go at racing. They were all painfully aware of the dreams that made men race in the first place, the effort and sacrifice a team made before it even arrived at the track. Everyone hated to see all those hopes dashed, that hard work go to waste.

Today was different.

They all grew silent as the roar of the engine reached them. They followed as the car climbed the banking in turns one and two. The pitch of the engine turned into a scream as it accelerated down the backstretch. Michelle found herself crossing her fingers as the driver charged out of the fourth turn, coming down to take the green flag. The motor was now in full song as the car flashed past the start/finish line.

The driver had a good run through turns one and two, not losing one iota of speed. Bubba stood beside Will, both men stone-faced as they watched the car push up off the corner and onto the backstretch. Jodell, Billy, and Rob all leaned on the rail, showing no emotion whatsoever as they followed the car speeding around the track.

Now, it was sailing into turn three, still right down against the white line, obviously making a fine run. Will could tell the car was flying as it hit the center of the corner. He forced himself to watch it all the way through the middle of the turn.

Suddenly, a loud boom echoed across the speedway as the engine in the car exploded. The driver wrestled with the wheel as oil from the blown engine spilled out a rupture in the block and beneath the rear tires. The car quickly looped once, then twice, before making a lazy arc toward the outside wall. The tires smoked as the driver stood on the brakes in a desperate attempt to keep the car off the wall, but it slid that way anyhow, finally hitting with just enough force to crumple the rear fender and trunk lid.

Among the group on top of the hauler, there was the usual sickening feeling as they watched a fellow racer in trouble, knowing the awful emotions he and his crew must be having at that moment. But an instant later reality set in, and the implications of the driver's misfortune really hit them. That car backing into the fence didn't get a finishing time. With three cars to go, that meant only one thing.

"We're in!" Will screamed in a burst of emotion none of them had ever seen from him before.

"Good job, good job!" Bubba beamed like a proud father.

"Yes, we made it. Can you believe it?" Will yelled as he grabbed Bubba Baxter, picked him up and danced around with him atop the truck. And that was no small feat!

Jodell turned and smiled at Billy. He took his offered hand, knowing how momentous the feeling must be for his longtime friend. It had been a long and difficult road for both of them, all the way back to their first race together in 1969, over thirty years before. This was clearly a brand-new chapter in their long careers.

Rob stood there, taking in all the goings-on atop the truck. But then, Michelle wrapped him in a tight bear hug and kissed him on the cheek.

They were going to go racing tomorrow! His first real Winston Cup race! The kid's face split in an ear-to-ear grin. When Will came dancing over to him, Rob joined in and made the jig a threesome. The impromptu dance was accompanied by lots of clapping and cheers as the celebrating began, even as the last of the cars were finishing their runs.

Will Hughes understood what a major milestone this was in his own career. This was why he had left Jodell Lee to crew chief for Billy Winton in the first place: to lead his own team to Winston Cup. He quickly scurried down the ladder to join the rest of the boys, to share the moment with the others who had worked so hard for this moment to happen. Donnie Kline waited at the bottom of the ladder where the two hugged each other unashamedly. For this crew, this moment was practically as good as a win.

Later on, making the field would be just another day's work. But not today. Today, it was truly something to celebrate. First races happened only one time in a career.

Once the reality of making the field had settled in, Rob couldn't quite understand what all the fuss was about. After all, he had never doubted that they would make the race. They had a car that was capable and, if it had been deemed the better plan, he had been more than prepared to take it out again for qualifying. Yes, he was glad he made the field, yet he could not understand why people kept coming over to congratulate him. Even all the strangers on the other teams. Jodell pointed out to him that most folks in racing were like family, that everyone actually wanted to see each other do well. All these folks were sincerely happy for Rob and the team. Today it was his turn and the outpouring of goodwill was genuine.

Jodell walked Rob down to the qualifying board where all the cars and their times were posted. A photographer came up and snapped several pictures of Rob standing there, smiling broadly, pointing at his time on the board. Jodell joined him for several more pictures before they walked slowly along the line of trucks back toward their own hauler. The old driver put his arm around the kid as he spoke.

"Kid, enjoy today 'cause this will be a big moment in your career that you'll remember forever."

"Aw, Jodell, this seems like just another day at the track for me. I did what I came down here to do. That's all."

"This isn't Grand National racing. Here, you're up against the best, and every week you're going to have to get better if you plan to stay at this level."

"I know, Jodell, but I feel like I can hold my own

against these guys. If I didn't, I wouldn't be here. I just don't know why everybody is making such a big deal out of it."

"I'll tell you why they make a big deal out of it. See that car over there?"

"Yeah."

"That's a two-time Winston Cup Champion loading his car up to go home. Tomorrow afternoon, he'll be sitting in his living room at home watching you race on TV 'cause he wasn't fast enough to make the field." Jodell paused a moment to let his point hit home. "I can tell you right now that it's eating away at his gut knowing that he won't be in that race tomorrow with the rest of you. That, son, is why you need to savor this moment."

Rob nodded, completely comprehending now. Right there in front of him, the joys and heartaches of this sport were perfectly contrasted.

Jodell's point had been made very well, but he stopped, looked Rob in the eye, and drove it home. "Enjoy the high points, son. The memories might come in handy when the low ones come galloping along."

Part **4**

MAKING NOISE

Noise proves nothing. Often a hen who has merely laid
an egg cackles as if she had laid an asteroid.

—Mark Twain

6

POSTMORTEM

It was a sobering experience, sitting in the shop the following Monday morning, still groggy from the drive home, reviewing the results from their first Winston Cup race. Gone was the heady thrill of lining the car up on race morning with all the stars, their race cars strung out there in front of 140,000 people. The nervous flutter in Rob Wilder's stomach as he walked across the stage at the drivers' introductions was nothing more than a memory now. So was the wonderfully loud roar of the crowd that had been, in fact, the combined force of thousands of voices, all of them cheering for him when his name was called.

But there was one person among those thousands whose cheers meant more than all the others combined. Christy Fagan had given him a good-luck kiss before he walked to the car. Then, she had waved to him from atop the hauler where she would be watching him. She was breathtakingly beautiful, and she had come a couple of thousand miles to watch him run his first race in Cup competition. That had to be a good omen, too.

Rob remembered vividly the command to start the engines, the feeling of power as the motor rumbled to life, the call over the radio from Will Hughes alerting him to the dropping of the green flag so far up ahead of where he ran that he couldn't actually see it yet. He could also still feel the sensation of acceleration as he mashed the gas pedal clear down to the floorboard; still relive the thrill of charging off into turn one for the first time, chasing cars driven by men who had been his idols but were now his competitors; still recall the excitement of passing some of those familiarly painted and numbered cars as he deliberately made his way closer to the front.

No matter what happened, no one would ever be able to take those memories away from Rob Wilder.

At that moment, all things were still possible. He had every intention of winning the race, regardless of where he started it. Winning his very first start in Winston Cup! What a glorious beginning it would be for the Billy Winton team! What a perfect lead it would make on all the sportscasts around the country that night!

But then there were the other memories as well, those he'd just as soon forget: memories like getting careless and bumping into the back end of the 33 car as he tried to make a pass, almost sending both of them spinning. Then the angry jolt to his own rear bumper a moment later, a shot aimed directly at his yellow "rookie stripe" as the driver he just shoved let him know how much he resented the contact. To both men's credit, though, they looked each other up afterward, and there were no hard feelings.

Just racing. Hard racing.

Then, finally, the persistent whine in the transmission that all too soon became a loud grinding noise in Rob's ears, the sickening smell of the burning grease in his nostrils, the bottom falling out of his stomach when the transmission finally shattered, forcing him to coast the car back to the garage for lengthy repairs. He remembered how it felt to sit there helplessly in the car, removing the shifter while the crew frantically worked to replace the smoking hot hunk of metal that been the car's transmission. The awful feeling of sitting there, parked in his broken race car as the laps were counting down out there on the track without him.

Once the repairs were made, all he could do was ride around the track trying to stay out of everyone's way, logging what he knew would be valuable laps as he built up his experience in the car. But as much as he loved driving a race car, Rob felt almost relieved when the checkered flag finally fell, putting an end to the most wonderful day in his life, to his most miserable day of racing.

Afterward, as they were packing up, Stacy Locklear came strutting by their garage stall. "What happened, rookie? Competition too tough for you up here?"

Rob bristled. "Seems like I remember passing you before my car . . ."

But, having dropped his little bomb, Locklear had quickly walked on. Billy Winton watched him go, muttering something about a "hen laying an asteroid."

Will gave Rob a quick punch on the shoulder. "Hey, cowboy. You know you're a threat when guys like him go out of their way to gig you. Take it as a compliment."

"Okay. I think I'll do that very thing."

"Besides," Billy added, "I hope we're never as proud of finishing nineteenth as he seems to be."

Rob nodded agreement, but his jaws were still white from clenching his teeth so tightly.

It was a rather inauspicious beginning to what he hoped would be a long and successful career. Still, he found it a humbling growing experience for all of them and a day that left every one of them hungry for a more successful outing.

To a man, they wished they could have gone out and raced the next weekend. Heck, the next day! But it would be February before they could make it right.

Now as they looked at the experience from all angles and in the bright light of hindsight, they could actually laugh at some of the things they had done wrong. They could easily see some of their weaknesses as a team, what they needed to work on before they headed off to Daytona for the start of the season in less than three months.

And with that, they drained their coffee cups, popped open the toolboxes, and went to work.

7

THE DUNE

A brilliant, warm morning sun bathed the shimmering Daytona crowd. They seemed almost as thankful for the respite from winter as they were for the start of the new racing season. Now, they breathlessly awaited the wave of the green flag that would signal the beginning of the first of the twin 125-mile qualifying races for Sunday's 500. Oh, make no mistake. The qualifying race wasn't the 500, for sure, but it was racing after three months without any. And the crowd was primed for anything it could get.

The flags along the pit road snapped in a breeze that rushed in off the ocean and the ever-present seagulls seemed to be as happy to be there, tacking and turning on the wind, as the mob of race fans were. It all added to what was already a sparkling, festive day at the stock car racing mecca, the huge superspeedway at Daytona Beach, Florida.

All along the tri-oval, the front grandstands were coming alive with eager spectators, on their feet from the time they'd arrived, eagerly awaiting the fall of the green flag on the first qualifying race. An entire winter's worth of anticipation was about to end for the fans, the teams, and the drivers.

Down on pit lane, the cars that recorded odd-number qualifying times sat stretched out in a neat row, their newly polished skins gleaming and sparkling in the bright sunshine. Many of the fans and not a few of the team members themselves had to check their programs since there were new teams, new sponsors, and myriad new paint schemes adorning the machines that were pushed to the line. Color blazed everywhere as the crews, in their vivid team uniforms, made last-minute checks and adjustments to the race cars.

For some, this was to be an especially pressure-packed day. This event each year used a unique means of placing cars in the field, a format that didn't rely totally on single-car qualifying speeds as most of the other races did. The final starting line-up and running order for the 500 was about to be decided in these two preliminary races. Teams without a provisional start to rely on, or those that had not posted top speeds during the more conventional time trials, were now faced with a most unpleasant prospect. They would have to race their way into the field through one of these qualifying races.

If they failed to finish in the top fourteen or fifteen, then they most likely would have to load their cars up several days earlier than they had planned and begin the long drive home, their season opener postponed for at least for another week. With all the money that had been spent and the endless hours work put in over the winter to create the specially built restrictor-plate race cars just for this track and this race, going home early was a particularly unpleasant thought. The battles for those last slots in the big race, the "transfer spots" as they were called, promised to be fast and furious and, in some cases, downright dangerous.

"Rocket" Rob Wilder was ready. The press that followed the Cup series had already picked up the nickname he had earned as an emerging star in Grand National racing, a name based as much on his speedy style as on his home in a small town near the "Rocket City," Huntsville, Alabama. Cameras had already found him this bright morning as he stood talking easily with his girlfriend, Christy Fagan, both of them casually leaning against his car on pit lane.

Though the cameras tended to dwell on the handsome young couple, they still managed to take in the brand-new race car the Billy Winton team had specially crafted for this race. One of the commentators noted how the youngster, about to line up and race like crazy to try to get a better slot in the first race of his true rookie Cup season, showed none of the prerace jitters one might expect. Especially in one so young, in such a pressure-packed position, and in what many had termed "The Super Bowl of Stock Car Racing."

No, Rocket Rob Wilder appeared totally relaxed, oblivious to the furious activity whirling around him like a freak February hurricane as the people on pit road scurried about in a final mad rush of preparations.

Rob simply smiled at the cameras, gave the reporters his best answers, and talked with Christy about school back in California, about her folks, about music, about the weather, about anything else but his chances of making the 500 at Daytona. He was just proud to be there at The Dune. That was the whimsical "code name" he and the crew had given the massive layout at Daytona when they talked about it over the winter. Do this or do that so they could take first place at The Dune come February.

The kid had plenty going for him at this place. The big track in Daytona was Rob's instant favorite from the minute he made his first practice lap around the giant speedway. He loved the towering banks and long straightaways, relished in his ability to run a lap flat out all the way around the circuit while pulling every ounce of power out of the motor. That sort of racing fit his driving style to a tee. He preferred driving the car as hard as it would go all the time. And that sort of foot-to-the-floor technique had served him well the last time he had driven this storied track to make one of the more memorable finishes in recent Daytona history—and that on a track that could provide reels of race highlights. Rob was nipped at the finish line by a bumper's width, costing him the victory in the Grand National race. It would take the photos later to show how heartbreakingly close the race had really been. One of those photos had made this year's official racing program publication and it was the talk among more than a few of the fans in the stands.

Now, as the start of the first qualifying race approached, Rob Wilder settled back and smiled broadly. Not only was he happy Christy had been there, but he also felt the total elation of knowing the long winter layoff was about over. Twin 125, the 500 itself, or a bunch of junkers on some dirt track somewhere, Rocket Rob was never happier than he was when a race was to be run and he was to be in it.

The young driver's easy air wasn't necessarily reflected in the demeanor of the rest of the Winton Racing crew. Their faces were hard-set, their concentration focused on prepping the bright red car bearing the brilliant silver number 52. The team had chosen that number in the off season. Their preferred Grand National number was already taken by one of the established teams on the circuit.

"That's okay," Rob had said. "That's how many races we'll win this year. Fifty-two."

"You dumb redneck," Donnie Kline had snorted. "We don't even run near that many."

"Then we better find some more to race in," Rob had quickly declared, unfazed. "I like the sound of it: fifty-two wins for the Ensoft number 52."

"Considerin' thirteen wins in a season is the modern-day record, I'd say that'd be quite a year," Kline had mumbled, shaking his head sadly at the naïvete of their young driver. "It might be in the papers and everything."

The cold hard fact beneath the warm Daytona sun was that on this day, the Ensoft team was in a tight situation. The only sure way for them to actually make the field for their first 500 was for Rob to race his way into one of the top fourteen finishing spots in this afternoon's qualifier. They had only posted the twenty-seventh fastest run in the time trials. That spot left no guarantee at all that they would be able to make the field. If there happened to be a big wreck in one or both of today's races, a wreck so big that enough of the faster cars were knocked out and had to use their times to get in, then there was a real chance the new 52 could be bumped. They, of course, had no provisional starting spot to fall back on.

No, everyone in the Ensoft pit knew that the only sure way for them to make the field was to race their way into it in the upcoming 125-miler. Rob had no doubts he could do it. Not surprisingly, Will Hughes was not nearly so confident.

The crew chief nervously barked orders to the crew over the two-way radios as they did all they could to leave nothing to chance. The car had to be perfect. The driver had to be perfect. The run had to be perfect. Anything less was unacceptable.

Billy Winton and Michelle Fagan had their own duties to perform, and they didn't require a pair of pliers or an air wrench. They were down at the end of pit road entertaining important Ensoft clients. They were located in one of the small grandstand suites overlooking the front part of the pit lane. A big contingent had flown in from Ensoft's corporate headquarters in San Jose to watch the race and mingle with another sizeable group of key customers. There would be a similar elaborate and expensive setup planned for the 500 on Sunday. That meant that making the race was going to be paramount for the young team for other reasons as well.

The officials began to clear pit road as the start of the race closed in. The Ensoft crew reluctantly moved away from their car and gathered over in their pit stall. To a man, they got busy with last-minute checks of all their equipment there.

"Load 'em up, cowboy," Will yelled to Rob, raising his voice to be heard over the din of the prerace activities spilling from the loudspeakers ringing the fence of the speedway. "You got to get out there and haul some mail."

"I guess that means I have to go," Rob said, sliding an arm around Christy's shoulders.

"Guess so. I wouldn't want to make you late for work," she replied, beaming at him as she looked squarely into his deep blue eyes.

"Will and the boys wouldn't like that one bit."

"No, they wouldn't. And I sure don't want to wear out my welcome around here. They might ban me from the pits or something."

"No chance. You're our good-luck charm," Rob said, gazing back into her eyes and momentarily finding himself lost there.

"I wasn't such good luck in Atlanta."

"Hey, who knows what might have happened when that transmission went if you hadn't been there." He struggled then to get himself away from the wonder of her eyes, back focused on the here-and-now and the reality of what he had to go out there and do in the next little while. "Well, I guess I'll see you in an hour or so."

"It's a date!" she said, stepping closer and into his arms. He pulled her tightly against him. "I'll meet you in Victory Lane."

"Perfect place!"

Rob hugged her close for a moment, then he kissed her briefly, hesitating to let her go. It took Will Hughes to finally break the spell as he shooed his driver on over to where the car waited. Still reluctant to let go of her, Rob dragged Christy with him as he crossed over to the race car. As he swung his right leg in the window, he gave her one last peck on the cheek. Finally, she stepped aside and out of the way as he slid down into the driver's seat.

She knew it was her time to fade into the background. Christy was well aware that Rob needed to get mentally ready to run the race, to focus all his attention on the car, the track, and the others he would be racing at nearly two hundred miles per hour. As much as she wanted Rob to think about her, she conceded this would be neither the time nor the place for that.

Christy stood a short distance away and watched Will help Rob get buckled into the race car. She marveled at how these two men could mesh their personalities so effectively at the start of every race when they were such polar opposites.

Rob was always confident and nonchalant, seemingly nonplussed by all the feverish activity around him. Will Hughes, on the other hand, appeared to her to be an emotional wreck, his manner bordering on open paranoia as he fretted over every tiny detail, circling back time and again to review the most minute part or setting. She could now understand why Clara Hughes, Will's wife, hardly ever came to the track to watch her hyperactive husband work. Of course, Christy realized she still had little idea of the enormous pressure Will faced every time the car's engine was started and Rob steered the machine out onto a racetrack somewhere. There were lives, careers, money, and much more at stake, and a great deal of the responsibility rested on Will's shoulders.

Christy also suspected that Rob might not yet realize or accept all the responsibility that he bore either. Or, if he did, he certainly managed to not let it bother him. At least not outwardly. She still worried about him carrying it inside, though, and wondered if it might someday explode. How would he handle that?

As she stood and watched the man she was growing to love more and more get set to go to work, she tried to chase those thoughts from her head. It was too glorious a day, too important a day to let that sort of thing occupy her mind when she should be thinking about how great it was going to be when they ran well in this qualifying race.

Settling into the seat of the race car, Rob finally began to allow the excitement to seep in. He began to think about the task at hand. The padding of the steering wheel as he placed it on its column and locked it into place made him all the more eager for the start to come. He adjusted the strap on his helmet one last time then did a radio check with Harry Stone, their spotter from the previous year who had made the jump to Cup racing with them. Will chimed in on the radio check, asking for a quick ten-four from everyone on their frequency, making sure there was good reception all the way around for everybody.

"All right, cowboy," he finally spoke to Rob. "I hear you loud and clear on this end. How you reading me?"

"Clear as spring water," came the immediate and obviously happy reply. "I just wish they would hurry up out there. I want to see what we got for 'em. My gas foot is gettin' a little bit itchy."

"Well, sir, you better scratch that itch 'cause we need

for you to run that good, smart race we spent all morning talking about."

"I know the drill: patience, patience, patience. I have been listening but that doesn't make it any easier. I just want to take this thing out and run her wide open and let the chips fall where they may.

Rob could already picture himself out there on that historic track, mixing it up in the draft with all the veterans on the circuit as they jockeyed for position. He liked the way that portrait looked!

"You just be ready to go when I tell you it's time to go. Then, and only then, you can let it all hang out. We will likely have us twenty or so cars in the lead pack and you know where we have to finish."

"I know. I know. And we'll do it, Will. Write that down somewhere. We'll do it."

For some reason, Will actually scripted out the words Rob had just spoken in the border of the note sheet on his clipboard. Shoot, maybe writing it down would make it so.

Billy Winton had slipped on his headset and was eavesdropping from his spot in the suite. He caught the last of the conversation between driver and crew chief. A broad smile crossed his face as he heard Rob's final comment. He loved the kid's confidence. And he knew it wasn't simply false bravado like so many who professed to be hard chargers but who then went out and drove timidly. Billy would not be at all surprised to see the kid at the front of the pack before the day was done. They weren't sure about the strength of the race car, but with Rob Wilder, they had a good chance of running better than the equipment might dictate. That kid was a natural. He could do things with a race car that Billy had witnessed from few drivers before him.

And the clincher was that the youngster loved this track. Couple Rob Wilder's amazing driving skills, his affection for Daytona, and his almost unnatural desire to win any contest in which he was entered, and Billy Winton knew they would either be up front before the 125 miles had played out or flat busted trying to get there.

Their guests were now making their way up from the suite below the small grandstand area, settling into their seats overlooking the pits below them. Michelle scurried around as surely as the pit crew down below was doing, making sure every detail had been covered, that the event went smoothly for these very important visitors. This was the beginning of a huge promotional effort for a new piece of software they were unveiling in conjunction with Daytona, and she needed everything to go perfectly. In her rush to accommodate all their VIPs, she had had little time to think about Rob or the race car or even the importance of the upcoming qualifying race. Only when she heard the thunder as the engines were started did she realize that it was almost time for the green flag to fall.

So far, so good. Rob had made a big impression on all the guests when he joined them for breakfast before the drivers' meeting. With only twenty-five or so guests, Rob was able to spend adequate time talking with each of them, impressing them as much with his knowledge of their business as with his descriptions of what it was like to be in a race car going a couple hundred miles per hour. Rob's eloquence and easy manner wore well on the corporate types and the young managers from Ensoft. Many of them were attending their first stock car race, meeting their first real, live, race car driver. They fully expected the driver to fit the "good old boy" stereotype, to talk with a twang about motors and tires and batteries. They were clearly impressed when the handsome well-dressed youngster could discuss operating systems, e-commerce, and software marketing concepts.

Next, the Ensoft logo golf shirts and bright red racing jackets were passed out, and they were an immediate hit.

Rob dutifully autographed hats for each person and for all their kids back home, too.

Now, well-fed but with a stock of snacks and drinks within easy reach anyway, the guests seemed to be having a good time. They had certainly perked up when the amazing, deep-voiced rumble of the collective engines thundered up to them. As the cars finally rolled off the line, the Ensoft group cheered wildly as their own car, the one that proudly carried their logo, rolled past them on the pit lane. The grumble of the engines vibrated the steel frame of the grandstand where they were standing, and they could feel the reverberation on their chests and faces. That only added to the growing excitement. For those viewing their first race, the closeness of the cars was exciting, stimulating, unlike anything else they had ever experienced. The smiles on their faces confirmed for Michelle that this little marketing investment was already giving a nice return. The customers were happy. Their own people were thrilled to be a part of all this.

All they had to do now was go out and make the big race. Michelle would not allow herself to think about failing, sending these folks home with a bad taste in their mouths, having a suite full of VIPs here on Sunday with no Ensoft car out there for them to watch.

No, if she allowed those thoughts to play around in her head, she might end up taking a big bite out of the cell phone she had to her lips at that moment, reporting back to Toby Warren and the execs in California about how well everything was going.

The car rumbled powerfully beneath Rob as the line of hopeful machines idled, waiting for the signal to fall in behind the pace car. Sitting back in the fourth row, Rob could see the whirl of lights up ahead, flashing on the top of the pace car. He looked across the gauges in the dash one last time before trying to find Christy standing over there behind the wall. He finally caught a glimpse of her, and she was waving to him. He raised his right hand to wave back at her but then quickly had to regrip the wheel tightly as the cars directly in front of him began to roll away in slow-motion pursuit of the pace car.

"It's about time!" Rob thought to himself as the car bounced gently down the pit lane like a trotter just coming up to a gallop. All the prerace activities were starting to get on his nerves. With the move up to the Cup Series, all the preliminary ceremony seemed even more interminable. The direct demands before the race on him and his time had been ratcheted up considerably now, just as he had expected they would. Not only did he have to keep the sponsor happy and make time for all their guests, but the mandatory drivers' meetings and introductions seemed to take eons longer than they had in Grand National. And certainly longer than in the tiny-track feature events where he had been running not quite two years before.

It seemed, though, that everywhere he turned, he was being pushed or pulled in one direction or another, leaving him with little time to concentrate on the race car or the upcoming contest. It seemed the only peace he had found on this trip was when he was with Christy Fagan or when he finally climbed behind the wheel of the race car. He wasn't complaining. He was merely aware of the fact that the distractions could have a bad effect on his concentration if he allowed them to do so.

But at least now, with the car finally untethered and in motion, he could put all that away as he guided his powerful machine out onto the racing surface, following the car that ran ahead of him by several car lengths. He stretched his arms, wriggled in the seat, then checked the safety belts one last time, making sure they were good and snug. The belts would keep him pinned tightly to the form-fitted driver's seat even when gravity and centrifugal force tried to rip him loose. The window net to his left sang softly in the wind as the cars began to pick up speed behind the pace car.

Rob chased off behind the line of cars as they followed the pace car down into the banking of turn one. He listened intently to the pitch of the engine and took comfort in the powerful roar emanating from beneath the hood. Even with the choking effect of the restrictor plate on the air flow pouring in from the carburetor, the engine sounded lean and powerful, ready to push the car at death-defying speeds out there on the giant speedway once the automobile had been given its head.

Rob goosed the gas, and the Ford lunged ahead obediently, threatening to gobble up the car in line ahead of him. He liked the reassuring feel under his foot, the instant response of his car as he applied even the slightest pressure on the accelerator.

The cars crossed beneath the flagstand for the first time. Now, settled into the driver's seat, Rob was completely ready to go, to begin this quest for real. He was impatient to show the others what he could do with the car in actual competition against something besides the stopwatch. Did he really have the mettle it took to compete with this elite group of drivers he now found himself surrounded by? He never had the opportunity to prove anything at Atlanta before his car broke. Or been given the chance to show what he could do when he had driven the fill-in role for Jodell Lee at Charlotte.

In a couple of more pace laps, Rob would finally be afforded his first real occasion to find out for himself and then to show everyone else.

Will settled in atop the pit box as Donnie and the rest of the crew scrambled around in a last minute minuet, preparing their stall for the first trip to pit road by their car. Will flipped through the pages on his clipboard, double-checking the calculations he had made on the various contingencies he and Rob had planned out back in the hotel room the evening before. He ran a last radio check between himself, Harry Stone the spotter, and the over-the-wall gang down below him.

"One lap to go boys! We got to be sharp and on the ball. We got to prove we belong here as much as anybody does," Will called around. "Rob? You got a good copy?"

"Ten-four. Like you're here in the car with me."

"Good. I want to make sure you can hear me over that engine old Joe Banker built for you."

"She's the sweetest-sounding thing I've ever heard, harmonizing like a choir of angels. It's all I can do to keep a rein on her right now."

"Well, cowboy, you're gonna have to keep that little filly under control. You can't win the race if you aren't around at the finish."

"Don't worry, we'll be there. All those hotshots in front of me are gonna know there's a new gunslinger in town by the time we're done," Rob sang into the microphone, then gave the steering wheel a slap for emphasis. His eyes never left the bumper of the car in front of him.

"Okay. Remember now that you probably aren't going to have many friends out there early on, so drive smart. All we need is a fourteenth here in the 125, and then we're in the real race, the one that counts. Try not to get hung out to dry on the inside. I doubt if anybody is going to try to pass with you when you go down there, and you could get yourself run off and left if you're not careful."

"If I'm fast enough and heading to the front they'll follow me. Of that you can be sure," Rob said, and just saying the words made him even more eager to get the race under way. He had no doubts at all that he could take the car to the front of the field, and if he got to the front, even the wary veterans would run with him. Those guys would have no choice then. Not, that is, if they wanted a shot at a good finish.

Will let the radio net go dead then, allowing his driver to focus on the immediate task at hand. The green flag was only a half lap away. It was time to go to work, time to see if the long winter's labor would bear early fruit or not.

With the cars now approaching turn three, Will no longer had time to pay attention to the flock of butterflies that had taken up residence in his belly. That was odd. He had never had such a bad case of the jitters before any of the many races he had been around before.

He adjusted the mike on the radio, trying to get it into a more comfortable position. Then he leaned forward and watched the tightly bunched field of straining, groaning race cars sweep together into the towering banks of turns three and four. He shook his head, swallowed hard, and gritted his teeth.

Billy and Michelle took a pause from talking politely with their guests to watch as the field came down to the start/finish line for the green flag. The distant racers were like tiny, colorful bugs from their perspective as they gazed off across the sea of passenger cars and campers that filled the infield between their position and where the race cars were riding the banking of turn three.

Michelle glanced nervously at the television hanging up in the corner of the suite. She watched the screen now as it gave her a better view as the cars gathered up even more tightly, closing up for the start. The camera panned back through the pack of cars, pausing briefly on the red Ensoft-sponsored car. Michelle couldn't help but smile broadly and pump one fist in the air as she watched Rob ease up closely onto the tail of the familiar car that ran in front of him, pull back, then swerve sharply back and forth to clean his tires of debris and warm them for the start.

Billy smiled, too, watching her excitement. It was infectious and had already spilled over to the folks who were sitting in the open air suite with them. Gradually, they were rising to their feet, realizing that the race was actually about to start, ready to watch the line of cars come charging directly toward them as they made their way down to the line.

Across the track from them they could already hear the soaring roar of the crowd in the long line of grandstands cheering as they awaited their favorites to come roaring past. Their noise actually drowned out the sound of the cars as they came down off the high banking of turn four, across the short chute, and headed toward the start/finish line in the tri-oval. They were still not under full power.

The covey of race cars seemed impossibly close together as they awaited the flagman's waving of the green flag. He stubbornly stood his ground and watched the progression of the two parallel lines of cars that were bearing down on him. The man was giving no indication whether or not he had decided to set loose the much anticipated melee or if he would make them go around again so they would behave themselves next time by. He was determined to make sure all the competitors were running orderly along behind the pace car as it led them down to the start.

Then, suddenly, as if he had thought of some other place he needed to be, the pace car's driver cut sharply left and steered his mount down onto pit road. The banner went high in the flagman's hand as he gave the dual line of cars a final squinted inspection. Then, once satisfied with the position of the two lead cars that were now pacing the field, he began to wave the flag vigorously in a blur of green.

Rob sensed more than actually saw the flag going up as he nosed his car as close up on the back bumper of the car in front of him as he could get without actual contact.

"Go! Go! Go!" came the frenzied cry over the radio from Will Hughes.

"Green! Green!" yelped Harry Stone from his spotters' position high above the grandstand.

Rob instinctively stomped down on the gas. The restrictor plate on top of the car's carburetor caused the car to bog down, to seem to hesitate, just as it was supposed to do, but every other driver in the field had the same sensation. This was the only part of racing at Daytona that Rob disliked. It felt as if a gigantic anchor had been tossed off the back of his car and was digging into the asphalt, trying to hold him back, no matter how furiously he tried to paddle.

The roar of the accumulated machines was unbelievable, though, and now the crowd noise was almost washed away by their earthshaking bellow. And sure enough, the rpms slowly came up in each car as the long conga line began gaining speed, snaking past the huge tower grandstands that overlooked the start/finish line in the tri-oval like a colorful reptile.

The brightly painted racers flashed sunlight off their windshields as they swept down toward turn one, still so close to each other that they appeared to be chained together in one long train. Nobody had yet achieved enough power to attempt a pass on anyone else. And even if they had, they likely would have waited a bit to make the move. That maneuver would have to wait.

Rob's eyes stayed on the car in front of him as he watched through his windshield, wary of any hint of trouble up ahead. All it would take now was for someone to miss a gearshift or make an ever-so-slight bobble. With the cars stacked up as they were, any hesitation would cause a tailgating driver to ram the rear of the other car and that would lead to a massive, grinding crash. In any race, it is the start or restart that everyone dreads—drivers, crew chiefs, crew, and knowledgeable fans alike. That's when they would collectively hold their breath and cross their fingers and, in some cases, say a small prayer. Only after the cars began to string out onto the track and get some separation could everyone breathe a little easier.

Now, though, the cars thundered into turn one still lined up in tandem, like a mule train in traces. Neither of the lead cars was able to pull ahead of the other by so much as a foot or two. Behind them though, a few of the cars in the outside line had pushed up toward the wall by the time they moved into turn two, trying desperately to gain a little advantage by the time the cars were ready to exit the turn and spill out onto the backstretch.

En masse, the cars continued to gain momentum down the long straight run. Then, finally, as they headed into turn three, the front-running car on the inside was able to push out to a car-length lead. By that point, it appeared that the inside line was the place to be as the cars shot through the corner.

The fans in the stands were still on their feet, waving, apparently screaming, urging the flock of cars along as they rumbled back around to pass in front of them once more. But this time, the noise from the wide open engines completely drowned out the cheers from the crowd, no matter how frenzied they were. As the field zipped by where Billy and Michelle and their guests watched, it resembled in both appearance and sound a squadron of fighter jets in close formation making a low-level pass. Michelle could feel the vibrations in the metal grandstand through the soles of her shoes. She gave out several whoops as Rob piloted the brilliant red car past their position.

If any of the visitors had taken their eyes off the track, glanced over and happened to notice the burning, intense stare and the incongruous broad grin on Billy Winton's face, they might have been startled. There was nothing else like being here in Daytona to race in February. To be in this sacred place during Speed Weeks and to be watching his own car racing in the 125 for a spot in the 500. Sure, Billy had experienced Daytona in February many times before in his long racing career. But that had always been from a totally different perspective. Here, now, it was *his* Cup car out there getting the green flag, *his* Cup team, which he had carefully built and nurtured, that was out there right now, racing for position. Instead of his usual relaxed and carefree manner, at this particular moment he was every bit as focused and intent as his young driver.

Billy Winton was ready to race. And he was just as ready to win. Today was as good a day as any to do that very thing!

Billy listened over his headset to the spotter as he guided Rob along, informing him when he was clear of another car he might be passing. Or to the familiar voice of Will Hughes, calling out a lap time to his driver. For now, his important guests would have to be left to their own devices. There was a race going on out there, and Billy had no intention of missing a second of it.

But a quick glance at the group confirmed that the visitors were doing just fine on their own. Every one of them was wide-eyed, some of them had their mouths open, as they watched the loud wild action unfolding before them out there at breathtaking speed.

Meanwhile, in the middle of the hurricane, Rob settled into as much of a routine as one could while whirling around a closed course doing 190 miles an hour with the bumper of the car two feet or less off that of the car in front of him. Cautiously, he began to move around a bit on the track, trying to get used to how the car reacted in the tight confines of the air that spilled off the car in front of him.

A car running at such speeds caused an effect that was almost like a powerful suction, pulling a trailing car along with it in what was known as the "draft." Two or more cars running in a close line would naturally be faster than a single car running alone on this track.

But now, the car directly ahead of Rob was not at quite full speed, and that had the kid itching to jump out of line to see what he could do. But every time he made a motion to pull down to the inside and try to make a pass, to try to pull out and go catch the other cars up ahead, he was forced to pull back in line. That was because the veteran driver behind him failed each time to follow, to pull out with him so they would both have the advantage of the draft. Without the extra push the following car would give him in the draft, Rob had little chance to pick up any spots ahead of him and ran a real risk of being passed by the veteran and anyone else who stayed in line back there.

That meant Rob was stuck for the time being, doing one of the things he absolutely hated: being patient.

Finally, suddenly, one of the cars ahead of him jumped down to the inside as they came off turn four. Rob sensed this was his best chance and jerked the wheel, taking a run at the car ahead of him. He had decided to take such a chance whenever it presented itself, with or without the help of the wary veteran who was likely unwilling to do much drafting with someone who wore the yellow "rookie stripe" on his rear bumper. As he twisted the wheel, he tried to push the throttle even farther into the floorboard, to open it another millimeter or so, although he knew it was already as wide open as he could possibly get it.

But the move worked! He used the draft of the car that pulled out of line in front of him to slingshot outward and get alongside the car he had been tailing since the green flag. The car he was now drafting with was making it a three-wide span up ahead, but Rob was still three car-lengths behind. He could only hope he was close enough to get enough benefit from the hole in the other air that the car was punching for him, so he could complete the pass and pull up closer.

Even at such tremendous velocity, the whole move seemed to unfold slowly for Rob as he gradually closed the distance on the race car ahead, as he passed several other cars in the process. He caught himself grunting loudly, making ugly groaning noises, urging the car along, willing it to move up closer to the racer he was trying to reach. The car seemed to be handling perfectly so far, and the Joe Banker–prepared power plant was definitely putting some horsepower at his disposal. Rob felt a shot of adrenaline run through him as he boldly continued to make the pass and saw the other familiar cars slide by to his right.

Upstairs in the radio broadcast booth, the play-by-play announcers duly noted the move, too, and immediately pronounced Rocket Rob as one of the drivers to watch for the balance of this qualifying race.

"Outside! Outside!" came the cry of the spotter over Rob's radio. That meant he couldn't pull back into line just yet, that there was still a car running to his outside that he might or might not be able to see in his mirror.

Rob charged toward the first turn, the car he was following still making it a three-wide phalanx on the track ahead of him. Still, he and the car he was drafting with held the preferred line going into the corner and that gave them the big advantage. The car caught in the middle and the one to the outside were struggling and slowly began to drift backward.

Finally the radio crackled in Rob's ears and he heard the single word he had been waiting for.

"Clear!"

He gracefully moved back up in line and tried to catch

his breath, to contemplate when and how he would pick off some more of these guys who were between him and the front of the field. He tightened his grip on the wheel even more, trying to hold the car steady in all the buffeting he was taking from the wind off the other cars.

"Good move, cowboy. Way to be patient," Will praised over the radio net. Rob had his hands full of jerking, twisting steering wheel at the moment and didn't bother to reply. "Ninth place," Will advised, letting his driver know what he had accomplished, that he was getting the job done.

But Rob knew he could lose the hard-won position much easier than he had gained it. With twenty cars still running in the lead draft, he was still only one slight wrong move from getting himself drop-kicked all the way back to the end of that bunch. The slightest of bobbles and he would have to re-earn what he had just taken plus more. Will was quite aware of the inexperience of his driver at this level. And he knew that such a costly slipup was not such a remote possibility.

It happened to veterans all the time. His rookie was not immune.

The laps began to wind off, and the front three or four cars began lining themselves up in single file. Running in line like that made them much faster than had they been racing side by side. Their unspoken alliance was quickly forming with one goal in mind: to stay in line and shake the others behind them, the part of the pack that was still racing two-by-two, trying to come on up and join them at the front. If they could do that, then they could simply run along together, put the rest of the field some serious distance back, then wait until the end and settle the final finishing order among themselves on the last few laps.

Inexperienced or not, Rob Wilder knew exactly what was going on up there. All he could do, though, was wish that the cars ahead of him would quit racing each other and fall into line so they could better run down the three or four cars at the front. If they allowed the leaders to break away, then Rob's shot at actually winning this race would be gone. Gone unless there was a caution flag, of course. With only fifteen laps finished, Rob still would have preferred to have been racing for the win, not the last transfer spot into the 500.

Down in the pits, Will carefully studied the speeds from each lap on the notebook computer that was sitting on the stand next to him. He was now contemplating what their pit strategy would be if there happened to be a caution flag in the next few laps. If there were none, the strategy was simple. They would run the entire fifty laps flat-out, no stopping. If there should happen to be a yellow flag, though, then the timing of the stop would be crucial in their decision making.

But that's what a crew chief did. He made those kinds of crucial, split-second decisions. It was clear, though, that those calls carried far more importance now than they ever did in Grand National.

Will ran the options through his mind, even as he studied the field of cars that passed him by. The tires were not falling off the car, so there was no need to get fresh rubber late in the race unless they needed the extra bite new tires would give them to try to get back inside the top fifteen. The car seemed to be handling fine, so no chassis adjustment was necessary so far, but, if there was a caution and they came in, he could always make a bit of a tweak. And there was, of course, plenty of fuel to run the distance, but they could take a splash if everybody else came in.

So that settled it. If they were outside twenty laps to go, then they would probably stop on a caution for tires, a tiny adjustment, and a swallow of gas. Inside twenty, there was no way they could afford to give up the track position unless they were running too far outside of the top fifteen and needed the boost of fresh rubber.

Meanwhile, Rob jockeyed to hold his newly won position on the track. He found another Ford from one of the multi-car teams that seemed to be running as fast as he was, and he latched on to its rear bumper, mirroring every move the car made. Working well together, the two cars slowly picked their way closer to the front of the field, passing a car here and there and holding off others who were as determined as they to move up.

Their charge toward the front was quickly acknowledged by radio and TV crews calling the race. A camera was now trained on Rob and the other driver and the director kept selecting that shot every time they passed someone else. The radio crew was hurriedly digging out Rob's previous record, his biography, so they could add color and shading to what they were describing down there on the track to their listeners.

Rob watched every move the driver in front of him made, almost like an apprentice observing a master at work. He knew already that the best way to learn how to use the draft on tracks like Daytona and Talladega was to get out and run around them with some of the best in the business, learning by following while locked on to their bumper. He had done that here at Daytona in his Grand National starts. Now, Rob Wilder mirrored the other Ford's every move over the last eight or ten laps or so.

The Ford Rob had been tracking suddenly pushed up to the high side, trying to gain an advantage in momentum by taking a higher line through the corner they were approaching. Rob didn't even hesitate. He steered right out on cue, using the wall of air coming off his front bumper to return the favor the lead car had been doing him, giving the other Ford in front of him a beneficial push.

Suddenly, as if coming from out of nowhere, another car moved up and tried to claim a spot in front of them that didn't even exist. The newcomer couldn't make the pass by himself and moved dangerously higher. His move squeezed Rob's buddy higher, toward the outside wall, and Rob had no choice but to follow him out onto shaky ground.

Rob was virtually certain the two cars ahead of him would collide as the track suddenly narrowed in front of them in the turn. The Ford ahead of Rob ran out of room and was forced to crack the throttle, allowing the other car to slip into line, and the kid had no choice but to do likewise. But still, he almost clipped the other car's bumper before he could slow.

That fraction-of-a-second's hesitation was all it took to send both of them falling back through the field as the lines of cars streamed by on their inside. It looked as if Rob and the driver of the other Ford had pulled over for a nice chat. In an instant, they fell from racing for fourth and fifth positions to struggling to hang on to fifteenth and sixteenth. Rob didn't have time to get frustrated or even to cuss his luck. He had his hands full, struggling to push his Ford back into line before he got booted even farther, maybe even all the way to the back of the field. Only when he finally got the car back into line and had cut his losses did he exhale, trying to catch the breath he'd been holding for what seemed like several minutes but had, in actuality, been only a few long, agonizing seconds.

Will watched breathlessly on the television monitor next to him as the cars ran out of room in the corner. He winced as he saw the two of them begin to get pinched up against the outside wall, and he instinctively knew one of two things was about to happen.

One would be bad. The other would be tragic.

"Hang on, cowboy, hang on," Will whispered out loud,

hoping the kid would have the experience to not force something that wasn't to be. Or that he would have the instincts to not tag the other car and wreck half the field.

As Will watched, he was certain that his first attempt at the 500 as a team crew chief was about to wind up in a heap of smoking, twisted metal and with a banged-up driver. Somehow, though, Rob was able to miraculously hang on to the car. But in the process, he had obviously had to ease off on the gas for an instant. Then, as the field drove right on by, the kid was helpless until he could find a space in the line big enough for him to squeeze the car back in.

To his credit, the youngster handled it perfectly, didn't panic, and finally slid in to lick his wounds and get ready to begin making his way back to where he had been only an instant before.

"Whew, that was close!" Will exclaimed, idly wiping his face with a shop rag as he watched the replay of the near catastrophe on the television. It was true. Disaster had been even closer than he had first thought. Rob had been only inches from touching the Ford in front of him. "How in the dickens did he keep that thing away from the rear end of that other driver? And out of the wall?" he asked the wind.

There was no answer.

He glanced down at the lap count. Twenty-two laps were already gone. It seemed like the green flag had dropped only seconds before, and the race was already almost half over.

But then, just as Will had started to breathe a little easier, all hell broke loose up the track several car-lengths ahead of where Rob was running. One of the cars suddenly clipped the rear of another as its driver tried to force his way back into line in a slot not quite as long as his race car. The touch was ever so slight, with just a hint of smoke from the contact itself. But insignificant as it was, at the tremendous speeds they were running, it was more than enough of a bump to send the innocent clipped car spinning sideways and immediately and violently into the outside wall.

Instantly, there was chaos on the track as the cars racing behind the spinning car began scattering in every direction, trying to avoid plowing into it. Blue, billowing smoke from the tortured tires immediately engulfed the track, totally obscuring the view of the oncoming drivers over half the field.

Rob was still working on getting his breathing back to normal from his own close encounter when he saw a flash of silver and a car up ahead of him quickly dart sideways toward the wall.

That wasn't right!

Rob instinctively twisted the wheel, his uncanny reactions kicking in immediately even as his conscious brain was still busy trying to compute what was unfolding up there in front of him. Then he watched through the windshield of the car directly ahead of him as the wildly whirling car shot straight into the wall. Rob held on tightly as the track immediately closed up in front of him, filled with spinning race cars assuming all different attitudes. Cars began to scatter in every direction around him, all of them looking for some way through the fray without getting caught up in it themselves.

Smoke and dust hung everywhere, obscuring Rob's vision as he shot for the last tiny hole he had spotted in the tangle of cars before it was gobbled up by the smudge. He jerked the wheel back to the right, pointing his car where some inner voice told him he might just possibly be able to thread the needle between another spinning car and the solid outside wall.

But that tiny opening started to close up on him frighteningly fast as well. A car had abruptly whipped around and now spun sideways in front of him as if it had been slapped askew by a giant, unseen hand.

It was too late. There was no way in the world he could save it now. He was about to crash hard into the spinning racer directly ahead of him, and there was not a thing he could do about it.

His Daytona hopes, his Cup Series debut, would all be dead.

Dead as his brand-new race car would be when he rammed it headforemost into the other hapless driver and then held on fiercely for the inevitable wild, wild ride.

Part **5**

THE PRIZE

Keep your eye on the prize. . . .

—from an old spiritual song

8

EYE ON THE PRIZE

is instincts had told him where to go and what to do. In an instant, Rob made up his mind to stay committed to what he was being told to do, no matter that he seemed doomed whether he did or didn't.

Common sense and pure logic screamed for him to crack the throttle, to climb hard on the brakes and try to skid away from the mess in some other direction. Or to try to slow down to lessen the inevitable crunch that was coming right at him at an unbelievably frightening speed.

But a voice far more powerful and primal than common sense or pure logic urged him to do something entirely different, something so seemingly foolhardy it might actually be laughable if he only had the time to laugh. No, the voice was telling him to hop back hard on the throttle and hold onto the wheel and go on through the tiny hole where he had started to go in the first place.

"Stay off the binders, kid," a strong insistent voice

seemed to be telling him. "Drive through. You'll get rammed from behind if you don't. It's your only choice."

Rob obeyed the eerie command, gripped the wheel and drove on without ever touching the brakes, without letting up more than a tiny bit on the throttle. But he still braced for the impact with the spinning car that he was now only a few feet from plowing into.

But then, just as the collision seemed inevitable, the gyrating car in front of Rob took an odd, unexpected carom off the wall and bounced right back up, miraculously banging repeatedly against the concrete instead of ricocheting back down into the kid's chosen path.

It was all Rob needed to squeeze past with a good inch or two to spare. But not a bit more.

The sharp, grinding impact he had fully expected, that he was already bracing for, never happened. A fraction of a second later, he broke out into the clean air, the smoke was in his mirror, the track was clear ahead of him, and he hightailed it on off after the leaders, not having lost much momentum at all.

He allowed himself a quick glance in the mirror at the track full of twisted racing machines he had just left in his wake. A brief wave of nausea swept over him but it quickly turned to elation.

He had actually driven through that mess? Lord knows how, but he had made it through!

The radio net was strangely silent as everyone tried to see what was happening out there in the bedlam that had been the backstretch mere moments before. Most teams were desperately looking for their own cars, hoping against hope that they had somehow not been among the wounded. All the Billy Winton crew members certainly were.

Then, the radio rattled and the voice was more a screech of elation. "He's clear!" came the cry from Harry Stone. "Lord, I don't know how, but he's clear and coming up to speed and ... lessee ... it looks like he's okay."

Rob sucked in huge gulps of sweet air as he tried to control his heartbeat. The thing was pounding like a piston after his two near-misses within moments of each other. Coming off turn four, heading down to the line, he finally let off the gas, slowing the car to take the caution flag that the flagman was wildly waving at him. It almost looked as if the flagman might think that Rob was unaware what a catastrophe he had just driven through. Ahead of him, the leaders were slowing, too.

Michelle had watched in horror as the wreck unfolded on the television screen. The replay was no better. The camera stayed focused on the crumpled race cars that were still coming to a smoky rest, the ones that had skidded down into the grass and stalled, those that were scattered across the backstretch. They neglected to show which cars might have been able to make it through the terrible accident or had managed to get stopped without harm.

She looked frantically for the distinctive red paint of their own car among the twisted sheet metal that had been strewn all the way from up next to the wall clear down and out into the grass at the bottom of the track.

Was that their car there on the screen, stopped dead, all smoking and crumpled?

Was that what was left of a scarred number 52 on its side?

The roar of the cars still running and approaching through the tri-oval made her hopefully look away from the TV monitor so she could scan the remaining field, desperately looking for Rob and the Ensoft Ford. The leaders shot by, taking the yellow caution flag that was being waved over them, but it was hard to pick out their car from the ones coming more or less directly at them.

The front six or so were running close together. Seconds behind that bunch came the stragglers who had been forced to negotiate their way through the accident. They took the caution in ones and twos, most already running at reduced speed.

Then, there he was. Rob was well off the pace as he came to the line but he was running. And he didn't seem to have been damaged at all.

"All right! Attaboy," she screeched, pumping her fist in the air and jumping up and down when she finally spotted Rob entering the tri-oval. The rest of the guests threw her funny looks. She realized then that she was the only one making noise. But she didn't care. She let out one more whoop and flashed a broad grin at Billy Winton.

"Yeah," Billy was whispering as he saw his apparently intact machine coming through the tri-oval. He was trying to maintain his own composure in front of their VIP guests, but it was hard to temper his elation. And he was also looking with squinted eyes for any signs of damage or a flat tire.

The silence over the radio net had caused him to momentarily fear the worst. Then, when he heard Harry's report and the following chatter on the radio, he could only sit down wearily and slowly shake his head from side to side as he waited for a look at his car.

How in the world had that kid found a way through all that mess? How in the world had he done it? And apparently without putting a scratch on the machine.

"How we looking, cowboy?" Will asked, almost afraid of what the answer would be. There were lots of things that might have gotten broken that wouldn't be apparent from a distance.

"I don't know just yet. Better give me a minute to get my heart back down out of my throat. That was a close one."

"Close? I'll say. We were afraid we had lost you when you dove into all that smoke."

"That makes two of us. I've never seen the track close up so fast. All I could do was close my eyes and hang on and feed this old Ford some gas. The next thing I know, I'm busting through into the clear."

Will was watching with disbelief the third or fourth replay of the massive crash on the television monitor, each of them from a different angle. The in-car camera on a racer behind Rob showed him something amazing. The kid had actually accelerated into the opening he had spotted on the track. Everybody else was on the brakes hard, skidding and spinning as if the track had suddenly iced over. But the kid stayed in the gas instead. And thank goodness he did. Another car was right on his bumper. If he had touched the binders, both of them would have kissed hard and gone whirling around right along with the rest of them. Or if he had hesitated even an instant, he never would have made it through the tiny opening he had found somehow right there in the middle of the massive crash.

"I got to ask you, kid," Will half-whispered into his microphone. "What made you think you could drive through that hole? And how did you know with all that smoke that there was a car coming up on you so fast from behind?"

"What car?"

Will shook his head and decided to let it drop for the moment. "How's your ride?"

"She's fine, I think. I think we managed to make it through without a scratch," Rob said, his voice wavering as the car bounced along. "Didn't look like our old friend Stacy Locklear fared quite so well."

"Serves him right," Will radioed back. "He started the whole thing just by being his usual impatient, overly aggressive self."

"I thought I caught a glimpse of his silver paint job up there where it all started but then I got kinda busy. I should have known it was him, though."

"Well, never mind him. Bring her in next time by after they open the pit lane. We're going to go for four tires and a can of gas."

"What about changes?" Rob asked.

"I think we'll try to drop a pound of air pressure on the right side, but that's all we planned to do. Do you want anything else?"

"No, that sounds good to me. This thing is practically driving itself right now."

Will grinned. The kid had just made two of the most amazing moves he had ever seen, all within one wild lap, and he was giving the car the credit.

"Good," Will said, then he called to the crewmen who made up the over-the-wall gang. "Four tires and a can of gas, boys! Paul, we want to do minus one pound on the right sides."

The spotter was watching the official who was standing at the entrance to pit road, waiting for him to drop the green flag he held to signal that the pits were once again open. While the cars were still passing through turn three, the official began waving the flag. Virtually every car on the track charged down onto pit road, their crews waiting to service their respective machines. With twenty-five laps to go and with that much debris scattered around on the backstretch, it was much too risky to forgo a pit stop now. Barring more trouble, the next run would likely be all the way to the checkers and it promised to be a virtual drag race to the finish.

"All right, cowboy. Watch your speed," Will advised. They didn't need a penalty for exceeding the speed limit on pit road either. "Look for the signboard. Remember, we're down toward the turn-one end. I'll call you in."

"Ten-four."

"Okay, here we go. Just follow the yellow car. He's going into his stall and we're a half dozen or so stalls in front of him. Here we go! Easy now! Easy!"

Rob guided the car smoothly in and to a halt, leaving the left front wheel sitting precisely in the box Donnie had taped to the pavement. The L-shaped tape markings made sure the car would be parked the correct distance from the pit wall so the crewmen would have enough room to work the jack and change the left-side tires.

The crew jumped over the wall while Rob was still two stalls away but closing the distance quickly. They had to be ready to go to work as soon as he brought the Ford to a stop. Donnie led the charge over the wall as he ran around to the right side of the car. He slid the jack under the frame at the exact spot that had been marked on the door as a guide. With two swift pumps on the handle, the entire right side of the car rose up into the air. Air guns whirred away, working on removing the lug nuts, their shrill whine almost drowning out the throaty roar of the idling engines. The tires where hoisted up and into place by the tire changers, then they were given a quick hit with the air wrench to secure their lug nuts.

A nearby official in his distinctive white pants and red shirt watched carefully, making sure every lug nut was put on and secured tightly, that the legal number of crew members were over the wall, that the car didn't accidentally run over an air hose when it pulled away. Any of those things could lead to a penalty that would virtually kill any chances they had of a decent run.

Quickly finishing up on the right side, Donnie let the jack drop while the crew scrambled around to the left side to repeat the process. The gas man had already completed dumping the can of gasoline in through the filler spout that was located high on the left rear fender of the Ford. That would be more than enough to finish the race and not too much to add unnecessary weight to the car. Donnie pumped the jack hard while the tire changers finished with the left-side tires.

Rob revved the engine a time or two to keep it from stalling as he held his breath, waiting to feel the thump of the tires hitting the pavement. Donnie watched intently as the tire changers worked, ready to drop the jack the second their chore was completed.

As the air gun hit the last lug nut on the left rear, Donnie twisted the jack handle and dropped the car. Rob, still sitting on ready, impatiently twisted the steering wheel ever so slightly and dumped the clutch at the same instant, being careful all the while not to spin the rear tires.

He steered around the car in front of him that was still being serviced, glancing in the mirror as he did, watching the other cars that had already finished their own stops and were now rolling down pit road toward him. It was truly a chaotic scene. A car shot by him on the outside while another, either not seeing him at all or believing he could slide in ahead of him, turned out directly in front of him. Rob found himself boxed in momentarily and was forced to jump firmly on the brakes to keep from driving hard into the rear end of the blue Pontiac that had pulled out in front of him.

Michelle watched the stop closely from her vantage point in the pit road suite. She was still amazed every time she saw the carefully choreographed ballet the crew performed during their pit stops. She had laughed at them the first time she watched them practice a stop back in Chandler Cove, running through all the moves out there in Billy Winton's driveway. But she soon learned how crucial a good stop could be and no matter how many times she watched the crew work, she was still spellbound by the quick coordinated work these men performed.

She followed Rob now as he took off, then caught her breath as he almost tangled with the blue car that pulled right out in front of him. She waited for the impact that, thankfully, never happened, then she breathed a sigh of relief as Rob drove on to finally cross the white line at the end of pit road and accelerate out onto the track.

Wow! Another close call!

Rob was perfectly content to be running in tenth spot after the round of pit stops. The youth and lack of experience of his pit crew showed in their stop. They were a full second slower than the lead group of cars had been and they had lost another half second in the near-collision. That was enough to have cost them two spots in the running order. Still, after the two close calls and a slower-than-desired pit stop, and the narrow escape coming out of the pits, they were still running in the top ten.

He had not lost sight of first place despite all. His eye was still on the prize.

Will was happy with the stop, too. The move up to Cup racing was a big step all the way around for him, the car, his driver, and his crew. This had been the very first competition pit stop for this particular group of crewmen, and Will was more than pleased with the effort if not the results. He didn't necessarily like losing positions in the pits and especially while under a caution flag, but, at the same time, he knew that with a few races' worth of experience and some more practice, the times on their stops would certainly pick up and be as good as anybody's.

Rob circled slowly, trailing along behind the pace car, trying to size up the competition that stretched out in front of him. The caution flag stayed out for a while as the cleanup of the big crash continued. That gave Rob a chance to finally catch his breath and stretch his stiffening neck. For a moment, he allowed himself to relax as much as he could and look over the drivers around and just ahead of him. It was still unbelievable that he was actually out here on the track at Daytona, and that he was competing with these guys. But he was certainly not intimidated by these stars of stock car racing. It was a wonderful feeling to know not only that he was here with them but that he was running competitively, not getting in the way of any of the legends, that he was actually passing some of them. Rob could only smile behind his face mask as he pondered the last twenty laps or so that would remain when the flag finally dropped again. He tried to anticipate what those laps might bring his way.

Will studied the computer, double-checking where they sat in the running order. The wreck knocked out five cars for sure and did damage to several others. Most of these unfortunate drivers had been among the fastest in the field. That should make their task of finishing somewhere in the top fifteen considerably easier. That also changed their strategy. Now that it appeared they should be able to make the race, they would have to drive smarter. Any kind of slipup or damage to the car could knock them from the biggest race any of them had ever run and send them to packing up for home.

"Okay, here's what we need you to do," Will radioed. "That wreck knocked out several cars in front of you. That leaves only sixteen or eighteen cars that can keep up with you." *Only* sixteen to eighteen! "We have to finish the race to make the field. Most of those that got knocked out have us beaten on speed. They'll fill the back spots on Sunday. We're going to have to race our way in if we're going to make the 500."

"Ten-four, Will. That I can do," Wilder answered assuredly. "No problem there."

Will went on as if he had not heard his driver's reassuring reply at all. "You're going to be smart and stay out of trouble. Don't be sticking the nose of that car where it doesn't need to go. We need to finish with the lead pack. Not necessarily ahead of the lead pack. With them. Understand?"

"Got you. But I have one question. What am I supposed to do when I'm riding along up there leading everybody else on that last lap? Want me to slow down and drift back into the middle of the field and hide?"

There was a moment's pause on the radio circuit.

"You just stay out of trouble out there," Will shot back, not totally appreciating the kid's sarcasm.

He had no time right that minute for his driver's humor or his usually appealing bravado. This was serious business, and they had to drive smart, not aggressively, to make the field. They could not rely on dumb luck. Not at this level. Driving skill requires far more than simply being able to drive fast.

"Okay, boss," Rob answered meekly.

He grinned, though, imagining the intense look on Will Hughes's face. Will worried too much. He would be okay. And he still had a shot at claiming the prize he craved in every race he ever ran: first place. First place had gotten much harder to come by since he had stepped up to Grand National—and it was going to be even more difficult now, running out here with the big boys.

Rob tried to get comfortable in the car, shifting in his seat, shaking his arms and legs. The tight safety belts didn't leave any room for his middle to move. His neck was already a little sore, likely the result of not being in a car over the long winter layoff. Or maybe from the sharp twists and turns and stops he had taken avoiding the near catastrophes of the last few minutes. Though he worked out often, there was still no substitute for getting out on the track and driving the car to get his body back into shape for racing.

All this time, Christy Fagan sat nervously in one of the director's chairs in the rear of the pit, watching the television monitor in the back of the pit box, listening to the give-and-take on the radio headset she wore. She grinned when she heard Rob's little joke and Will's curt reply. She had closed her eyes each time Rob seemed headed for disaster out there. In the little time she had known him and followed this wild and woolly sport, she had learned enough about it to know when something bad was about to happen. And she had seen a man she cared deeply for almost get himself involved in at least three calamities in the last five minutes or so.

But she tended to close her eyes each time things got tight out there. That's what she had done this time, too.

Now she looked up from the television screen when she heard the roar of the pack as it came thundering by, exiting the tri-oval.

The pileup on the backstretch left her with a bad case of twisted nerves, and she still shook slightly as she worked on controlling her breathing. Rob's voice on the radio after that mess out there had been a wonderful thing to hear. She still wasn't accustomed to seeing him drive that red car into a swirling mess of wrecking cars, getting himself swallowed up by the smoke. She would usually sit there, her eyes closed, holding the earphones tightly to her head until she heard his voice, heard him say he and the car were okay. Only then could she open her eyes and look for him to pass by or watch a replay on television of what had happened out there.

It was difficult for her not to worry about him when he was racing. He always told her, and always with a broad smile, that he would be okay, that the cars nowadays were as safe as they could make them. And she knew, too, the depth of his love for this sport. Racing was just about everything to Rob Wilder. Christy was also perceptive enough to know how wonderful it was for a man to be doing exactly what he most wanted to do. And she had to admit that racing had grabbed hold of her immediately.

Still, sometimes she wished the man she loved enjoyed writing computer software or playing a guitar, not riding a rocket at nearly two hundred miles per hour.

She absentmindedly wrung her hands as she waited for the restart. Now, she was more worried that he wouldn't make the race than she was about any more accidents. Surely that was all the banging and crashing they could cram into one simple 125-mile race!

Michelle chuckled as she spied on her sister from her vantage point above the pits, her binoculars to her eyes. She could see how flustered Christy was after the crash and Rob's close call. She nudged Billy and pointed to Christy. He grinned, too, but he also understood the rainbow of emotions she was likely experiencing. He had never married, but he had watched Catherine Lee and the wives of the other drivers go through the same agony and ecstasy that Christy Fagan was now experiencing every time Rob raced. And he strongly suspected that Christy was almost as competitive as Wilder. And that she was helping him drive the car in her own way from her director's chair down there in the pits.

Rob Wilder knew she was there, too. And he knew she was on his side. That made a difference to a man, a very special and crucial difference.

Once again, Billy Winton said a small, silent prayer of thanks for Christy Fagan.

The green flag fell once more, sending the swarm of cars racing off toward turn one. Rob ran up through the gears smoothly, hoping for a slipup by someone in front of him that might allow him to pick up a position or two. The tightly packed race cars sailed through turn one as the restricted engines brought the cars up to speed.

Rob looked down to the inside, already searching for an opportunity for a run on the car ahead of him. It was clear, though, he didn't have enough momentum just yet. He kept Will's admonition in the back of his mind, but he desperately wanted to jump out of line and try to make something happen.

Finally, he could stand it no longer and gently nudged the car down to the inside. A quick glance in the mirror confirmed what he already suspected would happen. The car behind him moved upward and filled in the hole he had just left, its driver poised to take Rob's vacated slot in line instead of pulling out and helping both of them draft by the car ahead of them.

"Come on, baby! Come on!" Rob coaxed, mostly under his breath, as he felt the power of Joe Banker's engine gradually pull the car toward the front, drafting partner or not.

He cleared one car and was almost past the second when something remarkable happened. The car he had just passed dropped down, slid in behind him, and, in the process, gave him a healthy, welcomed push. Rob shot ahead with the added boost from his new partner, bolting on past the car he had been passing and then picking off another car. As soon as he heard the word, "Clear!" shouted out over the radio, he drifted right back up into the long line of traffic, followed closely by the car that was pushing him along from behind.

Rob was confident he could have made the three-car pass without the assistance of the following car. But it sure had been a heck of a lot easier with him.

The kid studied the bumper of the car that now ran directly in front of him. He was lurking there temporarily, only waiting for the chance to make another move to get closer to the front of this long loud train.

With five laps to go, Rob found himself sitting in seventh position, riding along in an eight-car, single-file breakaway. A second pack held nine more cars and sailed along about thirty car-lengths back. They were still a threat, though. They had finally gotten in a single-file line and they were closing in on the leaders quickly.

The radio broadcast's color commentator summed up the situation for his listeners all over the world.

"If the leaders get to racing side-by-side over the next few laps, that second bunch is going to make it a sixteen-car draft for the lead. If that happens, then we're looking at a real shoot-out for both the lead and that last transfer spot into the 500, folks."

"I'll say," the lead announcer agreed. "This is shaping up to be a wild finish and one of these cars could easily wind up having to pack things up and head for home on Thursday night . . . not Sunday evening."

Even as they said the words, a couple of the front-running cars decided it was time to make a move, pulling out to try to help each other toward the lead so they could show the way the final few laps. That's all it took to allow the second cluster of race cars to come right on up and merge with the front pack.

"I tell you what, we have witnessed some impressive racing so far," the old driver doing the commentary said. "One of the most impressive is the job being done by young 'Rocket' Rob Wilder, now sitting there in seventh place. He has hung in there all race long. The kid seems to have the poise of a veteran with plenty more laps under his belt than this youngster has."

"After watching him weave his way through that accident earlier and get himself out the other side unscathed, I can tell you that I am thoroughly impressed, regardless of where he finishes."

"Well, I can't wait to see what the young kid can do over these last couple of laps."

"I think the key question will be whether his crew chief, Will Hughes, can keep the young man roped in and focused on making the 500. There's an awful temptation for a youngster to want to try to win the race and maybe lose far more in the process."

"I'll tell you this," the wily old veteran said, the admiration obvious in his voice. "If I was Hughes, I'd let this kid loose. I don't know if he has enough car or experience to mix it up with those two guys who are leading, but I bet they'll know who this kid is before this thing is finished."

Will sat hunched over, watching the TV monitor at his feet. He studied the stopwatch in his hand with every pass of the lead pack. He debated with himself about what he ought to do. Should he, indeed, cut Rob loose out there and let him do what comes naturally to him? Or should they simply play it safe, assure some spot in the 500 field? Or should they race for a better spot for Sunday's race.

While practically everyone else in the speedway happily watched the impressive show that was going on out there on the racetrack, Will Hughes agonized over his decision. As he watched the second group of cars drive right up and catch the lead pack he let out a long, anguished groan. He didn't need any more cars in the mix. If someone got overly aggressive, they could be in big trouble. And that would especially be the case if a couple of them got together and started another big pileup like the earlier conflagration.

Or if some of the cars in that bunch were as strong as they now appeared, they might actually pass Rob by and bump them from the race entirely. That was not a pleasant thought either.

Now was the time for Will Hughes to earn his salary, to justify the confidence Billy Winton has placed in him when he hired him away from Jodell Lee's crew to chief his own racing team. There was no one else to make this call and, right or wrong, they would have to live or die with it.

No use taking a poll. He knew what Rob's vote would be. Billy or Jodell Lee or Bubba Baxter would likely prefer to err on the side of caution. Whichever way he went, it would be up to Rob Wilder to follow through with the call and bring the car home. The truth of the matter was that, as the car's driver, the one closest to the situation, Rob had the ultimate say over what happened when it came right down to it. Will knew what the kid would decide. He would want to go to the front.

Win the danged race, and there'd be no debate whatsoever about a good starting spot for the big one come Sunday!

However they decided to play out the remaining half dozen laps, it would fall on Will to try to temper the young driver's enthusiasm, to make sure he drove smart. An intelligent driver won far more often than the guys with the faster cars. Rob's God-given ability and his smooth, smart driving style had attracted Jodell Lee's attention the first night he saw him run on the dusty little track in the middle of nowhere. But the kid had to take that skill and intelligence to a whole new level now. He just had a few rough edges that needed to be burnished with experience and with the tutelage of folks like Will Hughes and Jodell Lee.

As the cars flew into the third turn, sweeping through the steep slope of the sharply canted banking, the cars ahead of Rob seemed intent on breaking formation and mixing it up. Rob itched to pull out of line and have a go at them but he still heard Will's last words of instruction ringing in his ears. He felt certain he could take the 52 Ford to the front. He had felt the depth of her power. He craved a chance to learn for certain what he had for the leaders.

There would be four laps to go when they crossed the stripe this trip. Time was running out. Rob forced himself to lock onto nothing but the car in front of him. He had already made up his mind that he would follow that driver when and if he decided to make his own move.

Billy stood in the suite watching and waiting, dancing nervously from one foot to the other. The long string of cars rocketing past him had already begun to shuffle around. Their car stayed in line, though, crowding the bumper of the car ahead of it. The kid was doing a good job, exactly what his crew chief had commanded, but Billy could imagine what was running through the rookie's mind.

Billy grinned. If he had been sitting in the driver's seat of that bright red machine, he would be dying to do the same thing.

The radio had been quiet for a while except for Harry counting down the laps and giving Rob occasional bits of information about what was going on around him. But suddenly, there was Will Hughes on the net, and everyone with a headset perked up. They knew he was ready to set the strategy for the rest of this contest, and they couldn't wait to hear what it would be.

"Let's show these guys we came down here to race, cowboy. I guess it's time for you to introduce yourself to those boys at the front."

Billy smiled as he listened to Will's words. Surprisingly, he concurred with the decision. Though settling for a more sure position might be the cautious thing to do, they came down to this place to race, not to simply ride around and take what was handed them. If they fooled around and got themselves beaten by daring to go for the front, then so be it. There would be other days and other races, and they owed it to their driver, their crew, their fans, and their sponsors to run for the front, not sit back and idle.

The sixteen-car draft raced along in single file as everyone finally settled back into line for the moment. Drivers were dipping and weaving all along the queue, though, as they sized up the cars in front of them, trying to determine where or even if they would make a move. It appeared everyone was waiting on somebody else to be the first to step out into no-man's-land.

The veteran up front leading the race didn't care. They could stay lined up behind him for the rest of the race, and that would be fine with him. Better yet, they could get to dicing around, racing side by side, leaving him unchallenged for the point, and he would just drive right on off to the checkered flag and get this thing over with in a hurry.

Rob gripped the wheel a little tighter after getting the go-ahead from Will to cut it loose. Then, something fluttered wildly in his gut. Butterflies! All race long he itched to be given the go-ahead, to have the chance to race for the lead. Now when the nod came, he suddenly got swamped with a bad case of nerves!

The kid squeezed his eyes shut tightly then opened them quickly, gazing once more at the back bumper of the car in front of him. Somehow, he was now conscious of every bump and ripple in the track's surface passing up through the steering column and into his arms. His hands felt like they were made of lead. It was almost a struggle to turn the wheel as the car thundered back into the high banks of turn one. He momentarily fought the powerful urge to jerk the wheel to the inside to pull out of the tight line of drafting racers.

Where had his concentration gone? Where was his racer's edge that he usually had in him? Was it possible that he might not be cut out to compete at this level after all, that he had been fooling himself and everybody around him?

The questions ran through his mind like the signs and waving fans he passed around the speedway. Losing focus now at these speeds, with the tight racing that surely was about to get even tighter, was a dangerous thing.

For an instant, Rob considered simply holding his position in line and telling Will it was the best he could do, that he would settle for what they had and not take the risk. None of the other cars were jumping out of line. Why should he? With all their experience, they surely knew more about what was the best tack to take than he did.

As those thoughts circled in his brain, he rode along in the midst of the freight train of cars roaring out of turn four, heading for the stripe yet again.

Four laps to go.

It was crunch time, time to make a move if he ever intended to. But the young driver held his wheels straight, seemingly paralyzed behind the wheel, desperately trying to hold on and not risk what he had been able to earn already.

"Go! Go!"

The words rang loudly, fervently in his ears. But it wasn't the radio, and it was not a voice he immediately recognized.

Who was it? Where was the command coming from?

The car bored on through the wind, angling through the tri-oval. Then, there was the voice again, even more insistent than before.

"Inside! Move to the inside now! Do it!"

Then, he knew it was the right thing to do. The right time to do it.

"It looks like we're going to wind down to a last-lap shoot out," the lead announcer was saying. "It seems like nobody wants to hop out of line and run the risk of getting hung out to dry. They could find themselves falling all the way back to the end of the line and maybe even miss that final transfer spot."

"That's right. These drivers are all tightly focused on getting the car to the last lap." The old driver seemed to have a sudden thought, and he spoke it out loud. "But you know what? I'm not so sure if that is a smart move on their part. We haven't seen many passes lately, and on this race, if I was back a half dozen cars or so, I believe I'd be mixing it up, trying to get myself up as close to the front as I could. A couple of side-by-scrambles in the top five might give some of these other cars a shot at taking over the top spot. And, in my opinion, that's the place to be on that last lap."

At that very moment, Rob yanked the wheel to the left, pulling the car out of the safe, comfortable line and down to the inside. The Ford responded as if he had lashed her with a riding crop. Rob used the draft of the car he had been following to slingshot past him, as if he had just lit the fuse on a powerful, powerful rocket.

Rob Wilder looked nowhere but ahead. It was now or never. He had just made a brilliant or a bonehead move. The next few seconds would tell which. But one thing was obvious. He was running out there all by himself, and he would either pass the whole line of cars that had been ahead of him, or he would go skating backward, desperately trying to find a hole to crawl into and hide for the rest of the race.

"Whoa! Look at this!" the radio announcer sang. "We have a car moving down to the inside to make a pass. Who is that?"

"That's the youngster . . . Wilder . . . in the Ensoft Ford. It looks like he's not afraid to get out there and mix it up. And he obviously thinks he has a car that can go to the front."

The radio audience couldn't see the big smile on the old Cup star's face. He was proud of the youngster, and he felt a similar rush of adrenaline to what the kid must be feeling as he boldly whipped out of line and headed for the lead.

"This kid sure does have guts. And confidence to boot. Look at him passing cars on the inside. He has managed to push up to the rear of the fourth place car, and he's doing it all on his own."

"Without any help at all! Can you imagine? That's amazing. He may have a fast car, but if he stays out there on his own, then I'm afraid we're going to see the other cars start to go by him on the outside and he'll have to scramble to find a place to get back in line."

"I don't know. I like this kid's moxie. For a rookie here at Daytona in his first 125-mile race, this is an impressive showing of courage and confidence," the commentator said, the admiration obvious in his voice even as he tried to appear impartial to his radio listeners.

He was familiar enough with the kid from the previous year's season on the Grand National series. He had also heard whispers about the youngster in the garage from circuit veterans. This driver was not merely another of the up-and-coming open wheel hotshots that were now in fashion in Cup racing when a team wanted to hire a new pilot. No, Rob Wilder was more a throwback to stock car racing's heyday, when the new blood came from those who had been cutting their teeth already on tiny bullrings and wild-and-woolly Saturday-night features on out-of-the-way dirt tracks. He was more cut from the mold of Richard Petty and Buddy Baker and Bobby Allison, drivers who would run a race anywhere one happened to break out, no matter if there was prize money or not.

Sometimes, the old commentator thought, that youngster reminds me more of myself and some of the other old-timers than anybody I've seen come along in quite a while. He almost said as much into the microphone, but he stopped. He didn't want to jinx the kid, and such a pronouncement might be enough to do it.

Meanwhile, back down on the track, Rob could definitely feel the forward surge of the car ebb a bit once he got door-handle-to-door-handle with the Chevy that was running in fourth place. The momentum he had used to whip past the other cars seemed to quickly vanish once he found himself stuck in a side-by-side battle. Without someone following him, giving him a boost, he would soon be on a very lonely island out there. Still, Rob kept his foot jammed hard to the floor, coaxing every last ounce of power out of the engine, just managing to stay even with the Chevrolet for the moment.

Then, just when Rob was prepared to begin sliding back, looking for any kind of a slot to tuck into, a very familiar car, one driven by a several-time Cup champion, suddenly dropped down out of line and pulled right up on the rear bumper of the Ensoft Ford. Rob immediately felt the strong push of air behind him and his car nosed out ahead of the fourth-place car.

Rob held the preferred line going into the corner and he used the column of air off the snout of the champion's car to shove his own racer along toward the front of the lead pack. Rob wrestled the wheel mightily, holding the car down on the low line through the corner. The three cars ahead of him had to ease upward into the center of the banking as he quickly came up on their inside, almost as if he had been shot out of a cannon. Rob could only imagine what was going through their minds at that moment.

But he wasn't concerned about them. Now, he studied the open track that spread out before them, looking for slower cars that might soon be in his way up there. None. Nothing but open track. Then there it was, up there in front of him, ready for him to claim.

The lead!

Christy Fagan could hardly watch the television monitor as it all began to unfold out there, as the screen was filled with Rob and his red car, pulling down to the inside. She understood the draft well enough to know it was better to have a partner if he was to have any chance to gain much ground. She watched Rob quickly pull up next to the Chevrolet, then get stalled there, as if he simply couldn't find enough power to complete the pass, yet didn't dare back off and lose momentum.

She crossed her fingers on both hands and danced around in the chair as she watched and waited for whatever was to happen next. She hardly noticed when the network camera crew assigned to the pits eased up beside her and focused in on her beautiful but tense face, on her long blond hair blowing in the Daytona wind. Then they panned down to where she held her double set of crossed fingers in her lap.

She paid them no mind, keeping her eyes on the set until the shot returned to Rob and the action out on the track. Nor could she hear the director's words in the televisions crew's headsets.

"Money shot," he crowed. "Good job. Stay there. Money shot."

As she watched, she almost whooped when the former champ pulled out of line and slid down to tuck right in behind Rob. That was a good thing! She felt an electric charge of excitement run through her. For the first time this day, she thought that Rob might actually win this thing. And even as she felt the rush of exhilaration, the two cars, now working well together, began pulling up closer, just below the three lead cars.

Billy watched his driver slip out of the rocking chair and out into the fury, all of it happening just as the group of cars was roaring past where he stood.

"Yes!" he sang, clinching his hand into a fist and punching the air as Rob made his bold move.

Billy knew the other drivers were being way too conservative. They were all jockeying for starting positions in the 500 instead of trying to win an automobile race. They were being timid. Billy knew it. Somehow, the youngster out there in the brilliant red car had sensed it, too. Those front cars were not going to risk losing a top-ten starting spot in the big race just to capture a first in a qualifying event.

Billy didn't care. Neither did Rob. Barring a last-minute disaster, they would certainly make the field now. And his driver needed to experience what it would be like to be in the lead pack, to try to challenge for the win, just as he might be for real on Sunday. It would put a charge in his crew, give his sponsor a thrill to have the camera trained on the red car with their logo as it boldly dashed out for the lead.

This was racing! Dadgummit, this was racing!

Then, when Billy saw the experienced driver pull down and follow his own driver, he laughed out loud with the joy of what that seemingly minor move meant. His young driver had won the respect of at least one veteran out there. Enough respect that the former champion was willing to follow him wherever he went so long as it was toward the checkered flag!

Billy Winton continued to ignore his VIPs and glanced from the track to the television, whichever one offered him the best view of the final few laps. Things were quickly changing out there as the leaders exited turn two onto the long back straightaway. Stray seagulls dipped and dodged in the foreground, sunlight reflected off the lake in the infield, but Billy saw none of that. As he kept his gaze on the cars at the head of the pack, he could see that the second-place car had finally gotten brave. Or scared.

The driver had almost certainly spied Rob and his buddy charging up to his inside, quickly moving in on him and the leader when they likely were certain they had first and second locked up. He quickly made up his mind to dive down to the inside himself, directly in front of the red 52, trying to use the two hard-charging cars to propel him right on past the first-place car and take the lead himself.

Michelle Fagan had not sat down since the race started. Now, she jumped and cheered as the group of cars running two lanes wide charged in tandem toward turn three. She looked down from the monitor to quickly survey the pits. She saw Will sitting there amid all the jumping and cavorting that was going on, a study in serene concentration. Donnie, Paul, and the rest of the boys danced and twirled around the monitor or hopped up on the pit wall, trying to see everything as it unfolded out there.

Christy had both arms in the air now, fingers on each hand still crossed, as she kept her eyes on the screen. They were no longer closed. She had to see this.

There was an electric atmosphere all up and down the pit road as the sixteen cars jockeyed for position with only two laps to go. But the race itself was still a long way from decided. The front seven or eight cars now ran stacked two and three wide behind the leader, who was already trying to make his racer as wide as he could, fighting off the furious battle coming at him from behind. Clearly, Rob's move to leave the line and the former champ's driving out to join him had set off the competitive juices in these men. If the red car wanted to shake things up, then they had all seemingly decided to join the fray, to run for the lead. The packed grandstands, the television audience, and the listeners to the show on the radio were all loving it.

The leader skewed back and forth across the track, doing all he could to disrupt the air flow off his own car that was sweeping back to buffet the trailing racers. That also made it more difficult for anyone to pass him. Rob desperately wanted to make that pass to the inside of the leader but since the second-place car had pulled down in front of him, that route was effectively blocked for the moment.

As the field thundered down along the front grandstand, not a single paying customer was in his seat. The crowd stood shoulder to shoulder, cheering as one as the field shot past in front of them, the cars shifting, diving, darting, all of them now suddenly seeking a better position.

There was either going to be a frantic run to the finish or a massive pileup. Either way, the fans knew they were about to get their money's worth in a simple little qualifying race they would talk about for years.

"Two to go," Will called to Rob.

Rob heard the words, saw the flagstand slip past, but didn't take the time to reply and never once broke his intense concentration on the two cars in front of him and the dozen or so to his outside.

The spotter was silent, too, except for an occasional call of, "Outside. Still outside." Harry was determined to not let Rob forget that there was a long line of mean, fast race cars just up the track from him and even the slightest wiggle to the outside would set off a catastrophe. He knew there was no way the kid was going to try to pull back into ranks now. Not with the race on the line. But it was his job to keep reminding him, quietly but emphatically.

Rob followed the second-place Ford in front of him through turns one and two. The leader still sat a carlength ahead of the double wide line of cars that was furiously chasing him. Rob took a quick look down to the inside of the Ford as they came off turn two, then shot another glance in his mirror. His original drafting partner was still there, seemingly bound to his rear bumper, mimicking every move Rob made.

The second-place car's driver seemed to read Rob's mind and moved over to block any attempt to draft past him. Rob eased the wheel back to the right, considering trying to get by to the outside, but the Ford's driver moved over to block that route, too.

Rob was growing more and more frustrated. The cars in the outside line effectively kept him boxed in as the group raced off toward turn three. Farther back, the rest of the lead pack had now split up into their own skirmishes, effectively allowing the front seven cars to scramble for the win. This time, when the sixteen screaming vehicles swept into turns three and four, they had split up into two distinct bands separated by ten to fifteen car-lengths.

The second bunch would be fighting for the final transfer positions into the 500. The first squadron was gunning for the lead.

Each driver angled his way expertly for the best position as they collectively headed down to the white flag that signaled there was only one lap left to go. Will knew they had an outside shot at the win but the driver ahead of Rob was giving him fits. That was only natural. That driver had won scores of races, was one of the best in the business with a superbly prepared car. He would be hard to pass, and especially by a rookie like Rob Wilder in a brand-new race car.

And that would be an easy pass compared to getting past the guy who was leading! And they still had to consider all the others bearing down on them, too, as well as the former champ, still filling Rob's mirror. He wasn't trailing along just to enjoy watching the kid drive. He no doubt had designs on the lead himself.

But still, for some reason, Will liked their chances. Anything could happen. And it likely would.

Rob hardly noticed the white flag waving over them as they flashed across the stripe to begin the final lap. Will didn't even bother to call the last lap to his driver. Harry Stone simply said, "One to go," in a voice far more calm than he felt.

Will was certain the kid was driving as hard as he could, getting all he could from the car. Winning was all that mattered to him, after all, and he would be doing all he could to do just that. But they were about to run out of race as the gang of seven charged off toward the towering banking in turn one.

The wheel vibrated ominously in Rob's hands as he tried to dip down and shove his nose beneath the second-place car. The Ford's driver ran Rob all the way down to the track's apron as he tried to keep this young upstart behind him.

Rob would have none of it, though. He didn't care that he had watched the man win races on television, that he had almost asked him for an autograph the first time he saw him at a drivers' meeting. No, now he wanted the lead and the win for himself.

The cars shot through the sweeping high bank, making the transition down onto the backstretch. The second-place car suddenly pulled downward, making a feint as if he were headed that way, looking for the lead. The leader bit and cut over to block that route, taking the challenger all the way to the grass.

The cars running the outside line remained out by the wall, trying to stay out of any trouble that might break out and to see if they could get by on the outside if it should. Rob followed the Ford on its feint to the inside, then quickly nudged his car back to the right, trying to sneak up through the middle. In the process, they were suddenly a three-wide bunch at the head of the field.

Now, even the most unsophisticated observer could see that something had to give. There was simply not enough room for all those cars to run three across and seven deep through that upcoming turn without someone going astray. Rob rode along sandwiched between two other cars, what had been the second-place Ford and what had been, up until this sticky turn of events, the clear race leader.

But now, there was the most beautiful sight he could ever hope to see out his windshield as he nosed up even with the leader. Nothing but clear track as far as he could see into the turn.

But he could still see the former champ in his mirror. And he could only imagine the hungry grin on the man's face behind his full helmet mask.

"Look at that move down the backstretch by young Rob Wilder!" the announcer shouted into the microphone. He, too, had obviously been seized by the drama of the moment.

"That kid has shown he has a hunger to win," the commentator added. "That move up the middle took some guts. That youngster could just as easily sit back there and watch the others fight it out, assured of an excellent starting spot for Sunday. But I'm not sure 'sit back' is in Rob Wilder's vocabulary."

"I think we're seeing why he earned the nickname Rocket Rob. He sure looks like he's driving a rocket ship today."

Rob felt as much as saw the hole open up the middle as they raced wheel to wheel down the backstretch. He pushed the car into the narrow opening, splitting the two groups of cars that were racing on either side. Just as he had expected, the driver who had been tailing him for the last few laps, the one who had helped him get to this point, stayed right with him, trying to push both of them through the stingy gap they had found. It was a tough spot to be in though—three wide with a hungry former champion and three other desperate race car drivers right behind them, all of them aiming for the same thing that waited for them down there at the end of the lap.

The seven cars all seemed determined to occupy the same bit of real estate in turn three. Not possible—and they all knew it, but which would give way, which would hold their own, and who would survive this game of chicken at a 190 miles per hour?

Rob Wilder had already decided where he would fall in that quandary, and he rededicated himself as he set the car for the line he wanted to run through the corner. There was no way he was going to back out of the gas now. Not when he was so close to a victory.

The car on the outside found somewhere just enough momentum to push out to a lead of one car-length as they were diving into three. The new leader pushed his car high up into the turn, giving everyone plenty of room. The old leader, still hugging the low side of the track, could have used some space himself. He was rapidly running out of room at the apron. Rob saw no point in squeezing the guy, so he moved slightly up the track to give him room to race. Besides, if he hadn't, the Chevy might well have broken loose, careened up the track and plowed into his side, likely wrecking him and a whole raft of cars behind them. But the move up the banking killed his momentum and that let the three cars running nose to tail on the outside of him shoot on by.

There might have been a temptation then to surrender, to ease off, slide into line and cut his losses. But Rob's foot never lifted off the floor as he fed the engine all the gas he could get her to swallow. His buddy behind didn't hesitate either and continued to dance with the rookie he had hooked up with. That served to help Rob and his drafting companion get another good run on the three lead cars as they zoomed off the corner, all of them racing for the checkers that were already being held high over the finish line down in the tri-oval.

The front three cars stayed right out next to the wall. Rob waited a second until he felt the time was right, then tried to pick up the draft once more so he could get one last shot at the lead.

Finally, when he knew it was his very last opportunity, Rob swung wide going through the short chute, making his last desperate attempt at picking up a couple of positions. He held his breath, bit down hard, squinted his eyes, and held on as if he were riding an out-of-control Roman candle and really had no say about which direction the thing went. All he could do was keep his foot shoved to the firewall and the steering wheel straight.

But it was not to be. As the straining race cars flashed under the waving checkered flag, Rob was able to pull up even with the door handles on the third-place car. But that was it, all he could do as the cars shot across the stripe. The champ stayed with him all the way, locked to his bumper until they had whipped past the finish line.

An animated Billy Winton jumped and whirled as the tightly bunched pack of racers took the checkered flag, so close to each other a blanket could have been thrown over the lot of them. There was no way he could hide his excitement. Not only had they made their very first 500 at Daytona, but, thanks to his driver's skill and his crew's hard work, they would start somewhere close to the front on Sunday.

And they had put on one hell of a show. Yes, they had. One hell of a show.

9

VOICES

Fourth! Yes! Can you all believe that?" Billy Winton asked everybody within earshot as he reached for Michelle and proceeded to dance an awkward little jig around the suite with her. "We're in! We're in the 500, Miss Fagan!"

"Cool . . . so cool," was about all Michelle could manage. She was hoarse and out of breath from all the screaming.

Down in the pits below them, Will Hughes breathed a long sigh of relief as their car finally took the checkers safely despite the wild waltz it had been doing with the other cars out there. The Ford was still in one piece, and they had proved to themselves and everyone else out there that they had a car they could race with. Fourth wasn't so bad, either. It was mighty sweet reward for the winter's hard work. All the long hours they had spent prepping the car had clearly been worth it.

Christy Fagan was doing her own jig around the pits

with Donnie Kline and other members of the crew. It
looked for all the world as if they had actually won the
qualifier. The television crew was still right there, shoot-
ing her reaction to the wild finish.

Fourth place was winning, after all. They had accomplished their first goal of the week. They made the 500
and they made it in convincing fashion. Convincing for
their competitors, convincing for themselves.

Rob waited until the driver who had been tailing him
backed off before he finally cracked the throttle and began slowing the car down. The champ pulled up alongside him and gave him a wave that said "well done." The
driver must have sensed what a major boost this run was
to the young driver and his team. And with his own car
off just a tick today, the former champ was appreciative
to have been able to hitch a ride along with someone
faster, to claim a better starting position for the race than
he might otherwise have been able to get on his own.

Rob waved back and smiled. That veteran wasn't car-
ing that he had been drafting with a rookie. The kid had
no way of knowing that the former champion had
watched him in practice. It was obvious to the driver that
the kid could race, so he had not hesitated when he had
the opportunity to draft with Rob. Both men knew that
without the other, they would have been back in seventh
or eighth place or worse, certainly not fourth and fifth.

They coasted down onto pit road where the officials
were stopping each car at the entrance to the garage to
check the angles on their spoilers. Rob was cleared and
waved off to the gas pumps. When he stopped the car,
he was suddenly awfully tired. Sweat dripped from his
face and ran from his hair as he pulled off his helmet
and sucked in a deep draft of air. His arms still shook
from the tense grip he had maintained on the steering
wheel over the last half dozen laps, from the steady vi-

brations and constant bumps that were transmitted directly up through the steering column.

He flipped the buckle to the safety belts and let them drop off his tired shoulders. The window net came down while he was still fiddling with the wires to the radio earpieces. Then, the strong arms of Donnie Kline reached through the driver's-side window and literally plucked him out of the cockpit.

"Whoa there, Donnie. Hold on a minute. Let me catch my breath, wild man," Rob begged, sitting in the window, half in and half out of the car. The rest of the crew came sprinting up then, surrounding him, and pounding him on the back.

"Man, what a race!" Donnie crowed. "You should have seen the looks on everyone's face along pit road when you jumped out of line like you done and made that charge to the front. Whoooeee!"

"Just doing what Billy pays me to do, Donnie, that's all," Rob said, climbing from the window and standing there for a moment on shaky legs.

"Well, you left a lot of them superstars breathing your exhaust out there today, young'un. I think if you hadn't of pushed them, they would have been perfectly content to play follow-the-leader, boring us all to death, all the way down to the checkered flag."

"They might have done that very thing, Donnie, but I had no intention of laying back, sandbagging, settling. I think if I hadn't got boxed in by that blue car when he was in second, I could have taken them all," Rob replied, using his hands to show how the car moved right on over into his way and rudely cut him off.

"You should have just drop-kicked him out of the way," Paul Phillips added with a big grin on his face. Paul worked on several winning teams over the years. But he wanted more. That was one of the reasons he had grabbed the chance to join up when Will and Billy came calling. After today, he finally was reassured that the job change was a positive move. They could win with this car, with this team, and with this kid. Maybe not Sunday's race, but they could and they would win.

"I don't race that way," Rob said in all seriousness. Then his face broke into a big grin, too. "But that doesn't mean I didn't think long and hard about it a time or two."

Christy came running up then with Michelle and Billy following not far behind. She grabbed Rob, sending him staggering hard back against the race car. She locked her arms around him in a hug so tight he had to gasp for breath. Then, before he could dodge, she planted a long, fervent kiss on his lips. Rob ignored the catcalls of the crew and kissed her right back, loving the feel of her against him, of her arms around his neck.

"Here you go, Romeo," Michelle said when they finally broke the kiss. She passed him an ice-cold bottle of sports drink and a towel. "You might need to cool off after all that."

She had a slight smile on her face but an odd look in her eye. Rob couldn't help but notice it. Was she mad at him for something?

Interviewers, eager to get a word with this hot young driver, temporarily interrupted the celebration. Rob smiled and thanked all the right people and mentioned his sponsor and then colorfully recounted the last wild laps of the race. When the network crew walked up, Billy made sure that Christy was still hugging Rob, that her lovely face and the Ensoft logos on her shirt collars were in the camera shot. Billy had long ago noticed how the television cameras seemed to focus in on the handsome young driver and his beautiful girlfriend. And the sponsor logos were always in the picture by default.

Once the interviews were over, Rob looked around for Michelle. He wanted to talk to her, to find out if she was upset about something. He couldn't remember saying or doing anything before the race. As he looked through the milling crowd for her, he couldn't help but hear over the track loudspeakers an interview that was being carried from the radio broadcast. His ears perked up.

"Champ, tell us about that great fifth-place run you had today."

"Well, thanks, but we really weren't that happy with the car. It was off a notch or two today but we can fix that by Sunday. Listen, I just want to thank Rob Wilder. Without him, we would have been stuck way back in the field for the 500. We were able to draft with him those last few laps, and he pulled us to the front. We had ourselves about a tenth-place car and it looks like we got us a fifth-place finish out of it, so I think we can chalk it up as a good day."

"Tell us something about racing with young Wilder. A lot of drivers out there won't draft with a rookie. Especially one so young and inexperienced."

"He may be young, but I wouldn't say he's inexperienced. I saw him making moves out there today that a lot of these old-timers couldn't do. I'd rather race with him than some of the other so-called veteran drivers out there."

Rob couldn't believe what he had just heard. Here was somebody he'd idolized for years going out of his way to give him a compliment. He couldn't help it. He puffed out his chest proudly then went looking for Christy. Meanwhile, out on the track, the cars were already circling for the second 125-mile qualifying race.

A couple of hours later, Rob was still answering questions about the fine run he'd done earlier in the day. The second 125 was long since over, leaving the field for the 500 finally set. Christy, exhausted from the trip out from the coast, the long day at the track, and the emotional race had retreated to the comfort of the truck's lounge area while the boys finished up with the preparations for leaving the car overnight.

Michelle was tired, too. She had worked the suite and glad-handed their guests all day. Now, she walked over gingerly, her feet apparently aching, and joined Rob. The last few reporters had wandered off to find somebody else to pump for news.

He didn't see her coming. She came up behind him and wrapped her arms around him, squeezing him tightly. Rob, sure it was Christy, whirled around, his face inches from hers, ready to accept another kiss from her.

"Quite a race. Congratulations," she whispered in a voice he had never heard from her before. He jerked away from her embrace, a startled look on his face. She cocked her head. "What is it? You don't like me anymore?"

"Aw, Michelle, I thought you were Christy," Rob said, embarrassed.

"I thought I was your best friend. I don't get hugs anymore?"

"Michelle, you are my best friend," Rob said, and it sounded more like a plea. He had never actually thought of Michelle Fagan as a best friend, but, once he had said the words, he knew it was likely so. He had long ago lost most contact with his friends back in Hazel Green, Alabama. "And listen. You can hug me anytime you want to, okay?"

She didn't answer. She merely leaned into him even harder, letting him support most of her dead tired weight with his strong arms as he fell back against the race car.

As Rob tightened his embrace he felt a strange mix of emotions run through him. Was she trying to tell him something with her actions, her voice, the odd look in her eyes? Or was he imagining more than was actually there? It was almost like the voice he heard sometimes in the race car, the one that seemed to be telling him when to make his move. Except he usually obeyed that voice. He wasn't sure at all what Michelle Fagan was telling him.

He shrugged off the thoughts and finally released his hold on Michelle.

"Why don't you go on up into the truck and get something to drink?" he asked her.

"Good idea," she said. "And maybe I can get off my feet finally. You coming?"

"Maybe in a minute. I want to see how Jodell's team did today."

Rex Lawford had run in the second race, which had been a little less spectacular. Rob had been so busy with the reporters and accepting the congratulations of the fans and saying good-bye to the sponsor guests that he had not even seen how that qualifying had come out. Besides, he figured Will and Billy might already be over there in Jodell's garage space, all of them sharing what they had learned in the races.

As Rob double-timed alongside the team trucks, he heard a voice yell his name. He stopped, turned, and saw Jodell Lee himself headed his way, his step just a bit hesitant, the result of too many hard smacks into racetrack retaining walls.

"Where you heading off to in such an all-fired hurry, son?" Jodell asked when he was a bit closer.

"Over to visit with you, Jodell. I thought Billy and Will might be over there talking to Bubba, and I wanted to see how your car ran in the 125."

"Aw, we did all right. Eighth ain't nothing to brag about I don't guess. 'Specially when we got a car that's better than that. We needed a caution and we just didn't get one. If we could've pulled in long enough to drop a pound of air pressure out of the right sides, we'd have been fine. I guess those cats learned from that big wreck in your race and drove with their heads instead of their butts."

Rob laughed. And just then, he spotted the battered silver Pontiac of Stacy Locklear being loaded up in the hauler up ahead of where he and Jodell walked.

"It got a little bit tight out there. I had to close my eyes and let the old car drive herself through."

"I'm sure you had some help from somewhere on high. That was a tough one to get out of in one piece."

Stacy Locklear was standing there, propped up against the side of his hauler, forlornly watching his mangled car rise upward on the lift like some kind of offering to the racing gods.

"Yeah, and it was all so unnecessary. I don't know what he was thinking," Rob said, and pointed to where Locklear stood. "He was racing like it was the last lap, trying to squeeze into a spot that didn't exist."

"Some of them boys don't never learn, I reckon. Seems like they make the same mistake over and over. Now, there he is, loading up and going home because of it. It's a shame 'cause they had a decent car. Now him, his crew, his sponsor, his fans . . . they all lose without him ever running the race."

"I remember all that big talk he was giving me at Atlanta last year. Looks like he should have listened himself."

Rob caught Locklear's eye then as they walked close by. The sight of the kid brought an immediate deepening to the scowl that already owned the man's face.

"Hey, Locklear," Rob yelled, smiling. "Seems like . . ."

But immediately, Rob felt Jodell grip his arm tightly before the kid could go ahead and launch the wisecrack arrow he had strung and was ready to let fly.

"Easy now. That likely is going to be you one day, packing up and heading out of town early," Jodell whispered, so low Rob could barely hear him over all the noise in the nearby garage area.

Jodell slowed then and gave Locklear a wave of his hand.

". . . Seems like you had some tough luck out there today. Better luck next week, okay?"

Jodell was right, of course. Racing luck cut both ways, good guy or bad guy. It didn't seem to care whose day it ruined or made.

Stacy Locklear hesitated, then acknowledged Rob's wish with a nod. The two of them walked on and were out of Locklear's hearing when Jodell spoke again.

"That's it, son. Don't let guys like that get under your skin. They ain't worth the trouble or the knuckle skin."

"I'm not worried about him. I'd go fender to fender with him anywhere, anytime. And if he wants to tangle . . ."

"Never mind that. You waste time thinking about a guy like him and you let him win, regardless. That's how they try to get an edge, make you do something silly out there that lets him take you. Look, you're here to drive. Think about driving, not bustin' old Stacy Locklear's butt. And besides you know how they feel about fighting nowadays in the sport."

"Jodell, when I'm in the car, all I think about is driving. Driving and winning." He paused then. They were getting close to Jodell's garage stall. But there was something he had wanted to mention to Lee, something he wanted to ask him about. "You know, sometimes I have the strangest thing happen out there. It's like I can hear a voice, loud and clear as the radio, or just like you talking to me right here. It tells me what move to make on those last laps of a race. And sure enough, I do what the voice tells me to do, and it works." He stopped then and glanced over at the older man. What did he mean to do, talking to Jodell about such an impossible thing? Surely he would think Rob was crazy as a loon. But Lee was walking along, staring up at the awesome banking of turn three. "Am I losing my marbles, Jodell? Hearing things?"

Lee had slowed down his pace now, not quite so anxious to get back and see what Bubba and Rex were cooking up for the big race.

"What sort of a voice was it, son? Was it a fast, staccato voice with a deep mountain drawl?" Jodell asked him, as if the kid has just described some kind of rattle or squeak in the race car that he aimed to diagnose.

"Yeah, now that you mention it. There was a thick accent. How did you know?"

Jodell Lee had stopped now, stepping back out of the swirl of traffic all around them.

"Let me tell you a little story," Jodell said, and he motioned for Rob to join him for a seat on a nearby low wall. "A few of years ago, when they opened the big new speedway out in Fontana, California, I had to stop on the way out there to do an appearance in Nashville before I caught my flight out there. Well, I was rushing but things went smooth as could be expected, and I got to Los Angles right on time, rented a car, and set off on the drive out to Fontana. Forty or so miles from the airport, I imagine."

"We'll be out there later on. I'm looking forward to it," Rob offered, interrupting. He was already wondering where this was going when he mainly wanted to talk with Bubba and Rex about the Lee Ford and how it had handled for them out there on the Daytona track.

"Let me finish," Jodell said, throwing up his hand like a red flag. "Anyway, I got on the freeway heading toward the track. I'm late for the start of the first practice already because of the thing in Nashville and I'm driving along at a pretty good clip. Then, I remember wondering to myself about something we had been thinking about for the setup in the race car and that got me to thinking about my first trip out there. Neither Bubba or I had been married all that long, and we had flown Cath and Joyce out there, all the way from Chandler Cove. And buddy, that was a big trip back then. We picked them up at the airport and had a fine old time, like *The Beverly Hillbillies* or something, catching their first sight of the big city." Jodell had a faraway look in his eye and a slight smile on his lips as he talked. "It was a happy time. Cath surprised me on that trip with the news that I was going to be a daddy."

Rob studied the lines on Jodell's face, still wondering what this all had to do with his ghost voices. But something about the emotion with which the man spoke kept Rob from urging him on. Instead, he simply said, "Bob Jr."

"Right. Bob Jr. So anyway, I continue on out the freeway, and I remember hearing a voice. Well, not exactly a voice, but something that seemed to be urging me off the interstate. To this day, I couldn't tell you what it was. The next thing I know, I'm sitting out there on a big old chunk of concrete in the middle of a weed-strewn lot. And I realize I'm bawling like a baby." Now Rob was hooked. He started to ask a question, but he was silenced with another wave of the big man's hand. "And here's the wild part. I'm sitting there crying and all of a sudden, out there in the distance, I hear the sound of a race car in full song, running up through the gears. I could hear it coming around a racetrack just as plain as day. The quick shifts through the gears, that old engine squalling and singing when the driver gets back into the gas. This all went on and on as the car got closer and closer to where I sat. But remember I was in the middle of a big field, basically a construction site full of weeds and junk. Then, just when I thought that old race car was going to run over me without me ever even seeing it, I heard the most horrible grinding crash you could ever imagine. I must have jumped two feet off that slab of concrete, Robbie."

"Were you close to a racetrack, maybe? I didn't know there were any in Los Angeles except for the one way out there in Fontana."

"Yeah, sort of. I was at a racetrack all right. Or what was left of one, anyway. They had slapped up some kind of a housing development in one set of the turns. A shopping center covered up another couple of the far turns. The rest of it was covered with weeds and busted up concrete, what was left of a retaining wall."

"What track had it been?"

"Riverside." Jodell spat it out like it carried some awful curse. "It had been as fine a road course as I've ever seen. Dangerous, though. Damned dangerous. My buddy, Little Joe . . ."

Jodell's voice trailed off, and the man's head dropped. The memories clearly carried with them quite a burden on Jodell Lee.

Upon hearing the name of the track, Rob immediately realized what Jodell was talking about. Little Joe Weatherly, one of the early heroes of stock car racing, was killed at Riverside in 1964 in a crash into the wall in turn six. It was an easy lick compared to some the feisty driver had experienced in his long and noteworthy career. But Weatherly preferred not to wear the newer, more restraining safety belts. It was reported that he had them only loosely fastened that day. Jodell had been trailing him on the course and passed the crash seconds after it happened. He could see the car wasn't that badly damaged. But looks were deceiving. It had been a terrible shock to learn after the race that his friend had been killed in the accident.

Jodell cleared his throat and resumed speaking.

"Ever since then, I still hear the voices from time to time. They may be ghosts. Lord knows, there's plenty of drivers who believe in them along with all the other superstitions and black magic and such. Or they may just be voices in my crazy old head. But I do hear them, son. I never know when or where. I just hear them. And you know what? When they talk to me, I listen to what they're trying to tell me. Might do you a right bit of good if you'd keep on listening to them, too."

Rob couldn't believe it. Jodell Lee had heard the voices, too!

"You think they are the same people talking to us?"

"Don't know about that. But I do know one thing. I see things in you when you drive that I ain't seen in nobody since Little Joe and Fireball Roberts and crazy old Curtis Turner. I like to think they could any of 'em drive circles around most of these guys that run out here today. Just in case it is them, I think you'd best let 'em have their say and you listen."

Not another word was spoken. The two men stood and walked on over to the truck. Bubba was animatedly running through the day's races and setups with Billy and Will, sharing what he had observed in some of the other cars they had run against in the second qualifying contest. They had already worked through plenty of potential changes, but now, they all finally agreed on the direction they felt they needed to go on their respective race cars.

While the others talked, Rob found a quiet spot in a corner and sipped at a soda he had hooked from the Lee team's cooler. The odd talk with Jodell was still fresh on his mind. He thought little about the monumental race earlier in the day, even though he knew he should still be terribly excited over qualifying so well for his first start in the 500.

Instead, he kept replaying the voice over and over in his mind, trying it out, wondering if what Jodell told him earlier could possibly be connected. Then it dawned on him that it didn't matter. Whether it was simply intuition, his imagination, or the ghost voice of some old driver who had somehow decided to help him out, he would still listen, still obey the strange, otherworldly command.

If the voice helped him win, then all the better. He just hoped the bossy old ghost didn't expect all the credit when Rob ultimately put the Ford in victory lane on Sunday.

10

RUNNING

"C an't dwell on a race that's already been run," Billy Winton said. "Recap it, learn from it, then go on to wherever the next one is gonna be held. But go a little smarter, a little better prepared, and twice as determined."

That was fine with Rob Wilder. Will Hughes, too. There was no time at all to reflect on the 500 at Daytona. Another event was on the schedule the very next Sunday, this one in Rockingham up near the South and North Carolina border. It was a totally different kind of track, and they had to get another car ready to go there, to qualify, and to try to actually win this one.

The wonderful, heady euphoria they all had after the first 125-mile qualifying race had quickly given way to the cold, harsh realities of competition at the Cup level. Even with the confidence and knowledge he had gained in that race on Thursday, Rob realized in one big hurry that Sunday on the big track was a different day.

From almost the beginning, Rob found himself stuck in the middle of three-wide racing. But this time, unlike the finish of the 125, he quickly got shuttled to the back of the field as the two long lines of cars freight-trained right on by him on either side so fast he hardly had time to react. They were clearly unimpressed with his showing earlier in the week. Maybe they hadn't read the papers. At any rate, it was a helpless feeling, one that Rob was to encounter many more times during the day. For some reason, virtually none of the other drivers would draft with him. And, if they did, it was for only long enough for them to find a spot back in the big line and to leave him high and dry without anyone to dance with.

Time and again he fought his way up from the back of the pack to somewhere in the middle of the fracas, only to be once again caught hopelessly out of line and sent back to the end of the train to start the climb all over again. It didn't take long for Rob to realize that the yellow rookie stripe on his back bumper was a big factor in keeping him from getting to the front. Not having any partners out there was putting him at an insurmountable disadvantage.

Hot, tired, frustrated, and exhausted as he was, Rob managed to bring the red Ensoft Ford home in sixteenth position. It hurt, though, that he had a car much faster than his finishing position turned out to be.

Rob couldn't understand all the smiles on the faces of the crew in the garage after the race. Why were they so happy? Even Will, of all people, was smiling.

Billy finally pulled his young driver aside and had a chat with him.

"Look, Robbie. You went out there in your very first 500 and got yourself a top-twenty finish at Daytona. There was another dozen and a half cars that would have loved to have your spot. Another several thousand race car drivers all over this country that would have given their firstborn to trade places with you. And Lord knows how many millions of folks watching on television that'll go to sleep tonight dreaming they got a chance to drive and finish so strong down here. Yeah, you might have flubbed a few times. We missed a couple of times on the pit stops, too. And maybe we didn't have the car exactly right. But we can fix all that. And that's what we're gonna do starting first thing in the morning."

Billy's logic was flawless, but Rob still didn't really feel much better. After the qualifying race, he had been confident of a top five, if not better. He was sorely disappointed with the final result. Any way the finishing order appeared, it was still a loss for the 52, and its driver hated to lose.

Billy told Rob and anybody else who would listen how delighted he was with his driver's disgruntled reaction to the good run at Daytona. He wanted him to be disappointed, hungry for his first win at this level, dissatisfied with anything less. Billy Winton was in this game to win, too, not ride around at the back of the pack and stay out of trouble. He would prefer sitting on his porch back home, enjoying the spectacular view of the mountains, than to come to a place like Daytona only to race and not be competitive.

But he recognized that the finish was better than a lot of drivers, car owners, fans, or journalists ever would have expected. They were still a growing threat in many people's eyes, and he hoped that they would show it even more emphatically at Rockingham.

They managed to qualify in the top twenty-five at The Rock, guaranteeing a spot in the field after only the first day of timing trials. That was important for three reasons. First, some pretty good teams would go home after the second day of qualifying because there were more cars trying to get into the race than the field would hold. And second, it left them the rest of the practice sessions to work on their race setup instead of qualifying. And finally, it would also allow Rob to get precious track time.

But this time it was racing luck that reared up and bit them.

They finished two laps down to the leaders after a cut tire late in the event. All and all it was another good run and, for the second race in a row, Rob brought home a race car without a scratch on it. That was no small accomplishment on a track like Rockingham.

That was also a big boost for the crew. They were able to continue to focus on getting cars ready for the next weeks' races instead of having to beat and bang on damaged cars even as they tried to get others prepped for the track. Will and the boys were still in the process of getting the operation ramped up, getting all the pieces in place for the full season. Emerging unscathed from the first two races was a luxury they definitely needed.

They could also concentrate on getting qualified for each of the races all the way through the Atlanta event. That would earn them an all-important provisional starting spot they could fall back on when they inevitably had trouble qualifying somewhere along the way. Rob would be seeing so many of the tracks for the first time, and they would unquestionably need to spend the provisional spot somewhere down the road. They needed to make the first four races. That's when the provisionals were awarded based on the current year's point standings instead of the previous year, when Rob had only run the one Cup race.

Rob found the step up difficult on a personal level as well. The demands on his time were even greater than before, more exacting than he had even imagined. The days of working in the shop, crawling around beneath the cars, helping the crew out, were all only a pleasant memory nowadays. He truly enjoyed turning the wrenches with the guys, getting to know even better each of the cars he would race. Now he spent more time in an airplane or in hotel rooms than he did in his own apartment. There was always an appearance scheduled for here, and interview there, charity work at another place. In between it all he was supposed to carve out enough time somehow to test, qualify, and race the car.

Lots of days he looked forward to actually getting to the racetrack on Thursday or Friday, simply so he could slow down a bit and relax and maybe actually get some grease under his fingernails. The cities and towns he rushed through the rest of the week melded together into a blur of airport concourses, convention centers, morning television shows, and rental car counters.

One reporter asked him what his biggest challenge was.

"Figuring out how to turn on the hot water in all those different hotel bathtubs," he said with a grin. But he was mostly serious.

Also, it seemed he spent far more time with Michelle Fagan these days than he did with anybody else, including Will and Billy and Donnie and the rest of them. That didn't seem quite right somehow. But usually, if he was on the road, then she was right there with him, making sure the particular event went off without a hitch and that they managed to get to the next one on time. He did appreciate her, but he had to wonder how she could keep this pace and still run the marketing department back at Ensoft.

At least he could find some time to himself when he climbed into the race car and took it out on the track. Michelle could never drive away from her cell phone.

As for Christy, Rob had to winnow out what time for her he could from his breakneck schedule. Most often it was a quick call to her, trying to catch her between her classes or the part-time job she had taken interning with a legal firm in Los Angeles. That call usually was made on his own cell phone, emanating from an airport or along a stretch of highway somewhere. Or it came after he had set the hotel room alarm clock to wake him up at two in the morning, the three-hour time difference factored in so he would be more likely to catch her.

Sometimes he would forget which city he was in and would have to check the telephone book in the nightstand so he could tell her where he was. Christy at least pretended not to mind the short, disjointed calls, even when they sometimes came several times a day. She was happy to have a few minutes to talk with him.

"I'll take what I can get, Mr. Rob Wilder," she told him more than once. "And you remember, my sister is keeping an eye on you for me."

Michelle was actually about the only thing that kept him on solid footing with this drastic change in his lifestyle. She was his secretary, keeper, friend, confidante, and boss lady as she kept him shuffling from meetings with sales reps to autograph sessions at retail stores to media interviews, doing it all usually with a firm hand but mostly with good humor.

He could only imagine how many hats, T-shirts, collectibles, or Ensoft software boxes with the photo of him and the car on the package that he had signed already. And that's not to mention the supply of glossy pictures Michelle seemed to never run out of. But she did keep him going. Somehow, she seemed to always find a way to keep his spirits up, whether it was with a pizza at midnight or a joke when she called his room to wake him up at six A.M. However she did it, she managed to keep him intact until she could finally deliver him to the next racing venue in time for him to climb into the car and get to work.

Of course, the one sure way for Michelle to pick him up was to get her sister on the phone. She would pretend to be calling work, then suddenly announce that she must have a wrong number, tell Rob to take the phone and apologize, and it would be Christy giggling at him from the other end of the line. Or when Rob would get crabby, she would hit the speed dial button on the phone and toss it to him like a hot potato or a hand grenade.

"Time for a 'Christy-fix,' " she'd announce, and wrinkle up her nose at him. "And not a second too soon."

Still, Rob caught the same odd look in Michelle's eyes when he would talk with or about her sister. Was it jealousy? Envy? Pure old sibling rivalry? Was she being protective of her kid sister, worrying about her involvement with a man who obviously had another powerful love in his life?

Or was he imagining the whole thing? One thing was for sure. He didn't have the time or the opportunity to dwell on it much at all.

The races came and went with Las Vegas following Rockingham. Rob was amazed once he saw all the bright lights of Vegas.

"I bet that one hotel there has more lights in its sign than we had in the whole town of Hazel Green," he remarked in awe.

"Wait'll you see this place," Billy said as he turned into the broad entrance of the Bellagio.

But when they got out, it was Rob Wilder who attracted all the attention away from the bright lights and sparkling fountains. A gaggle of racing fans spotted him, and he spent the next twenty minutes talking with them and signing autographs while the rest of the party waited patiently, even though they were already late for their dinner reservations.

Besides the race, the best thing about Las Vegas was that Christy could drive over from Los Angeles and spend the weekend. She and three of her friends from school showed up on Thursday night. While she pulled Rob off to spend a few minutes alone together, several of the crew members struck up an immediate friendship with Christy's buddies. Billy had brought the crew out a day early as a reward for all their hard work over the winter, and they were feeling especially frisky. The men's accents, their good looks, and their clear willingness to have a good time fascinated the young women. And the several single men in the bunch were obviously fascinated by the girls in general.

Billy looked at Will and shook his head as Donnie and the boys ushered the young ladies through the casino and out the front of the hotel, supposedly off to see the sights of Vegas.

"I want y'all to show me one of them places where Elvis slept," Donnie Kline was saying as they disappeared.

Billy Winton was actually a little jealous of his bunch. He, Will, Michelle, Christy, and Rob had the dinner scheduled at the Bellagio with a group of Ensoft distributors. Sometimes he still longed for the old days when racing was about all they thought about until they finished at the track. And by then, it was time to start looking for a good time. Too often now they traipsed from track to hotel to personal appearance and back and not too many other places. Billy could only imagine what damage some of the old-timers like Joe Weatherly or Curtis Turner or Tiny Lund might have done during a race weekend in a town like Las Vegas.

The Vegas track was large, flat, and fast. It presented a new set of challenges to the team. Rob had raced it the year before in the Grand National event, but the extra power in the Cup cars gave the race car an entirely different feel from what Rob had experienced then. As it turned out, they spent the entire race chasing the car's setup, never quite getting it to Rob's liking or to maximum speed. Still, the kid gained valuable experience racing on the flat surfaces. Most of the newer speedways on the circuit were basically flat cornered and the race, though disappointing, would prove to be time and effort well spent before the year was over.

Soon, the Ensoft team had made the races at Atlanta and Darlington, too. After those contests, they were twenty-first in the point standings. Not great, and certainly disappointing by the standards Rob Wilder had set for himself before the year started. But their ranking was not bad at all, considering they were still learning the new Cup cars and getting acclimated to the tracks. Most of their competitors had been driving these places for years. Their finishes were midpack for the most part, not bad enough to be totally discouraging but not good enough to crow about either.

It was obvious to all that they were showing the growing pains of a brand-spanking-new race team. But something else was clear to anyone who observed what they were doing. Rob Wilder was demonstrating a plethora of promise. The team was gelling, the cars were getting stronger, but the driver was a racing star waiting to happen.

They actually led their first laps under green at Darlington when they got out of sequence on a set of pit stops. Still, Billy Winton beamed with pride as he saw his car's number flash to the top of the scoreboard for those few laps. Rob was too busy wrestling with the car even to realize he was the leader. It was a surprise when Harry Stone calmly gave him the news on the radio.

Still, Darlington left Rob with an unquenchable thirst for the front of the pack. At the end, they gambled with the air pressure in the tires in a last ditch attempt to get Rob back up there where he wanted to be in the waning laps. The car developed a push at the end, the nose trying to head for the outside wall when Rob tried to steer it through the corners, and that left them falling out of the lead lap with twenty more yet to go. Still, they managed a top-fifteen finish, and that was no small accomplishment at the storied "Lady in Black."

People were noticing: people in the pits, reporters, fans. A surprising number of the fans already wore ROB WILDER #52 T-shirts and hats, and the merchandise vendors were quickly ordering more. There was even talk of "Rookie of the Year." Rob pointedly ignored that sort of thing. He figured if he won, everything else would take care of itself. If he didn't, there was no point even thinking about it.

The team approached the race at the Bristol track with especially high hopes. It was almost right there in their backyard, and that gave them the opportunity to spend two days testing there. The car was specially designed to run on the tight concrete racing surface. The crew added stiffeners to the framing in numerous places in an attempt to keep the car from flexing under the strain of the impossibly high speeds they would run on the track's tightly banked corners.

The tests were heartening. The car was lightning fast. And they were able to back that up with their first top-ten qualifying run of the season. Ecstatic, Rob called Christy three times to tell her how well they had run in the time trials, how he didn't think he would be able to sleep until they could run the race itself.

"We're gonna get a win, Chris," he told her, his confidence clear on the transcontinental telephone circuit.

The tight turns and narrow one-groove racing surface had tempers flaring and normally cool race car jockeys swapping paint in retaliation before the race was forty laps old. Will spent much of the first hundred laps on the radio, doing all he could to keep his young charge calm and under control. Beating, banging, and fender-rubbing was par for the course at Bristol. A driver had to ignore it and stay focused on the task at hand, on surviving the brawl long enough to take the prize at the end. Even some of the experienced drivers had trouble doing that, though. They weren't as accustomed to the close quarters battering and shoving as their predecessors had been. The old drivers had mostly cut their teeth on such narrow, short tracks—but the drivers had fewer opportunities to experience such races anymore. There were plenty of red faces and colorful language on the radios before the race was more than a few laps old.

Bristol was certainly not a forgiving place. One wrong move by someone, and there would be an accident that would inevitably sweep up a whole slew of good cars before anybody knew what had happened. By the time an accident occurred, with the surprising speeds they ran here on such a short spiral of racetrack, it was usually simply too late to get on the brakes and get the car stopped in time to avoid contact with something or somebody. The only hope would be that the driver would have enough spacing to react, to be able to find a hole in the melee and squeeze through it before the narrow track closed up on top of him.

Rob fared relatively well, all the way up to about the 400-lap point. This track reminded him so much of the dusty little asphalt ovals he had driven since he was fifteen years old. They were, at that point, only one lap down and working on a long green flag run. There was still time to get the lap back and, with a little luck on caution flags, they might actually have a chance to challenge for the lead.

But then, a bout of impatience by another car that was running many laps down to the leaders triggered a massive pileup along the backstretch. Rob shot for a hole in the midst of the spinning cars and almost made it. But then, he was clipped in the rear end and the impact was enough to nose the right front of the car into the outside wall.

It could have been worse. He could have hit the wall

more solidly. Some other driver could have bulldozed right into him and ended the night entirely. As it was, Will and the boys were able to fix the car on pit road and they lost only one more lap during the caution period. That, of course, was far too much ground to make up in the amount of race remaining. And the toe-in was knocked out of whack in the brush with the wall so any hopes of a spectacular finish were done.

The Texas race was strikingly similar to the one at Las Vegas. The experience there helped somewhat but, try as they might, they just never were able to quite get a handle on the race car. Joe Banker's engine put out plenty of power, but the car seemed to have a mind of its own coming off the track's broad, flat corners. They chased the setup the entire weekend, changing shock combinations, working with the front end geometry, shifting around the weights in the frame rails, and even trying some goofy things they knew had no hope of working.

"It's like trying to pick up mercury with tweezers," Will announced.

No one laughed. It was true.

Still, they managed to finish well enough to stay just outside the top twenty in the point standings. And everyone was still in good spirits, confident about their chances as they packed up and began thinking about the upcoming race at Martinsville.

Everyone, that is, but Rob Wilder.

On the plane ride back from Texas, Rob allowed the frustration to show on his face, in the way he slumped in his seat, his face resting sadly in the palm of his hand. Billy rode in the copilot's seat while Rob was in the back with Michelle, Will, and Donnie Kline. Michelle and Donnie were asleep in their seats almost before the plane's landing gears had lifted off the runway.

"What's wrong, cowboy?" Will finally asked.

"Nothing."

"Gotta be something. Your face looks like it's about to cloud up and rain."

"Aw, Will, I was just sitting here thinking, that's all."

The kid shifted around in the seat uncomfortably. He had driven a full race already that day. He had to be tired and sore and half-dehydrated. But Will knew none of that was what was really bothering the youngster.

"Thinking about what?"

"Nothing, really. I guess I'm just tired from the race. Long day."

"Yeah, I think everyone's tired." Will nodded at Michelle and Donnie, the two of them sleeping across the aisle from them. Donnie's snoring was already rivaling the drone of the airplane's twin engines. "It was a frustrating weekend for all of us. We're going to have ones like that, though."

"I guess so. I just find it hard to take when we run that bad, though. Am I not telling y'all all you need to know to set the car up right? Is there more I can do?" Rob asked.

The kid gazed out the window as he asked the question, watching the lights of some little East Texas town slip by beneath them. He seemed perfectly willing to shoulder all the blame for the afternoon's disappointing finish.

"Rob, listen to me," Will said, suddenly straightening up in his seat and tapping the youngster's knee. "This is a team effort and all of us are responsible for how the car runs. It's all of our jobs to give you the very best car we possibly can. Once we do, then you have to get out there and make things happen. If the car is not there, it doesn't matter how hard you drive it. At this level of competition, if you are off even a tick it'll seem like a ton 'cause these cars and the guys who drive them are so good. This is the NFL, the NBA, and the major leagues all rolled into one."

"I know. And that's where I want to play."

Rob was now looking directly at Will. The spark in his eyes was clear, even in the darkness of the plane.

"We had a good car today," Hughes continued. "We just didn't have the best. There was nothing you could do with it out there on the track that would make one bit of difference."

"That's what I find so frustrating. I'm used to taking a car and making things happen, even when it's not perfect. I used to be able to find a way, you know? When I can't, then I figure it's gotta be my fault."

"Maybe on those little, old tracks you used to run back there in Podunk. Even at the Grand National level, that was possible sometimes. Not here. The cars are too good. You have to drive smooth and smart and consistently. Some days, you're not gonna win. Or even come close. But when those days happen, you gotta suck it up and squeeze out the best finish you can. Believe me. Sometimes, the best race you'll ever run will be to stay in the top twenty-five. Mark Martin, Dale Jarrett, the Labontes, Jeff Gordon? They run to win. But sometimes they're racing for points as much as anything. They know what their cars can and can't do. If they can't win, then they want as many points as they can get."

"I guess the points are important, all right," Rob said, but there was still something bothering him. He looked down at the toes of his tennis shoes for a moment, then back at Will. "But you know what? I still want to win more than anything else in the world."

Will could feel as much as see the intensity on Rob's face, the same intensity Jodell Lee had identified in the youngster, the same drive and desire the kid had shown when he did the test drive, auditioning for Will and Billy at the track at Nashville. It was heartening to know the kid still had the fire burning in his belly, that their showing so far this year had not damped the coals of competition.

"I know, I know. Look, there are two races every week. One of them is for the checkered flag. The other one is for the points. If you tend to win one, you're likely to be pretty doggoned good at the other."

"I'm sorry about whining to you, Will. But I'm hungry for a win. And maybe a little bit too impatient for my own good."

He was staring out the window again, watching the stars popping through the fabric of the night sky.

"You wouldn't be worth a thing to us if you weren't! We're still a young team. We've just begun to sort things out back at the shop. We're all still learning what kind of commitment it's going to take up here. You have to remember a few things though. We've made every race so far. Some folks been at this a lot longer than we have had to pack it in early already. And we're not going backward either. We're making progress every race, whether you realize it or not." Will tapped the kid on the knee again. "You mess up, Billy and I will let you know. You don't do what we think is best for this team, you'll not have to guess about it. But if you'll stay focused, drive smart like you know how to do, then maybe the racing gods will eventually throw a little luck our way. When they do, we'll be ready to take it and run with it."

The kid's grin was visible in the glow from the plane's instrument panel lights. With all he had accomplished for them so far, with all the skill and guts the youngster showed out there among men much older, it was sometimes easy to forget that he was only twenty, a veritable baby.

"I hear you, Will. You can count on me. I just don't want to let y'all down after all the confidence you put in me, letting me have this ride with so little experience, so young and all. Shoot, there are guys who would pay you to have this ride."

"You can take this to the bank, cowboy. We don't want any other driver in the 52. You're the one that's meant to be there."

"Then you can count on me, Will. I hope you know that."

He hit his palm with a balled-up fist for emphasis. Donnie Kline snorted at the slapping sound then resumed his buzz saw noises.

"I know we can. We're a team. Remember that. You and me and the rest of the boys. And none of us cotton to losing races any more than you do!"

Across the airplane's narrow aisle, Michelle Fagan listened to the talk with eyes barely shut. She actually enjoyed hearing Rob's self-doubts exposed sometimes. It only made her think more of him. And always, when he did open up and talk with her or Will or Billy or Jodell Lee, the conversation ended with a renewed commitment on his part to redouble his efforts to win. It seemed he would always emerge even stronger and more confident.

Now, she could close her eyes again and let the welcome sleep overtake her once more, lulled back into a deep slumber by the comforting hum of the King Air's turbo props.

Part **6**

THINKING

No one is thinking if everyone's thinking alike.

—General George Patton (and one of
Billy Winton's favorite expressions)

11

MARTINSVILLE

The car sped along through mostly light traffic as it made its way out of Greensboro, its quartet of occupants quiet now as the gentle rolling hills slipped past outside. They were still thirty miles or so from the Virginia state line, a lot closer to their destination than they had been but not there yet, no matter how much they wished it so.

Rob Wilder was bone-tired, his right hand still sore and aching from all the autographs he had signed that afternoon at the car dealership near High Point. Michelle Fagan made no pretense of trying to stay awake. She dozed in a corner of the backseat, her purse for a pillow. The pretty young publicist from Lee Racing's lead sponsor had taken Michelle's lead, and she, too, was curled up in the other corner of the rear seat, eyes closed, sleeping as best she could.

Jodell Lee was at the wheel of the rental car, whistling softly through his teeth as he drove, obviously thinking deeply about something as he pointed the car northward toward Martinsville, Virginia.

The racetrack would open the following morning, and Rob wanted to be there at first light. It would be his first visit to the historic half mile at Martinsville. The young driver was excited at the prospects of getting a chance to tackle the long straightaways and the tight flat turns. Rob actually preferred the big, fast superspeedways such as Daytona. There was nothing else on the planet, except maybe piloting a fighter jet, to match the sheer speed and excitement of those places. Daytona was the one track he always cited as his hands-down favorite for that very reason. But he always looked forward to running on the shorter tracks, too.

From what he had seen of Martinsville in Billy Winton's vast library of videotaped races, the place most resembled the track back home in north Alabama where he had first learned to race. He couldn't wait to pull his red Ford out onto the track's surface. He ached to run in the tracks of the legendary drivers he had grown up hearing about, that Jodell Lee still talked about, told stories about as if they were next-door neighbors or part of his golf foursome every weekend.

The two drivers had done the autograph session as a favor to a longtime friend of Jodell's. The dealer wanted to do a "New and Old" promotion for new and used cars and Rob and Jodell certainly fit the bill. Rob jumped at the chance to join Jodell in the appearance. He knew it would offer another chance to be around the man, to have time to glean more information from him. He learned so much from the big man every time they were together, he often thought of it as going back to school with a particularly good teacher.

And it wasn't just racing tips he picked up either. It was enlightening to watch Jodell work the crowd, greet his fans, making every single one of them feel as if he or she had had a private audience with their hero. Jodell was always talking about how it was the fans that gave him his job in the first place and that he always did his best to show his appreciation to them. To thank them for spending their hard-earned money and, in so doing, affording guys like him and Rob the opportunity to go racing for a living.

Rob was a willing and eager pupil whenever Jodell dispensed advice, solicited or not. The hastily scheduled appearance at the car dealership gave Rob precisely what he was looking for: a chance to meet some new fans in a hotbed of racing activity plus an entire afternoon to pick the veteran's brain about how to best attack the tricky speedway at Martinsville. Rob used any free moment during the afternoon to ask questions. Jodell patiently obliged and offered the kid more practical knowledge about the task ahead of him that weekend than he could ever have gotten from any other source.

Wilder had hoped to do even more talking on the drive up to Martinsville, but the car had been quiet for a while and he hated to push any harder. Jodell, almost fatherlike in his pride, had already given tips to Rob on all the different nuances of the track. He described which lines to take through each of the turns, where the braking points would be, precisely how to feather the gas to get the absolute most momentum coming off the corners, the best places to pass another car. He detailed a hundred other little things that could not be found anywhere in any manual describing how to best conquer Martinsville.

But now Jodell seemed preoccupied, his mind lost in some other unrelated thoughts, so Rob was watching the countryside, listening to the roar of the wind, biting his tongue. He actually jumped when Jodell suddenly cleared his throat and began to talk.

"So, I been thinkin'. You have to realize that the fastest car all day don't necessarily win at Martinsville. It would be a lot bigger factor if the brakes would only hold out. The whole race will boil down to which of the front-running cars have the most brakes left at the end. Usually does, and that's the paradox here."

The big man had only been considering what else he needed to tell the kid. That's what he had been thinking about ever since they left Greensboro behind.

"What do you mean by 'paradox'?"

"Well, you really do need a good car first of all. Don't misunderstand me about that fine point. But you also have to be easy on the brakes all day long. It's easy to get tempted to drive the car a little harder into the corner if you got some power to play with, and then you tend to use just a little more of the brake pedal to pass somebody or stay up with somebody else. But you do that and before long, you'll begin to boil the brake fluid and feel the pedal start to get all squishy and not do you much good a'tall. That happens and any chance of getting a good finish or even winning is gone like the wind."

"I understand that but what's the paradox?" Rob asked again.

"Let me finish," Jodell said, taking one hand off the steering wheel and holding it up like a traffic cop. "The paradox is that you got to have lots of motor power and lots more of stopping power to win. One thing's for sure. You have to stay on the lead lap at Martinsville. Have a bad pit stop and get behind or make a mistake and get passed by the leader and any driver could get desperate. There's a strong temptation to overdrive the race car, trying to come up through the field and get back or stay on the lead lap. To do that, most people are naturally going to be too hard on the brakes. No binders, no victory. Get a lap down and short of some kind of a miracle, you won't even be able to get within hollering distance of the guys who are leading the race."

"I think I see what you mean," Rob said, nodding his

head slowly up and down. He knew a race car driver's most thoroughly instilled rule is to always push the car as hard as it will go. But Jodell was telling him that doing it that way at this track would be highly counterproductive. The question was, how do you avoid burning the brakes up while you're trying your darnedest to outrace all those other guys to stay on the lead lap and have any chance of winning. "So how do you get around it, this paradox?"

"First you have to drive smart. All day long. You have to leave your temper in the toolbox in the truck. You won't be needin' it this day. You can't get all hot and bothered either when somebody passes you and you start racing them just for the heck of it, to show them they shouldn't be doing that or maybe because they've bumped you a time or two out there. You just let them go ahead on and you go about your own business of catching up patiently. That is why a lot of the hotheads in Cup never seem to run real good here."

"Like Stacy Locklear for instance?"

"He's a walkin', talkin' demonstration on how not to win a race at Martinsville! Watch him and do the danged opposite and you'll be fine," Jodell snorted. He mentioned a few run-ins Rex Lawford had had with Locklear and his silver racer on this and a couple of other tracks over the last couple of years. "That so-and-so could be a pretty decent driver if he'd just use his head for something more than to separate his ears from each other.

"See, you got to approach this place like old Darrel Waltrip used to in his heyday. You'd not notice D. W. all day then all the sudden, with a hundred laps to go, there he'd be, sittin' up front and with a fresh set of brakes and it was 'see you later.' He'd blow by you like you were sittin' still. The next time I would see him, he'd be down there in Victory Lane pickin' up his trophy and his prize money and the kisses of the race queen. I reckon Richard Petty is about the only one ever came close to mastering this place like old D. W. did. He could flat get around this place."

"Sounds like Will is going to need to do a lot of talking during the race. There's no way I am ever going to remember all you're telling me, Jodell."

"Hey, kid, you'll do fine. As long as you keep your wits about you and save those brakes, you've got as good a chance of winning as any of the rest of these yahoos. Just drive her smooth as silk like you know how to do. And don't force any issues out there. Save 'em for the pits afterwards if you can even remember what they were. Then, when you get down to the last fifty laps or so, you can throw caution to the wind, forget about how red-hot your brakes are by then, and let it all hang out."

"So when I get inside fifty laps, and while I can still see the leaders, I fully intend to run the brakes and tires right off the car," Rob said emphatically, visualizing how it might be to run ragged-edge laps on the Martinsville track.

"If your brakes are used up enough that the crew has to drag you to a stop in Victory Lane, and if the danged things are still smoking when they hand you the trophy, then I'd say you drove her just about right." Jodell told Rob then about one of his several trips to the winners' circle there. "This is one sweet place to win a race because you know you took a good car and you drove it the best you knew how to bring it home at the point. Car and driver, together. That's racin', young'un!"

They talked about other things then, keeping their voices low so the two women in the backseat could rest. But Rob Wilder found it difficult to concentrate on what Jodell was saying now. He kept running through his mind what it would be like to race on this throwback track, how wonderful it would feel to have his first Cup race win come at the same place where so many great drivers had shown their true talent.

Jodell suspected the kid was losing interest in his stories. But he knew full well where the youngster's mind was. He could remember his own first trip to Martinsville when he was not much older than Rob. The big, heavy cars they ran then and the brakes that were practically the same as those on a passenger car always made for a long afternoon. But it had been so much fun, too. So much fun.

Jodell steered the rental car around some slower traffic and, before he even realized it, they were driving past the entrance to the speedway, giving Rob his first glimpse of the towering new fourth-turn grandstand. Jodell gave Rob a nudge on the shoulder to point out the track, but he had seen it already. The young driver's eyes were wide.

"There she is, kid. Probably one of my favorite tracks in the whole world."

"She's beautiful!" Rob marveled, taking in the towering steel structure of the grandstands. It didn't look much like the speedway he had seen on Billy's tapes at all. They had obviously given the place a new look over the last couple of years as the racing magazines had promised.

"Rob, I got to admit," Jodell said as the speedway finally disappeared behind them. "I'd give just about anything for one more race on that old lady. I got a throttle foot that's itching something terrible, and I do believe that would be the only thing that would soothe it."

Rob watched Jodell as he still checked the rearview mirror for any kind of glimpse of the speedway they had passed. The old driver had called him "Rob" instead of "kid." Maybe Jodell finally saw Rob as a full-fledged race car driver, not an eager but green kid.

He studied the deep lines crisscrossing the retired

driver's face, each like a ring on a tree stump that measured the years. The intensity was certainly still there on that countenance, the almost fanatical desire to race and to win. It was clear in the set of the man's jaw, the clench of his teeth, the competitive fire still burning in his clear gray eyes that the hunger to take one of those steel beasts out onto the track and push it was still gnawing at Jodell Lee.

What would it be like to race against Jodell? Rob wondered. What if he coaxed the old man out onto the Martinsville track and raced with him, allowing him to show him in the most logical way all the lessons he had been sharing with him?

And if it came down to it, could Rob actually beat him? He liked to think so, but he certainly wouldn't make book on it.

After a quick dinner with Michelle that he hardly tasted, Rob spent a restless night at the hotel. He went back to her room to watch a movie on television, but he couldn't concentrate on the show's silly plot and clueless characters. He finally excused himself and went across the courtyard to his own room.

He couldn't keep Jodell's ideas about running Martinsville out of his head. If only Will were there, they could go over the setups for tomorrow or something else to occupy his racing brain.

He kept seeing himself, zooming into the corner, nursing the brakes, maintaining momentum. But sometimes the car he was driving in his head was something out of the sixties, something like Jodell must have driven. What must it have been like back then? How different it must have been when there wasn't such a commitment to sponsors and fans and newspeople. And he wondered what it would be like to race against Jodell in his prime or some of the other greats he had only seen in the grainy films and washed-out black-and-white photos on Billy's wall.

He finally fell into an uneasy sleep. But soon he was dreaming about racing on the flat track with the likes of Richard Petty, Cale Yarborough, Jodell Lee, and Buddy Baker.

He was out of bed and showered before the wake-up call came from the hotel operator. Then, with only a quick stop for a sausage and biscuit, Rob made it to the track before it even opened. He was sitting there at the gate, waiting for them, when the crew drove up in the hauler.

The tractor trailers for all the teams sat in a long, meandering line waiting to cross over into the infield of the speedway. Finally, the gates swung open, and the line of trucks snaked in. Rob was already studying the racing surface as he walked through the gate alongside their own truck.

The turns looked more suitable for a quarter-mile track than a half-mile one. The straightaways on each side appeared to be more like a couple of drag strips running parallel to each other, ending in two sharp, relatively flat, banked corners on each end of them. Now Rob understood what Jodell was talking about. This configuration looked like it could put plenty of white-hot pressure on a car's brakes. The long straightaways allowed the cars to achieve impressive acceleration before the drivers would suddenly have to hop on the brakes to slow the cars down enough to make it through the corners. Otherwise, their centrifugal force would send them rocketing toward the outside wall. It was the rapid acceleration and deceleration that put so much strain on the engine and the drivetrain and the poor, suffering brakes.

Rob walked over the track to where the new pit road had replaced the set of old pits. There had been two sets of pits at one time, one that ran along the frontstretch and the other around on the backstretch. Racers would now enter pit road just before heading off into turn three. The pit stalls themselves stretched all the way around the arc of the speedway, then the pit lane dropped the cars back out onto the track at the beginning of the back straightaway. Pitting on the back set of stalls had always been a huge disadvantage at Martinsville. At least that worry had now been eliminated.

But, as Rob surveyed this tough old track, he reminded himself that he had plenty of other things to be concerned about. And he couldn't wait to get out there and start learning what to look for and how to handle the challenges as they came up.

When they had the car off the hauler, had it all primed for the first practice session, Rob was in the car and getting buckled in before the crew had stopped pushing it to the line. Once out on the track, he did what he always did in his first run on a new track. He quickly fell in behind one of the veterans and followed his line, studiously watching how he attacked the corners. Rob tucked right up on the rear deck lid of the car, inches off his rear end all the way around the track. The veteran didn't even seem to notice or care that he had a shadow. He kept his car right down against the white line at the inside of the track, only a few inches away from the curbing that ran around the inside of the concrete strip in the corners.

Each time they entered one of the turns, the veteran would drive slightly deeper, get into the throttle a half second quicker than Rob, pulling away a few car-lengths. Only the power being generated by Joe Banker's motor let him pull back up even again as they rumbled off down the two long straightaways.

Will picked up on the power in the motor from the very first lap. The kid would just have to get used to saving the brakes. It looked like they would be going through several sets of them before the weekend was over.

Rob continued to run laps even as the veterans began to come in and start making changes on their cars. He was quickly getting a feel for this old lady. With each lap around the half-mile speedway, he got faster and faster, gaining confidence in how to handle his braking going into the corners. It didn't take him long, either, to pick up on how to feather the gas in order to keep from breaking the rear tires loose coming off the turns. The urge was to hammer the gas coming out of the corners, but he saw quickly that that tended to cause the rear wheels to spin. Rob soon found it was much better to ease back into the throttle gently instead of jamming his foot to the floor.

Will studied his young driver, seeing for himself that he was learning tricks with every circuit. He timed the kid along with some of the other cars and saw the results of his schooling right there on the watch. Rob was, thankfully, a quick study and learning fast.

Finally he signaled for Donnie to bring him in so they could check over the braking system, to see how they were holding up. The last thing they needed was to have a brake failure and put the car hard into the wall. He didn't want to have to go to a backup car. That would put an awful strain on his young team, and at a track where they had never run. They had plenty of practice time between then and Sunday, and if the worst happened they could likely get it done. But Will preferred making the original car better rather than scrambling and scratching to get a backup ready to run.

Rob eased out of the gas on the backstretch and pulled the car way down to the inside, out of the way of those still practicing at full speed. He steered the car into the entrance to pit road, coasting around to where the crew waited. Later, he would practice race speed stops. This time, he only wanted to get down to the pits so they could take a look at the brakes and tires.

Donnie quickly jacked the car up while Paul Phillips and the others started placing jack stands underneath the car. Michelle was there, passing him a towel and a cup full of ice water. Someone handed the tire temperature sheets to Michelle and she delivered them through the window to Rob with only a quick glance at all the figures on the pages.

"How was it?" Michelle asked, yelling to be heard over the din of a revving engine several stalls down from theirs.

She needn't have asked. Rob had a broad grin on his face when he lifted the face cover of his helmet. The wide, flat track obviously suited him just fine. He confirmed it as he took a look at the tire temperatures.

"I love it. 'Chelle! This place is just like the places I used to race on back home." He took a big drink of the water and winked at her. "I'm gonna win this thing. Just watch. I'm gonna get a win this time."

"You looked good out there. Even Will seemed to be pleased."

"Where is he anyway?" Rob asked. Will was usually close by during practice, overseeing every tiny bit of preparation on the car.

"He's on top of Jodell Lee's truck with Bubba Jr., timing cars and doing man-type stuff," Michelle said as she took the cup he passed back to her. She poured him another drink.

Rob kidded her all the time about being the highest-paid water girl on the Cup circuit. It was likely true. She had vowed to hire someone else to handle all the minutiae of doing the PR on the racing team, but the truth was that she had come to love it so much she hated to give it up. And until she decided differently, she was more than happy to be there to hand him towels and pass him ice water. That, in its own little way, was how she helped them win.

"Timing cars?" Rob asked.

"Yeah, they're trying to figure who's fast and where the grooves are on the track today."

Rob wondered why Will wasn't waist-deep beneath the hood of the car, the way he usually was. Instead, it was Paul Phillips who was barking out orders as the crew worked frantically under the front end. Even Donnie Kline seemed to be taking orders from the newest member of the crew.

It was Donnie's voice on the radio in Rob's ears. "Okay, pipsqueak, let's make another run. We need to work on dialing this thing in now. Paul wants to know whether or not you got a push in them corners. We'll call you back in when we're ready. Remember, the car should be able to turn through the corner without you having to steer it with the brakes."

Donnie slapped the hood with his open hand as the crew members finished removing the fan that was hooked over the radiator, then he closed and latched it and motioned for Rob to refire the engine. The kid steered the car down the pit lane and back out onto the track, anxious to get back out there. It felt to him as if he had been running here all his young life. He kept the car high through turn three as he built speed, then pushed her hard coming off the corner, loving the feel of the torque from the engine as it kicked in.

In the pits, Donnie and Paul stood watching. Paul had worked for several teams over the years, teams with more than a half dozen victories on this track between them. That was why Will had Paul directing the work on the car this morning while he was on top of the Lee team's truck, honing their strategy for the race. And that was why Donnie Kline and the others willingly followed his direction. Additionally, one of Paul's areas of expertise was braking systems, and everyone knew that knowledge could be of great value at this track.

Rob cranked off a dozen or so quick laps. He could already feel the differences resulting from the changes Paul made the last time in. The car felt good beneath him. Real good. No push at all. He dived down into the first turn, setting the brakes, wheeling the car through the center of the corner. Then he raced down past the old back pit area, boldly turning things up a notch. He liked the feel of the car and didn't hesitate to drive the next couple of laps hard.

Over the next hour, they brought the car in and out of the pits several times, making minor changes to the handling, working mostly under the front end and especially on the right side. They made several changes to the track bar on the rear end, moving the body around, trying to get the right feel for Rob. The last thirty minutes of the session, Will was back, and he and Paul worked shoulder to shoulder under the right front, trying several different shock combinations.

Later that afternoon, the teams slowly pushed their cars out to the qualifying line and strung them out like ants. It looked odd to see such fast, heavy machines being shoved along by their crews, then left sitting motionless, deathly still and quiet. But soon, they would be anything but static.

The final times Rob posted from the morning practice session had been fast. Paul's help had been invaluable to Will in getting the car set up right. The question that remained was whether Rob had had enough practice time out there so he could manage that one perfect lap that it would take to get a top qualifying spot.

At least that was the question in everyone else's mind. Rob Wilder had no doubts at all.

They were going off twelfth in line with many of the pole position favorites stacked up at the back of the line.

With almost fifty cars at the track and trying to make the field, it promised to be a tense qualifying session. Some well-funded teams wouldn't make it. It would be that simple. The track had grown hotter now in the afternoon sun, enough so that it would be a factor in qualifying. Those who had not allowed for that eventuality would be at a disadvantage.

To a man, the Billy Winton team figured they had done all they could to get ready. The speed was in the car. Their young driver seemed to have a good feel for the track. They weren't necessarily after the pole. They only needed a starting spot toward the front of the field. Track position would be crucial during the race. A good starting spot would take a lot of pressure off the driver, not making him have to use the brakes harder in the early going. The drivers at the back of the field would be forced to do just that in an attempt to keep from getting lapped in the early going. With forty-three cars on a half-mile track, there would be a real threat of getting passed by the leaders after a restart should there be an early caution flag.

As he waited to mount up and ride, Rob stood next to Billy and Jodell Lee, listening to the retired driver as he gave him a last set of pointers on getting a good lap. Confident as he was, Rob figured another guideline or two might come in handy.

Just then, the first car roared to life and took to the track.

"Remember now to not even think that you're out there trying to qualify," Jodell was saying, an arm around Rob's shoulder. He used his other hand to point into one of the track's corners. "Just go out there and try to run the smoothest lap you've ever run. Resist the urge to drive her deep into the corner then depend on the brakes to 'whoa' you down. You'll think that's the faster way but she'll push up on you in the center of the turn and that'll be that. A couple of tenths is all there'll be between the pole sitter and last place."

It never occurred to Rob or to Lee that Jodell had a driver of his own who would be out there shortly trying to run a quicker lap than Rob did. From their first Cup race against him and Rex Lawford, Jodell Lee had treated the kid as if he was merely another team in the Jodell Lee stable, not a very worthy competitor. He had discovered Rob after all. And besides, he liked the kid, seeing in him a young version of himself. That was more than enough for him to have a solid vested interest in how the youngster's career unfolded.

"I know what you mean, Jodell. I go flying off down that straightaway and I just want to drive her in there as deep as I can. But don't worry, I'll be smooth. When I ran a good smooth lap in practice, the car just seemed to pick up. You could tell the difference," Rob added as he zipped up his driving suit. It was time for him to climb into the 52.

Billy watched him cross over to the car.

"How will he do?" Billy asked Jodell. He knew the old driver had kept his usual close watch on Wilder throughout the morning practice session. Billy was still unsure how the kid would do. He knew this was a tough track, especially for a driver who was impatient or who liked to force the issue. Rob fell into those categories sometimes. But he could also be as smooth a driver as anyone who had come along in a while.

"If I was a betting man, I'd put my money on him," Jodell answered without hesitation. "He won't get the pole, I don't reckon. He ain't had enough laps here yet. But give him a few years and he'll own this place."

Billy nodded. Those were powerful words coming from someone who had won more than his share of races on this tricky, tight old track.

Rob set his driving gloves up on the roof of the car as

he adjusted the sleeves of his suit. He looked at the cars ahead of him and spotted the silver-colored Pontiac of Stacy Locklear two cars ahead of him. Locklear had his back to Rob as he prepared to climb into his own car.

Rob swung a leg in the window of his own car, glancing Locklear's way one last time. The driver turned and shot his trademark glare at Rob, a welding torch of a stare that seemed strong enough to burn right through sheet metal. Rob only smiled and nodded in reply, as pleasantly as if they were the best of friends.

Will stepped over to help him get buckled up. It was time to concentrate exclusively on the task at hand. There was a race to be run, and this qualifying lap was the first step toward the checkered flag on Sunday. Rob thought of nothing else as he placed the wheel on the steering column, snapping the clip, securing it into place.

The qualifying laps of the other cars went by quickly. Rob hardly got settled into his machine when Will called for him to fire the engine. The motor grumbled obediently to life at his touch on the starter switch. Rob pushed the shifter up into first gear, ready for the official standing in front of the Ford to wave him out onto the track. His gaze stayed straight out the front windshield as he mentally reviewed his brake points. He subconsciously tapped the brake with his right foot feeling for the amount of play in the pedal.

Will stepped back from the car an instant before the kid was waved out onto the track. Rob rolled down pit road, already accelerating quickly up through the gears. He needed to have the car yodeling at full song before he entered turn three. Once there, he charged hard into the turn, willing himself to be as smooth as he possibly could. He got back in the gas and shot down toward the green flag and where it waved in the flagman's hand. He flashed across the stripe, starting the clock on the timed run.

His hands and feet worked in perfect unison as the car hurtled into turn one. His left foot pushed solidly on the brake pedal while his right foot feathered the gas. His strong arms twisted the padded steering wheel, forcing the car right down along the curb ringing the inside of the strip of concrete that covered the inside lines. Back in the gas, the car raced down the backstretch, parallel to the railroad tracks that ran just beyond the narrow grandstands.

Rob set the car going into turn three, again working the brake pedal and the gas together. He resisted the urge to take the car the slightest bit deeper into the corner, even though it seemed to be the faster way. Instead, he braked normally, trying to keep the rhythm he had been running.

Keep your head, he thought. Think.

Off turn four, he pushed the car right out against the outside retaining wall as he crossed back over the stripe.

And just like that, his qualifying lap was over.

He killed the motor as the car sailed into turn one, then pulled way to the inside as he coasted down toward the entrance to pit road. The lap felt fine, but how fine? He shrugged his shoulders in reply to his own unspoken question. He had done all he could.

Jodell and Billy watched the lap with expert eyes, following the car all the way around the track, all the while listening to the pitch of the engine. Any slipup on the track would be announced by the sound coming off the headers. But when the kid flashed beneath the checkered flag, there was a wide grin on both men's faces.

"Good enough for you, Bill?" Jodell whooped, slapping Billy on the back. He turned and walked away before the time even flashed up on the giant scoreboard sitting on the back of the trailer in the infield.

"We'll have to wait and see. . . ." Billy started to reply and then realized Jodell was already several stalls down the way, headed for his own pits. The time reported over the loudspeaker was good, the third fastest so far, and a little more than a tenth of a second better than their fastest practice time. Billy could never quite figure out how Jodell could tell a lap time so accurately without a stopwatch.

A small celebration had broken out by the time Billy and Will had crossed back over to where Rob had pulled the car to a stop. They had gotten the smooth lap they needed. The time should be good enough for a top-ten starting spot. There were still some good cars sitting on the line, but, based on the practice speeds, the 52 should still be in decent shape. Donnie and Paul were trading high fives when they walked up to the car.

"Paul, you sure know how to set up a car for this place," Will called out as he unhooked the radio from his belt. He put the radio and headset up on the rear deck lid, then gave the car a gentle pat. "Man, you were fast out there!"

"Do you think it might be fast 'cause of the driver?" Rob asked, managing to keep a straight face as he climbed out of the machine. But then he broke into a massive grin. He sensed then that he had likely made an almost perfect run. At least near perfect for this place.

"Yeah, we'd have the pole if you hadn't slipped up high over there in turn one," Will deadpanned, winking at Michelle.

"Push up in turn one? Are you kidding! I was so smooth going into that corner I could hear all the other drivers going 'ooooh.' "

Will grabbed Rob around the neck, trying to get him in a headlock. The two of them scuffled for a moment, urged on by the hoots and howls of the rest of the crew. Will finally let him go.

"Okay, I'll have some mercy on you," Will said, actually thankful for the chance to catch his breath.

"Mercy? I had you on the ropes, old man," Rob said, then suddenly lunged for Will again.

Will sidestepped him deftly, doing his best bullfighter impression. That move drew another appreciative cheer from the assembled spectators. Billy watched the good-natured horseplay from a safe distance. He knew it was a sign of good chemistry between driver and crew chief, a factor that was often missing on many of the other teams on the circuit.

The celebration was to be a short one for Rob Wilder, though. Michelle hustled him on into the truck to get cleaned up. There was an appearance later on at a local mall, where he was scheduled to meet with fans and sign autographs. There was an interview with a local television station to be recorded before the start of the appearance. If they could get away from the track and to the interview on time, there was even the chance they could get a live spot on the early evening sportscast. Michelle had worked hard to get the interview set up. It would be a big boost for the mall appearance if they could make the early news and encourage all the race fans that were already in town to come out and join them.

Rob balked. He wanted to hang around to find out where they ultimately finished in the qualifying order. A top-ten starting spot would be a major coup for the young team. Rob was eager to see if they had made it, but Michelle would have none of that.

"You finished where you finished, okay?" she fussed as she half pushed him back to the lounge. "You can hear about it on the radio. Now you get your butt in gear and be ready as soon as they open the crossover gate."

"Come on, Michelle. It won't take me a second to get ready. I want to watch the 3, the 24, and the 43 qualify anyway."

"No way, buster. It took me the better part of a month to get this interview set up. This is the top-rated station in this market. Their only condition was that we had to be there on time. Miss their deadline, and we'll get shoved back to the eleven o'clock news instead."

"We have almost an hour and a half. We'll make it easily."

It was a small town, after all, and the mall was only a couple of miles away.

"It may take us that long to get out of here once they get finished qualifying."

"Okay, okay," Rob said, surrendering.

Fifteen minutes later, a freshly showered Rob Wilder emerged from the changing room, still tucking the tail of his golf shirt into his pants. He glanced out toward the track where he could hear the solitary whine of another car making its timed run. He combed his hair as he tried to see how the rest of the session was going. Michelle was standing there with Billy and Donnie as they watched the scoring monitor.

Rob quickly determined that they were still in the ninth position with nine cars still left to qualify.

The 2 and the 6 cars were among those still to make their runs. Both machines had been very fast in the early practice. Will rubbed his hands together anxiously as he watched each of the last few cars roll off. The 2 car blistered the track, producing the third fastest time of the session.

Finally, the 6 made its run. Michelle had forgotten the urgency of their schedule as she watched along with the three men as the veteran made his lap. Even she was able to see that the car was flying. Each of them held his breath until suddenly, there was the slightest hint of a bobble as the car dived into the third turn. Michelle heard the men exhale in unison and she knew something had happened. The driver apparently tried to push the car a slight bit deeper into the corner than he should have. That slight wiggle, almost imperceptible to the casual fan in

the stands, was enough to drop the car down in the final
standings. The 6 car's speed was still good enough for
eleventh, but that left Rob sitting in tenth with three cars
yet to go.

"I'll take tenth starting spot," Billy said, turning to Rob
and shaking the kid's hand. "Congratulations, young'un.
You did a fine job out there. You drove with your head.
Thinking. That's what we need."

"Thanks, Billy," Rob said, almost embarrassed by
Billy's praise. After all, he was only doing his job, driving the car as fast as he could.

They knew now they would be in the top ten. The cars
that were left would likely struggle to make the field.

As those last drivers made their run, Michelle was
dragging Rob toward the crossover gate. The pit reporter
for the television network stopped them, though, seeking
his reaction on making the top ten in his first appearance
at Martinsville. Michelle stood to the side, giving him
signals to hurry up as he patiently answered each question posed by the reporter.

Then, finally, they hustled through the crowd, heading
for the parking lots. Michelle hopped behind the wheel
of the rental car and sped toward the exit. Thankfully,
the traffic was light and that allowed her to quickly negotiate the narrow side street on which the track sat and
pull out onto Highway 220, the main road that led into
town. That's where they encountered heavier traffic,
mostly the fans who had left the track once their favorites
had made their qualifying runs. Michelle bent over the
wheel and began to weave in and out between cars, doing
her best come-from-the-back-of-the-pack imitation.

"Whoa! Don't you think you can slow down now? We
still have forty-five minutes," he said nervously. He held
on to the handle above the passenger side door with both
hands, his eyes wide with fright.

"I don't want to take any chances."

"Well, I don't either. As a matter of fact, I would like to still be in one piece," Rob said, closing his eyes now as Michelle pulled out of line and whipped around a group of slower cars.

"Just sit over there and ride nicely. You act like you've never darted in and out of traffic before."

"I have, but it's in a race car with a nice, safe roll cage wrapped around me. Right now, I'm feeling kind of vulnerable and . . ." Rob hushed fussing and braced himself against the dash as she slammed on the brakes to stop for a traffic light.

Finally, much to Rob's delight, they pulled into the parking lot of the mall. He had hardly had time to unbuckle his seat belt before Michelle was hurrying him again. They jogged across the parking lot toward the mall entrance but a couple of kids, ten or eleven years old at the most, spotted them. The kids headed them off and begged for autographs. Rob patiently fished out of his pocket the pen that Jodell had taught him to always keep with him. He scribbled his name on a couple of the postcards from the box he was carrying. Michelle shot him a pointed look while nodding toward the door where the television crew would be waiting, but Rob took his time, patiently answering the excited kids' questions.

They finally got inside and found the television crew finishing their setup. Introductions were made and the crew signaled they would be ready for Rob in about five minutes. Michelle steered him over to a nearby chair.

"Sit!" she ordered.

"What for?"

"Because I told you to!"

She stood there between his lanky legs while she searched around in the oversize purse she carried.

"What are you looking for?" Rob asked innocently.

"Shut your eyes," she commanded.

"Oh, no! No, you don't. No way."

"Shut up and sit still," she said, producing her makeup case. "If you keep squirming around, you're gonna have this stuff all over you."

"I'm not gonna have any of it on me."

He started to get up but Michelle pushed him back down onto the chair. She began to apply the makeup, turning her head sideways like an artist beginning work on a blank canvas.

"Quit being so silly. Don't you remember doing the commercials you did? You have to have some makeup on or you'll look like a ghost during the interview. We don't want your adoring fans to think you're sick or something," Michelle teased. Still, he squirmed and wiggled around in the chair as she worked on him.

"You guys ready?" the sportscaster asked as he wandered over to check on them.

"I think we have him about as pretty as we can get him," Michelle replied, stepping back to observe her handiwork. "He look okay to you?"

"Yeah, not bad for a race car driver," the sportscaster answered.

Rob didn't bother to comment. He sat there glumly, hoping none of the dozens of curious onlookers who had gathered would notice that he had had powder slapped all over his face.

The taped interview went smoothly and with enough time left that they were able to make the spot on the early news. That made Michelle happy, and so was the sportscaster who now had a good clip for the lead-in to the piece he was doing about all the preparations going on for Sunday's race.

But the instant the taping was over, Rob dashed off to the restroom, anxious to wash his face before anybody else saw him.

The autograph session went smoothly, too. Or at least as smoothly as any event can go when there are far more fans there than anyone anticipated. Hundreds of people turned out, causing the mall security folks to call for reinforcements and leaving Rob Wilder sitting there long after the two hours the session had been scheduled for had passed. That was something else Jodell Lee had counseled Rob about, and he took the advice, staying until the last fan had a chance to visit with him.

He actually enjoyed the attention of the fans and his willingness and patience was quickly enhancing his reputation as an accessible driver. That, in turn, was helping draw legions of new fans that showed up every week at the racetrack, wearing a T-shirt with his name on it, yelling his name, asking him to sign a 52 hat. He still did a double take when he ran into someone wearing a shirt with his likeness on it or presented him with a picture of himself, asking him to sign his name on it.

Michelle wanted to talk on the way back to the hotel. Talk about racing, about appearances she had scheduled, about important people who would be showing up at the various stops on the tour that lay ahead. But Rob sat there, all scrunched down in the seat, for once unconcerned with Michelle's erratic driving, mostly ignoring her monologue except for an occasional grunt to let her know he was still awake.

Already, the next day was shaping up into something special. It was a feeling he'd had since he arrived in Martinsville. It was almost as if the stars and the planets were aligning, coming together for him. All he would have to do the next day would be to drive that gleaming red race car the best way he knew how and he might actually get himself a win.

His first win in his first year.

"What you grinning about? You making fun of my driving?"

Michelle was scowling at him.

"No. No, no. I just had a happy thought, that's all."

"Well, don't let me interrupt your happy thoughts. I merely assumed you would be interested in some of the plans we have for you."

"Oh, no. That's fine. I'm listening."

But before she was even cranked up and running again with her news, he was gliding out of four, taking the checkers, and looking for Victory Lane.

12

LOOKING FOR VICTORY LANE

It was a beautiful early Sunday morning sky, the cool of the previous evening already being chased away by the sun as it cracked open the eastern sky. There was a promise of a warm, dry, early spring day, the man on the radio forecasting a temperature in the mid-eighties, "A perfect day for running that race over in Martinsville," he declared.

After the fireworks of the previous afternoon, it looked as if race day would be hot in more ways than one. Tempers had flared in the "happy hour" practice session the day before. A crash late in practice left everyone involved pointing fingers at each other and several teams postponing their confrontations while they unloaded backup cars off their trailers. Still, a couple of the drivers needed to be separated before their shoving match turned into a good old-fashioned pit fight. Each blamed the other for the stupid move that caused the accident in the first place.

Donnie Kline was one of the crewmen who jumped in

to stop the fracas. After all, it was threatening to break out directly in front of their truck while Rob was coasting in from his last run to seat the brakes. Rob noticed a strange look on Donnie's face as he held one of the angry drivers in a quite effective bear hug. It looked almost like disappointment, as if the big man would much prefer to let the drivers go at it for a bit, as if he would actually have loved finding himself in the middle of a good scrap instead of playing the role of peacemaker.

Rob got a reminder of the previous afternoon's brief brawl as he walked through the pits on Sunday morning, just after the garage opened. There was Stacy Locklear's crew, already at work, making a few hurried last-minute repairs to their car. Rob was still surprised it had not been Locklear involved in the preempted fight the day before, even though he scraped a fender avoiding the fracas out on the track. No, for once he wasn't involved with the shoving match, actually steered clear, kept his nose clean, which was way out of character for the usually combative driver.

Rob looked away as he walked on past. Despite his dislike for Locklear, he didn't wish bad luck on anybody. Racing was just too tough a business these days. He hated to see such things happen to anyone. Even to Stacy Locklear.

Rob grabbed a can of soda from the lounge inside the hauler then stepped back outside to watch his own crew go through a far more pleasant routine than the silver car's crew was faced with this day. They were working through the regular but meticulous process of prerace preparations and checklists, not beating and banging on their racer to try to get it shipshape for the contest.

Just then, Rob glanced across the infield and spied a lone figure high up on the track itself, standing with his back up against the wall in turn one. But the man looked very familiar. Intrigued, Rob walked that way, climbed over the low wall separating the front pits from the racing surface, crossed the smooth pavement, and continued on over to the transition leading into the turn.

"Morning!" Rob called, and tipped the can of soda in the direction of the man who was leaning there.

"Morning, kid!" Jodell Lee said, then took a deep breath of the clean morning air and pointed at the robin's-egg sky. "Man, this is going to be one fine day for racing."

"Going to be a beautiful day, that's for sure."

"More like perfect. Look at her!" Jodell said, waving his arm at the sweep of the speedway. "I love to look at this place from over here. Rarely had the chance when I was driving 'cause I was always trying to get around her as fast as I could manage. Better than fifty years of history here at this proud old lady, you know. Mr. Earles sure knew how to build a racetrack. None of these other cats have ever come close."

Jodell stood there quietly then, listening to the slight breeze as if he might actually catch the grumble of engines lingering in the air from some race long since run. The kid took the opportunity to study the old driver's lined face. The message there was clear, as if Rob could actually look inside and read the man's soul. There was a stock car race about to be run in this place today, and Jodell Lee would have given about anything he possessed for the chance to strap himself into one of those machines and hurtle around this strip of asphalt one more time.

Rob could almost feel the sorrow and turmoil that Jodell undoubtedly endured at each race he attended nowadays. It was especially ironic that something that gave the man so much pleasure could, at the same time, cause him pain, too.

No doubt about it. The fire still burned intensely inside the man. The fierce desire to race and to win that had always been so much a part of his makeup was still there.

And it was likely as strong as it had been those many years ago when he ran that very first race on the old track carved out of a cornfield out on Meyer's farm. As Rob quietly stood there beside him, he thought he could almost understand the helplessness that Jodell must be feeling. The skills and strength that had made him one of the best to ever run the circuit were fading now. That was a given. But the desire? The drive? They were as intense as ever.

Jodell's numerous encounters with racetrack retaining walls and other race cars over the years had taken their toll, too. What the collisions had not swiped, old age was now angling for. The reflexes were more than a little bit off. His eyesight was not quite as sharp as it once had been. The raucous roar of the racing engines had long since numbed his hearing. But it was an inevitability that Jodell Lee clearly didn't want to face. Rob suspected that if it had not been for the fear of what his wife, Catherine, would do to him if she found out, Lee would still stubbornly climb into a race car on occasion and take it out for a spin.

Now, standing there beside him in the warm, early-morning sun, Rob could clearly see the pain in the man's eyes, the hopelessness on his face.

"Let's take a walk," Jodell finally said, setting off on a slow stroll through the wide expanse of the turn. Rob followed silently, knowing that whatever Jodell might say would be well worth hearing. "Look at that transition there between the asphalt and the concrete. You got to have the nose of your car up on the quarter panel of the other old boy's car through here if you're gonna make an inside pass with the money on the line."

Rob mimicked the move with his hands to show Jodell he understood. He studied the transition and the near dearth of banking in the corner. It certainly looked different standing there on the track than it did from the car, zooming through at speed. An outside pass would be difficult at best and next to impossible against a truly fast car. Somewhere in his mind he had already known this, but Jodell was bringing it to the forefront, confirming it was so.

"The only way to pass late in the race is to outbrake somebody entering the corner right here," Jodell said, pointing down at the pavement at their feet. "That's why you have to save the brakes all day long. When it comes time for the run to the checkers, you're going to have to really lay on them hard if you want a shot at winning. Burn 'em up early in the race, and you can forget about it."

"I'll be easy on them. Don't worry."

Rob looked around the speedway now toward the towering grandstands at the far side. As he stood there, he thought he could feel some of the same affection that Jodell must have for this place. And he thought he could understand, too, why it was so difficult for the retired driver to be so close to it and not be able to do the one thing he most loved to do.

Some day, Rob knew he, too, would face that inevitability. But he quickly shook it from his head. That would be a long time coming.

And he wondered, too, if Jodell ever took these walks with his own driver, Rex Lawford. He had never seen him do so, but he wouldn't question him about it. He was thankful for the counsel. The knowledge Jodell imparted on his little strolls was invaluable.

They walked slowly on around the track, stopping this time between turns three and four, and looked back toward where the diminutive set of suites once sat atop the concrete grandstands that ran the length of the far turn. As they ambled along, Jodell continued to offer Rob tips about how to navigate this tricky old track. And all the while, he kept pounding home the same theme: "Save the brakes!"

Then, Jodell paused again, stepped up to the outside retaining wall and leaned there. Rob followed, leaned there next to him, but neither man spoke. For an instant, Rob thought something might be wrong with Jodell. He had quit talking and merely stood there as if listening for something. But he seemed to be okay, only oddly preoccupied as he stared off at the wide expanse of the track.

Then, suddenly, Rob heard something. It sounded for all the world like a race engine roaring way off in the distance, out there beyond the grandstands and parking area. He cocked his head sideways and tried to get a better direction on the noise. Was somebody driving a car that loud to the racetrack? Was the slight breeze playing tricks with an engine that might have been cranked up over there in the garage?

But now, it was rapidly growing louder, getting closer. Rob looked around wildly, trying to pinpoint the origin of the sound.

Jodell's face was blank, his eyes still squinted as he surveyed the speedway, watching for something, someone.

Didn't he hear it? Rob wondered. Didn't he hear the race car coming in their direction. The man had lost most of his hearing, true, but the engine noise was loud now and rapidly getting louder.

And by then it sounded even more like a race car in full song. But not exactly one of the modern engines like the one in his red Ford. No, it was more like what he figured the older cars had sounded like once upon a time. Like the cars that might have circled this very track twenty, thirty, maybe even forty years before.

Then, the din was almost there. Rob's head swiveled about, looking for the car, but there was not one anywhere to be seen. Pit road and the track itself were empty. The thing had to be circling just beyond the retaining wall. Or was it somewhere else?

All the time, Jodell simply stood there, not moving,

smiling slightly, leaning nonchalantly against the wall he had kissed so many times.

Now, the awesome roar seemed to be directly on top of them. Rob thought he could feel the ground shake beneath his feet from the power of six hundred horses thundering by only inches from where they stood.

Then, as quickly as it had come, the noise was gone, replaced by more mundane sounds, the distant revving of an engine down in the garage, the shouts of early arriving race fans out in the parking lot, a couple of guys yelling to each other as they swept the pits.

Rob felt a chill down his spine and realized that cold sweat had popped out on his brow and upper lip. He stepped away from the retaining wall and glanced back at Jodell. The old driver still stood there, as if he might still be in a trance.

But suddenly, he turned and walked away, his slow, slight limp (the relic from some previous encounter with a concrete retaining wall) even more pronounced than usual.

Rob followed along silently, his hands stuffed deeply into his jeans pockets to hide their trembling. But then, at the exit from turn four, Jodell stopped dead, turned, and looked back at Rob.

"You heard it didn't you?"

"Yeah. Yeah, I heard it. What in the world was it?"

"Who knows? Might have been a helicopter bringing in the television crew, coming in low behind the wall to keep from dustin' them boys down in the pits. Mighta been that old helicopter all right." And then, there was that look again on the old driver's face. "Or maybe it was one of the boys who got called home too early, before they got to enjoy one more run at Martinsville. Maybe he came back to look for Victory Lane one more time." Jodell turned then and started on toward the garage. "Don't matter. You're gonna have a whale of a race today if you keep your wits about you, son."

"But . . . wait a minute!" Rob yelled, still rooted to the spot. "What does it mean?"

Lee stopped again and turned back to look at the kid over his shoulder. "When you don't hear it anymore, you'll know your time has passed."

"But you still hear it, don't you?" Rob asked, even more puzzled than before, not considering how cruel the question might have sounded.

"Yeah, I do." He grinned broadly, taking no offense. "I do hear it sometimes. So maybe . . . just maybe . . . I still have what it takes." With a wave of his hand Jodell put an end to the conversation. They each had teams waiting for them. It was time to go run a race.

Rob still felt chilled when he got back to the truck, even though the morning temperature had climbed nicely. Michelle met him at the entrance to the hauler, and she was animated, clearly excited about the upcoming race. But she took one look at him and put her hand to his forehead in a motherly gesture, feeling for a fever.

"You okay?"

"Sure. Why?"

"You look a little pale, kind of tense, that's all."

Rob Wilder never got prerace jitters. He only turned restless when he couldn't climb directly into the race car and crank it up and go run. And today would not be a good day for him to suddenly develop the yips. She figured he would be especially confident this morning after the way the car was running in the happy-hour practice the day before.

"I'm fine. Jodell and I just took a walk and he gave me some tips, that's all. I guess I was thinking about what all he told me and not paying attention to anything else."

Michelle knew him well enough to know he was tap-dancing. Something was bothering him. Family maybe? She knew so little of his background, but that was the only thing she could think of that might rattle the kid. That or something to do with racing, and so far as she knew, everything was going very well at the track. She only hoped whatever it was wouldn't affect him during the race.

Then a sudden thought occurred to her. "You talk to my baby sister last night? Everything all right between you two?"

"Yes, as a matter of fact I did," he answered quickly, thankful for the change in subject. "She's fine. Wonderful, in fact. And everything is great. Said she wished she could be here but she's studying hard for that big exam she's got on Monday. I'm gonna call her in a little while. Want me to tell her anything?"

"No," Michelle answered curtly and with a flash of something disturbing in her eyes. "I've got to go check on the hospitality tent. I'll see you before the start." And she turned on one heel and was gone in one big hurry.

What in the world was all of a sudden wrong with her? He shook his head and once again promised himself he would quit trying to understand the female of the species.

He walked on toward the back of the hauler to get into his driving suit but he stopped as he passed a mirror.

"You do look a little flustered," he told the image staring back at him. Sure enough, he was still a bit pale, his eyes a tad wild.

Heck, he thought, you better be thinking about winning this blamed race and stop looking for ghosts. Except, of course, for the spirit that sometimes rode alongside him in the race car.

No, he'd welcome a visit from that spook anytime. And especially today.

He just might need him to show the way to Victory Lane.

13

INSIDE PASS

The cars were lined up in tandem, stretched out two-by-two along the pit lane, waiting patiently for "The Star Spangled Banner" to finish. Rob stood there among the rest of the crew on pit road after the drivers' introductions, his hand over his heart, half singing the song.

Bubba Baxter earlier stopped by to help himself to a sandwich on the way back from the morning's drivers' meeting. Between big bites of the sandwich, he had given Rob still more advice on race strategy, and the word "patience" was contained in most every sentence. Before he left, he pilfered himself one more sandwich and left Rob with a final thought.

"No matter how tight the racing, you can't afford to lose your temper. I know it's hard to do out there when it gets dicey. But like I preach to Rex all the time, if somebody gets to rubbing fenders with you or butts you in the back end and spins you around, just suck it up, turn the thing straight, and get on with your business. You get mad or try to rub somebody back, all you'll do is beat yourself. You lose concentration on what you're out there to win, and you'll beat yourself every time."

"That's what I keep hearing," Rob answered.

Bubba Baxter didn't talk much, but when he did, he always said something worth listening to. The big man owned more wins at Martinsville as a crew chief than anybody still racing.

The flags all around the speedway whipped briskly in the southerly breeze, and the sun had already driven the temperature up high as the crews stood lined up alongside their cars on pit road. The tremendous throng of fans packed the grandstands ringing the track, and they were all on their feet, giving a hearty roar of approval as the last notes of the national anthem were played, as thousands of colorful balloons were released from the infield. It was a festive atmosphere that mostly hid the nervous tension swirling along pit road among the drivers and teams.

Michelle gave him a quick hug, then he shook hands with the crew and climbed into his gleaming, freshly polished machine. Once settled into the cockpit, he blanked out everything else and concentrated purposefully on the task at hand. He sat five hundred laps away from his first win. A powerful confident feeling seemed to settle over him leaving him certain that somehow he would emerge victorious at the end of this warm afternoon. Yes, there was plenty of racing to do in the meantime. And the odds were definitely stacked against a young, inexperienced rookie, and especially on this tight old track. But Rob knew he had the talent. He knew, too, that he had a car that could lead. With a favorable nod from Lady Luck, this could be his day.

While he waited for the cars ahead of him to roll off the line, he stared straight ahead out the windshield. Will tugged at the window netting, making certain it was secured tightly.

"Gentlemen, start your engines!" came the cry over the public address system.

Rob reached over and flipped the starter switches with his gloved left hand and the perfectly tuned engine jumped to life, maybe as ready as its captain to set sail on this quest for victory. He scanned through the gauges, making certain the readings for the oil pressure and amps from the alternator were what they were supposed to be. He looked to his left at the car beside him, the one that would be running to his inside when they took the green flag. Then he made one last check of the cockpit before the field got the signal to move off. Will slapped the windshield and gave Rob the okay signal. Rob, in turn, flashed him the thumbs-up sign, signaling everything was ready from inside the race car.

As he walked to his spot behind the pit wall, Will checked all around the radio net, making sure everybody was hooked up and working and had good signals and reception. He instructed the crew to make last-minute checks of their assigned pit areas to ensure that all the parts and equipment were in place and ready to go. Ten sets of fresh Goodyear tires sat neatly stacked at the back of the team's pit.

Michelle walked along with Billy, then climbed to the top of the Jodell Lee Racing truck to watch the event with Jodell and Bubba. From there they could see the action all the way around the track. Michelle quickly claimed one of the director's chairs, knowing the guys would spend the whole race leaning against the railing that ran around the observation deck. The starts of races always made her especially nervous. Everybody was all bunched up tightly and all eager to push their way up to the front, and they dashed and darted wildly all over the place. It was even more treacherous at a smaller track like this one. Anything could happen when all those cars tried to fight it out for the critical inside line.

Rob and Will were actually talking on the radio about that very thing as the cars were taking to the track. Starting tenth, Rob would be stuck in the outside line. Will reminded him that it would probably take at least a hundred laps before there was enough spent rubber on the track for the second groove, the outside line, to come in. Anyone stuck on the outside line after the first couple of laps would be in real trouble before the crowd had even settled into their seats. Before the outside groove was available, it would be next to impossible for even the fastest cars to hold a position for long out there.

Will strongly reminded Rob of the urgency of getting down into the inside line at his earliest opportunity.

"Get down there when you can or you'll be seventeenth or eighteenth before you know it," he said. "But be careful doing it. Better seventeenth than wrecked up."

"Ten-four."

Rob needed little more encouragement. Jodell Lee and Bubba Baxter had made the same point.

The cars rolled around the speedway behind the two pace cars that were effectively splitting the field in half. The pace cars moved for a while at the pit road speed limit to allow the drivers to mark their tachometers. They would have to use the rpms on their tachometers to judge if they were within the allowed speed on pit road. These race cars did not carry a speedometer. The different rear-end gearing used by the various teams meant each car had a slightly different rpm level when running at the required speed. Rob noted the rpm on the Ford's tach and called it out to Will, who entered it in the proper spot on his clipboard. It would be one of Will's jobs to remind Rob of the reading to maintain each time he brought the car down pit road. There was a stiff penalty for speeding into the pits: a stop-and-go that then sent the driver to the end of the longest line of cars out on the track. That could be a real race killer on a short track like this, a place where track position was so critical to maintain any hope of winning the contest.

The lead pace car finally rolled beneath the flagstand for the final time. The lights on its top went out as the flagman signaled one lap to go. Rob glanced at the crowd in the grandstands along the front straightaway. They were all on their feet and likely would be for a while. Though he couldn't hear their screams and shouts, he could almost feel their excitement. Some drivers claimed they never noticed the crowd. Rob certainly did. He loved to feed off their excitement. Now, he grinned as he shifted slightly in his seat to make sure the safety belts were good and tight, then stretched both his arms and tightened his grip on the steering wheel.

"Let's go, Big Red," he said out loud. "Rocket" Rob Wilder was ready to get on with the upcoming five hundred laps.

He eased tightly up on the back bumper of the yellow Chevrolet that rolled along directly in front of him. All throughout the field the cars pulled in tight on one another in preparation for the start. Two-by-two they rolled through the third and fourth turn under the towering grandstand packed with cheering fans. They came down toward the line watching for the green flag to fly in the starter's hand.

"Green! Go!" crackled Will's voice through the earpiece inside the full-faced helmet Rob was wearing. Instinctively, he stomped on the gas, hanging on the rear deck of the yellow Chevy as the cars charged down across the line.

Still in two lines, the field ran down into the first turn, but everyone was jockeying for position already, the cars on the outside desperately looking for an opportunity to drop to the inside. Rob jammed hard on the brakes for the first time, trying to hold on to his position as Harry Stone constantly called out the position of the car on his inside. He twisted back and forth on the wheel, trying to keep the Ford as low on the track as the race car to his inside would allow. He feathered the gas coming off turn two as he tried to use the torque of the engine to outrun the inside car down the back straightaway. Then, quick and firm on the binders again, Rob outbraked him going into the corner. The inside car bobbled slightly as he got on the gas a bit too hard exiting the turn. That gave Rob the very tiniest of openings and it would be there only for an instant.

But the kid saw the chance and he took it. He shot down to the inside in front of the other car.

"Clear!" Harry cried, but Rob was already safely tucked in and setting his sights on the next car in line.

Behind him the field had begun to bunch up as a couple of slow cars insisted on running side by side, effectively blocking the way for some of the faster cars that had already been charging up through the field. There was pushing and shoving going on between drivers all the way through the field and the first lap was not even in the books yet. Some of it was unintentional in the close quarters at the start. But then, some of it was very much on purpose.

By the time they had recorded a half dozen laps, tempers were already growing thermal. Something would have to give, or it was going to be a very long race.

Will watched anxiously from his perch atop the pit box as the cars all through the field jostled for inside positions. Right in front of him he spotted a puff of tire smoke from a couple of cars rubbing together. Tempers and brake fluid would be both be boiling soon, he thought. Hard, vicious side-by-side racing was going on all the way around the track. It was much too early for the drivers to be racing each other so hard, but then, track position was critical.

So far, the battle behind them allowed the leaders, who faced a clear track ahead of them, to start to pull some distance ahead of the rest. Rob was settled in the single file line that included the top twelve cars or so. He now ran in eighth place and was perfectly content for now to ride around right there, saving his brakes, letting those behind him swap paint, as he tried to get a better feel for the track's characteristics in the early going. He remembered well the prerace advice he picked up from Jodell.

The silver Pontiac of Stacy Locklear was running back in the thirtieth position. Those eavesdropping on Locklear's radio channel had heard him declare rather vehemently that he had a car that was much faster than the one directly in front of him.

He had already given the car's veteran driver several bumps in the rear end, trying to tell him in no uncertain terms that he was in the way, to move over and let him by. But apparently the message wasn't getting through, and Locklear was growing dangerously impatient. More than one scanner-listener in the stands winced at the language coming from the silver car's driver.

Locklear gave the car in front of him another shove, this time much harder than the ones before. The forty-year veteran in the front car raised and shook his fist to let the younger driver know he didn't appreciate the pops in the rear. Hard as nails, the cagey old veteran was not about to be pushed around by someone the likes of Stacy Locklear, who, in his opinion, couldn't drive a tricycle, much less a roaring, snorting racing machine. After all, the circuit vet had driven longer than anyone else now in the game, and he was certain that he was as fast as Locklear, if not faster. There was no way he was about to give the brat in the ugly silver car an inch of racetrack without him earning it the old-fashioned way. Let him pass if he was that fast. If not, he could just stay back there where he belonged.

Locklear finally ran out of his notoriously limited patience waiting on the old driver to move over and finally drop-kicked the rear of the camouflage-painted Chevrolet as they roared off into turn one. The veteran had no choice. He had to stand on the brakes, trying to hang on to his car as Locklear, still running hard, ran the nose of his car up under the rear of the Chevy. Metal crunched and scraped as the rear wheels of the Chevy were actually picked up slightly off the pavement. That was more than enough to send the Chevy spinning out of Locklear's way.

But Locklear had to struggle to hold on to his car to keep from losing it himself as he and the rest of the field sailed by the spinning car. The caution flag appeared in the starter's hand as the old veteran's Chevy came to a halt in the middle of the turn. Locklear picked up speed, trying to stay on the lead lap. Will had watched the questionable move Stacy made and he knew the old veteran would likely be a bit upset.

When Locklear came back around, Will smiled and shook his head. There was a tiny stream of water dripping from the front end of the silver Pontiac.

Locklear pulled the car down onto pit road with a cloud of steam fogging from beneath the slightly crumpled hood. In his impatience to pass, he managed to plant just enough of the front of his Pontiac under the rear end of the other car to crack his radiator. Depending on how the cautions fell, it would take at least a hundred laps in the garage to get it repaired.

The old veteran fared much better. Except for some crumpled sheet metal on the rear bumper and a set of flat-spotted tires from the spin, he was no worse for the wild ride he took. No one else had hit him. Sometimes it was good to be near the end of the field!

Rob used the race's first caution to catch his breath and reflect on how the car was handling. But the calm in the middle of the storm also allowed him an opportunity to take note of how warm it was getting inside the Ford, and they were barely twenty laps into the race.

"Okay, cowboy, we did a good job there on the start. How's she handling?" Will asked as the field slowly circled the track under the caution. The safety truck was out sprinkling drying compound where Locklear's car dropped the water from the radiator.

"The handling is perfect. Wouldn't change a thing right now. We going to get tires?"

"No, we'll have to stay out with the leaders this time. There's no way they'll come in now and let everybody else catch up."

"Who all is coming in?"

"I'd say anybody in the back quarter of the field will pit. With the single-file restart, they're going to get killed anyway, so it doesn't hurt them to come in. You're running in eighth, so we have to do what the leaders do."

"You're the boss," Rob said as he pulled up closer to the seventh-place car in front of him. Of course Will was right. He usually was.

Rob held his left hand out the edge of the window and tried to deflect some fresh air into the driver's compartment. It was really getting hot now that they had slowed down.

"How you doing on those brakes?"

"Barely having to touch them."

"Just make sure you save some for the end. They're getting ready to give you the 'one lap to go' sign next time around. Just keep on doing what you're doing and then we'll race 'em in the last hundred laps."

"Roger!" Rob answered, punching the mike button with his right thumb. He couldn't wait!

On top of the truck, Billy smiled as he listened to the

exchange. Rob was once again showing the skill, smooth-
ness, and savvy they had first noticed when he drove the
initial laps for him and Will at Nashville.

The rookie driver was also quickly attracting attention
from the television people high up in the booth. They
were already speculating. Was the good run the result of
luck or did the kid really have a car that could hang
around all day and contend at the end? And, if so, was
the handsome youngster a good enough driver yet to
bring it home?

The green flag fell once again and that sent the field
charging off into turn one in a long snaking single-file
line, dust flying, their combined engines deafening. The
rear cars in the field were over half a lap behind the
leaders as they took the start. It would not be long before
the front-running cars would have to start dealing with
lapped traffic. Up front, the race leader got a good jump
on the restart and quickly put several car-lengths between
himself and the second-place car.

Rob quickly settled right back into his rhythm as the
laps began to reel off. He was able to get his nose right
up on the rear of the car in front of him, but, try as he
might, he could not get a good enough run on him to get
a fender alongside going into or out of the turns. Rob
could tell his Ford was the stronger of the two cars, but
the driver ahead of him was an expert at protecting his
line.

"Patience."

He could clearly hear the word spoken in Jodell Lee's
syrupy east Tennessee drawl. In Bubba Baxter's low,
slow twang. In Will Hughes's direct, clipped voice.

And so he waited. Waited for the proper opportunity.
It finally came when he got a good run coming off turn
four. That allowed him to get the nose of the Ensoft Ford
up alongside the back edge of the rear quarter panel on
the other car. He stayed in the gas an instant longer than

he normally might have, trying to drag race the other car down into the first turn. Rob was forced to stand hard on the brakes but they held, and he was able to outbrake the outside car going into the mouth of the turn. He twisted the steering wheel mightily, hoping and praying that the car would stick as he placed the left-side tires right down within inches of the curbing.

· The driver of the car on the outside was not willing to give up the position without a fight. He held his line, not trying to cut down on Rob at all but desperately trying to keep him from gaining the advantage. He tried to make the outside line work so he could hold on to the spot but in the process, the two cars rubbed together ever so slightly, neither driver giving an inch.

Finally, with Rob having the advantage on the inside, he was able to pull ahead of the other car as they came off the corner.

"Outside, still outside," Harry Stone sang sweetly, his voice surprisingly calm on the radio. But then, there came the word Rob was waiting for. "Clear! You're clear, Robbie!"

With those words still ringing in his ears, Rob allowed · the car to drift out toward the outside wall as he set his line more naturally for the next corner. From where he stood on top of the truck, Jodell couldn't help but pump his fist in the air when he saw Rob complete the pass as if he had been doing this Cup racing thing for years, not months. The kid was tough, and he was definitely learning fast the way to get around this track in the shortest amount of time. Once again, Jodell caught himself following the red Ensoft car as it circled the track and taking his eyes off Rex Lawford, his own driver in his own dark blue car.

Rex was struggling early, though. His Ford seemed to be running well on short spurts of ten or fifteen laps, but he fell off quickly with the longer runs under the green flag. Jodell couldn't help himself. His driver was doing all he could, but the kid was fun to watch.

The heat continued to build inside the cars. Even with the second caution after about a hundred laps, and with the quick trip down pit road, there was hardly a chance to cool off at all. The pit stop was so short Rob had little chance to enjoy much of the cool drink at all from the bottle that was passed in the window to him. The sweat rolled down his face inside the helmet mask. The blower attached to the "cool box" was supposed to send cold air through a hose attached to the helmet and across his face, but it seemed to only be sending warm air his way. Either the dry ice had dissipated or the system was malfunctioning somehow. But whatever the reason, it was like riding in a passenger car on a summer day with the heater on full blast and the windows rolled up tight.

By the time the infield scoreboard showed two hundred laps had been run, Rob thought he knew what a pot roast must feel like. And he said as much on the radio.

"Hang in there, cowboy," Will urged. "Not as far to go now as it has been."

He was still running in the top ten. The car remained strong, needing only minor adjustments on the first few pit stops. And still, practically everything Rob did out there on the track was to stay where he was in the lineup and to save the brakes for the end. He felt he had a good shot at pushing the car closer to the front, certainly into the top five. The car was strong and he felt supremely confident in his ability to navigate this track.

But every time he found himself wanting to ram the car a little too hard, those voices would appear in the back of his head and tell him to take it easy. There would be time soon to spar with the race leaders.

Now wasn't the time. Not now.

Michelle was actually finding it difficult to follow only Rob around the track. It seemed as if there was something going on everywhere out there, like watching a multiring circus with death-defying acts performing all over. The steadying hand of Bubba Baxter on her shoulder kept her turned in one direction or another while he pointed with a crooked finger to wherever he felt she needed to be looking. She'd turn to watch and the next thing she knew she had lost Rob in the jumble of cars strung out all around the speedway. Sometimes she felt as if her head was on a swivel and that, along with the thunder of the race engines and the constant roar of the fans had her head reeling.

Billy and Jodell stood calmly atop the truck, elbows on the top railing and feet propped on the second in identical poses. They might just as well have been standing on the pier on Jodell's fishing pond back in Chandler Cove, waiting for a nibble. They seemed oblivious to all else as they tracked their own two cars, studying them through senses honed from years and years of hard-won experience. Their faces showed no emotion as they watched the cars circle, their concentration broken only occasionally when one or the other of them would click his stopwatch as he timed a car.

As Rob brought the car across the start/finish line for the three hundredth time, Jodell finally turned toward Billy and nodded toward where the red car dashed off into the first turn.

"The kid has a shot you know," he said, raising his voice loud enough to be heard over the eddy of noise that surrounded them.

"Yeah, he's running a good, smart race today," Billy agreed. "If his luck holds, we might get us a top ten."

"He's gonna do a lot better than that. A lot better than that."

At that very moment, Rob likely would not have agreed with Mr. Lee. He had been able to hang on in the top ten all day but he was starting to get even more uncomfortable inside the car. He felt as if he were boiling in his own sweat, and it was all he could do to keep his concentration focused on driving smoothly through the corners. He had to fight the impulse to charge into the corners and then stomp on the brakes as he tried to catch up to the bumper of the Pontiac running in front of him.

His head was pounding, his stomach was churning, and he felt faint, the track swimming out there in front of him. His arms ached from the constant strain of sawing back and forth at the steering wheel. His left leg was beginning to cramp up from the near constant pressure he was applying to the brake pedal. The tight, narrow turns did not allow him more than an instant to relax. He had to consciously force himself to concentrate, to put his pain and discomfort out of his mind and try to ignore his misery.

In lap 340, several cars got together in the center of turns three and four. One car had slammed hard into the side of another, rupturing its radiator as well as the oil cooler, sending a thick stream of liquid across the track. Two of the cars were damaged too badly to move under their own power while several others managed to pull away from the scene of the catastrophe, dragging loose sheet metal as they went.

The caution flag was a godsend for Rob Wilder. He actually whooped as he saw the yellow lights beginning to flash as he raced through turn one.

"Caution, Robbie. Caution. Crash in three," Harry announced. "Track's open."

There was no acknowledgement.

"Okay, cowboy, how we doing out there?" Will asked. There was a pause with no answer. "Talk to me Robbie. How we doing?"

Another few seconds passed before Will finally heard the squelch on the radio broken by Rob's signal.

"Hang on a second. I need to catch my breath," Rob

answered, and anyone listening could hear how weak his voice was, how hard he was trying to suck in deep gulps of the superheated air.

As long as he was racing, he could close off much of the discomfort, but now, slowed by the yellow flag, he became acutely aware of everything around him. And the most obvious thing was that he was roasting. He reached up and yanked the hose to the malfunctioning cool box off his helmet. Better no air at all than having his head inside an oven!

Billy got a worried look on his face when he heard the transmission. He could tell by the tone in Rob's voice that the kid was in trouble out there. A fast race car and a chance to win could help a driver fight off nausea or a headache. But heat was another story. It could steal a man's strength, rob him of all reasoning, and send him to the pits as surely as a bad crash.

"He's cooking in the car, Jodell," Billy said, leaning over, yelling into Jodell Lee's ear. "The darn cool box must not be working. It's just burning him up. Looks like that'll put an end to our top ten run."

Jodell looked over at his old friend and winked.

"It'll take more than heat to slow him down. Y'all just got to keep him calm and focused."

Jodell pulled down his own headset then so he could listen in on what Bubba Jr. was telling Rex about their pit stop.

Billy appreciated Jodell's optimism, but Lee had not heard the kid's voice on the radio, had not heard how he was struggling to breathe. Michelle Fagan certainly had, and she had a horrified look on her face. She turned to Bubba Baxter to see what he thought about what might be wrong, but the big man was gone already.

One of the wrecked cars had died right at the entrance to pit road, effectively blocking it, so for the time being, the pits could not be opened to the rest of the field until the car was moved. Bubba had climbed down from the truck and headed quickly across the small garage area to where Will sat atop the pit box. Will was still trying to talk to his driver without too much success. It seemed Rob lacked the strength to speak more than a few words at a time.

"Pits are still closed. You okay?" Will said into his headset microphone.

There was a pause that lasted several seconds before a ragged answer came.

"I think I climbed into somebody's microwave oven. And I think I'm just about done."

"Just catch your breath. There's still a car blocking the entrance to pit road so it will be another couple of laps before we can bring you in. We got four fresh tires and a couple of cans of 'go juice' ready for you."

"Better make that a bucket of ice water, or we're not gonna get very much farther." The kid's voice was thin and wavering.

"Hang in there. We're up to sixth, and there'll be less than a hundred and fifty laps to go when we get the green. How are those brakes?" Will asked, trying to keep Rob's mind on the car and the race and off the heat in the cockpit.

"Just as tight as they were on the start," Rob answered, perking up a bit.

"Good. We need to keep on saving them. We've kept the leaders in sight all day. We can bring this thing home."

"Ten-four," Rob confirmed as he slumped back as far as he could in the seat. He stuck his left hand out the window again, trying to scoop any cool air he could find into the cockpit of the racer. But what he found seemed about as blistering as the dry, scorching air the cool box hose had been blowing into his face.

The cars circled the track for another two laps while

the wrecker was getting hooked up to the foundered car that was blocking pit road. In the meantime, Bubba Baxter came into the 52 car's pit at a dead run. He grabbed the first small towel he found and threw it into the water cooler then picked up one of the supersize drink cups and filled it up with the icy cold water from the cooler's spout. He said something in the ear of the tire carrier and pointed at the giant cup of ice water he still held. The tire carrier nodded and tightened his clutch on the tires he held under each arm. Bubba stood next to the wall, waiting for the call that the pits were open.

"All right, boys, we got to make a quick stop," Will was saying over the radio. "The cream has risen to the top of the heap here, and we can't afford to lose any spots. We're going for four tires, two cans of gas and a half round of wedge out of the rear. Let's make it quick. We don't want him to have to pick up any spots he's already earned out there."

Will got the signal then that the pits would be opening the next time the leaders came by. He stood up on top of the pit box to find where Rob was on the track.

"Okay, cowboy. Pits are now open. Bring her in this time. Watch your pit speed."

"Ten-four," was the only response, and it was weak.

Physically, he was totally exhausted. Mentally, he still thought he had a shot at winning if he could stay conscious. It was going to be a long hundred-plus laps to the finish. The car was perfect on the long, green-flag runs and that's what they needed for the rest of the race. They would have to stop one more time for tires, but if they could stay green for the last fifty laps or so, they'd have as good a chance as anyone.

Rob followed the car ahead of him onto the pit lane. He forced himself to watch his speed closely, especially after the other car peeled out of line and darted into his own stall. Rob strained to see the signboard that would be waiting for him all the way down toward turn one. Finally he caught sight of the red and blue board held high for him, guiding him in like a beacon. He brought the car in to a perfect stop right on the marks taped on the pavement.

Donnie Kline led the charge over the pit wall even as Rob closed in on his pit. The jack was shoved under the car, and Donnie gave one quick pump on its handle, raising the right-side of the car up off the pavement enough for the tires to be swapped. The tire changers quickly dropped to their knees, popping the lug nuts off with a whine of air wrenches. The carrier shoved the fresh tires into the waiting hands of the changers who placed them onto the lugs and quickly bolted them in place before dashing around to the other side to repeat the process.

Rob went ahead and moved the gearshift into first so he would be ready to scoot away as soon as the jack came down on the left side. The water bottle was in the window almost before the car stopped. Rob gratefully accepted it, flipping the visor up on his helmet so he could get a long drink of the cold liquid. He tried to wipe away the sweat from his face with his gloved hand. But it was useless. More perspiration popped out immediately and little rivulets ran from his soaked hair and into his eyes.

Bubba retrieved the towel from the cooler and grabbed the giant cup of water he had poured. He watched the right-side tire change, waiting for the tire carrier to come running back around when the changers were finished. Bubba shoved the towel and the ice water into the waiting hands of the tire carrier. He stepped over to the race car's window and stuck the ice-cold cup of water in. Rob reached for it instinctively, but before he could get it, the tire carrier dumped the contents of the cup down the front of Rob Wilder's driving suit.

The driver yelped as the cold water ran down his chest

and belly. But then he broke into a broad grin. The carrier dropped the cold towel in on Rob's knee as he backed away from the window.

The jack came down then, and Rob popped the clutch, hit the gas, and twisted the wheel as he accelerated away. Once he blended back in with the other traffic, he took the wet towel and wiped his face and neck.

What a relief! He felt better then than he had at any time in the last two hundred laps. He was smart enough to know the respite was temporary, but, temporary or not, it would certainly give him a better shot at actually finishing this thing.

"Thanks for the towel and the ice water, Will. I feel a hundred percent better now."

"What?" Will asked. But there was Bubba Baxter, standing at the foot of the toolbox, flashing him a thumbs-up before he turned and wandered on down to his own pit. "Okay, cowboy, we're going to need us one more stop before the finish. You're sitting in seventh. It is about time to turn the wick up a little bit."

"Hey, I'm ready to go," Rob called back, and his voice was noticeably stronger after the stop.

"Let's take it easy until we make that last stop, then we can cut it loose."

Rob let the radio go dead as he tried to stretch some of his aching muscles. The cramp in his leg was so painful that he had barely been able to work the clutch on the pit stop. Now he tried to reach it to massage it but had to settle for flexing the leg, trying to get blood to circulate.

"One to go till green," Harry called.

"Ready!"

"Remember the plan," Will chimed in. "We got what it takes to get us a good finish but we need you to take us there."

"Gotcha!"

Bubba Baxter angled his way back up to where Will sat on the pit box. Will waved him up into the other seat on the box. Bubba nodded, then climbed up and joined him. With Rex Lawford already several laps down, there was little he could do for his own team. Here, with Will, there was still a race to win, and he might just be able to offer some help.

Rob tried to take in deep breaths of hot air as the twin line of cars rolled slowly through turns three and four. Once again, Rob ran his car right up on the rear bumper of the Ford that was now running in front of him. He goosed the gas, trying to stay mere inches off the back end of the other Ford. His own car lurched forward as the field hit the exit of turn four.

The green flag flew high in the starter's hand one more time, and the leader surged ahead by several car-lengths, buzzing on past the lapped car that had been down to his inside. Racing off into the first turn, he quickly moved down to the inside, leaving the lapped car to separate himself from the second-place car. The lapped traffic was soon giving fits to the cars running from second on back.

Rob threaded his way carefully through the lapped cars, trying to make some progress while being sure he didn't get caught up in somebody else's accident. It took another dozen or more laps before he was able to clear the last of the slower guys. Now, he could turn his attention to trying to run down the leaders.

The four-hundred-lap mark came and went. Rob was working hard, doing all he could do to pass the yellow Chevy that was running in fifth place. The two of them had been battling furiously for the spot over the last eight or ten laps. Rob could get a fender underneath him as they rumbled down the straightaways, but then he would get outbraked every time they dived into one of the corners together. The heat was starting to work on him again, too, and he had to work on maintaining his concentration. He kept reminding himself what all could happen if he lost focus, if he allowed his attention to wander. And all of it was bad.

Finally, he yanked the wheel hard coming out of turn two and once again got down to the inside of the yellow car. And as he had done several times before, he managed to outpower the Chevy down the backstretch, pulling almost even on his inside. This time, though, Rob used his brakes harder at the turn, driving the car deeper into the corner than he had before. He pulled ahead slightly in the center of the curve, then used the horsepower of his Ford to ease on past the other car as they headed out of the turn and into the frontstretch.

Fifth place was his! Now, without even pausing to congratulate himself on the move, Rob set his sights on the fourth-place car.

The front six or seven cars were still running in a single-file line with less than a third of a lap separating first from seventh, the leader ahead of number two by five car-lengths. Third and fourth were racing hard for their positions. Rob trailed them by a half-dozen car-lengths but he was closing on them rapidly.

"Good move out of the corner, cowboy. Way to go."

Will decided to take the time to compliment him on his capture of fifth place. The kid deserved the praise. He had been patient then took the pass when it was the proper time. There were good drivers in Cup racing who had trouble doing what the youngster in the 52 had just done.

"How many laps to go?" Rob radioed back.

Will shot Bubba a concerned glance before he answered. Bubba shook his head and held up a hand, suggesting that Will might be best to ignore the question. They didn't need their driver thinking about how much longer he had to endure the heat. And the question had confirmed that the kid was still mighty uncomfortable in the car.

"You're as fast as the leader right now. We're going to stop in about thirty laps if there's not a caution. Once we stop, then you need to cut it loose."

"Ten-four," came the raspy, barely audible reply.

The lead group was coming up now on a sizable knot of cars, many of which were racing hard for position. Trailing the back of the pack of the cars they were approaching was the repaired silver Pontiac of Stacy Locklear. Locklear's car was still slightly slower than the cars around him, the result of the damage from his accident early in the race. Still the driver hogged the inside line, forcing the leader to pass him on the outside. The leader made it past unscathed but glanced over and scowled at him as he went by.

The second-place car pulled up next to Locklear as they went down the front straightaway. He surged ahead as the cars dived into the first turn.

Locklear seemed to take the attempted pass personally, though. Suddenly he turned into the driver that was trying to ease on past, bringing the sides of the two cars together hard. Then they scraped together a second time, sending up a puff of tire smoke where someone's tire rubbed sheet metal on the other vehicle.

The driver of the second-place car decided to floor it, to go on past before he got jammed again, and he managed to finally clear the silver Pontiac before its driver could do any more damage. The third- and fourth-place cars' drivers apparently saw what trouble the other leaders had had with Stacy Locklear, so they didn't hesitate. They picked their spots and bulled on past him, even as the flagman was showing the silver Pontiac the "move-over" flag.

Locklear simply ignored it.

Rob, too, had seen the stubborn driver cause the others

problems. He studied the silver car carefully, then, unlike the others, decided to try to get by on the inside of him. But it seemed every attempt Rob made was blocked by Locklear, as if he and the 52 were fighting for the lead.

Locklear was a good hundred laps down. Why didn't he just move over and let the faster cars pass? Or was he determined to ruin somebody else's day because his had gone to seed?

The struggle to get past the guy was beginning to cost Rob time on the track, though. The sixth-place Chevy had already closed back to within a car-length of him while the front four cars were pulling away alarmingly fast.

Billy watched as Rob tried to make the pass on Locklear time after time. He was concerned because he could tell that his driver was beginning to get impatient, was almost certainly thinking about pushing the issue. Jodell watched the kid carefully, hoping he would have sense enough to give a reckless, dangerous driver like Locklear plenty of room.

Rob wrestled with the car as vigorously as he did with his own emotions. It seemed every lap was more difficult than the next. The only thing keeping him going was the knowledge that his lap times were as fast or faster than the leaders' were. The steady announcement on the radio of his lap times helped Rob maintain his focus on the track, on taking the car to the front.

When it was right, he would take the pass. When it was right.

He closed in on the silver Pontiac of Locklear yet again, hoping against hope that the jerk would finally realize how foolish what he was doing would appear to the fans, that he had nothing to gain by knocking someone else out of the race. Surely Locklear would see how much faster Rob was than he and he would move over and let him go on by.

He should have known better.

Now even more weakened and distracted by the heat and frustrated by Locklear's stubbornness, Rob fought to keep his mind on the task at hand. He got a fender up alongside Locklear as the cars cleared turn four and stayed there halfway down the front straight. But once again, the Pontiac chopped down hard on Rob as they raced into the next corner. That forced Rob to back out of the throttle once more and jam hard on the brakes to keep from colliding with him.

"Whoa!" he howled, certain the two cars were about to slam together and go spinning off into the brilliant afternoon sun. At the last second, though, Rob managed to brake just enough so Locklear could slide back up and in front of him and hold the spot. Rob yelled at him: "Idiot! What are you trying to do?"

Of course, nobody, and especially Stacy Locklear, could hear him at all. But it made him feel better to scream at him, to vent some of his building rage.

Rob patiently set the car right back on the bumper of the Pontiac as the two of them raced through one and two yet another time. Locklear knew that Rob could not afford to be reckless, to foolishly risk ruining a good run. And he likely knew, too, that the youngster would not take a chance retaliating against him either.

Rob settled back in line. But when he glanced up ahead, he could see that the distance between him and fourth-place car, a span that had been manageable a few moments before he caught Locklear, was now growing infinitely greater. He had to do something or settle for fifth place in a race he could and should win!

Finally, he gave the Pontiac a slight tap in the back end in the middle of the straightaway where it would do no damage. He was merely serving firm notice that he should move over and let the faster car pass. Locklear showed no inclination to honor the request, though. He continued to make his blocking moves, holding up the entire parade behind him.

Okay, that's it, Rob finally declared to himself. He had checked the mirror and saw the sixth-place car was quickly closing in on him. And out the windshield the leaders were driving away from him.

He drove the car deep into turn three, trying to out-brake Locklear. Using that momentum, Rob then got a run on the Pontiac, but this time he was on the outside. With the power in the motor, he pulled even with him in the center of the turn. He deliberately kept Locklear pinched down low, knowing his engine would bog down under the stress. He knew his own engine could handle it and basically, he was simply outpowering the silver car.

But again, just as it appeared Rob would clear him, Locklear deliberately jerked his to the right, darting up the track to just catch the rear of Rob's car. But even with the jolt of contact, Rob Wilder did not hesitate. He charged right on past Locklear.

Now, assuming he was safely by, he was about to set his sights on the fourth-place car when all of a sudden, he felt the rear of the car start to go around. It felt as if he had hit a patch of ice as the car looped around, spinning 360 degrees. A huge cloud of tire smoke quickly obscured the track all around him. The trailing cars immediately began to stack up as they darted and braked to miss Rob's spinning car. In an instant, one of the other cars was turned around as someone wasn't fast enough getting on the brakes and booted him in the back end.

Rob was alert enough to kick in the clutch as he felt the car shoot out from under him. Somehow, he had the presence of mind to know to keep the engine running. Amazingly, he was able to get the car stopped with its nose pointed toward the first turn. For a second, he was disoriented by the suddenness of the spin, the blinding smoke and screeching of tires all around him, and the intense heat in the cockpit. He fully expected to get rammed hard and he instinctively braced for the impact even as he tried to get his bearings.

Will was watching his television monitor as Rob raced down the backstretch. With Rob now faster than the leader, they were looking at a real shot at winning this race. Bubba was helping him calculate when they needed to stop for the final time, assuming there was not another caution period. He could tell his driver was having trouble with the silver Pontiac but he knew Rob could eventually get by him if he was patient. But then, as the cars hit the corner, he studied the lap count on the computer that was resting between himself and Bubba, and, when he looked up, the Pontiac flashed in front of their position without Rob on its tail anymore.

Will's stomach fell. Where was Rob? He frantically looked back toward the far turn and saw the tire smoke and the spinning cars.

All hell was breaking loose back there and the leader was already hitting the backstretch. Will squinted, desperately trying to find their bright red Ford somewhere in the bedlam that had most recently been a well-ordered bunch of race cars.

Then, he saw him. Down by the wall, pointed in the right direction, but surely stalled. And maybe damaged.

"Get it moving! Come on, kid! Come on!" Will was screaming, pleading out loud. But somehow, he had forgotten to hit the mike switch. And when he jumped up, the radio headset and the transmitter on his belt were ripped off. He frantically reached for them, looking for the microphone switch, yelling all the time, as if, somehow, the kid could actually hear him way over there. "Get 'er in gear. Get 'er cranked. You got to go. The leader's coming."

Rob was still trying to figure out what had happened

when he heard the words "get this thing in gear" and "leader's coming" ringing in his ears. He shook his head to clear the fuzziness and quickly threw the shift lever up into first gear then let out the clutch.

The engine was still running! Thank goodness!

She pulled away strongly at his command. And before the smoke had cleared, before the dust had settled, before all the other cars that had been spinning all around him had even come to a rest, he had spun the tires and accelerated away from the mess. Still trying to gather his wits, he rolled across the start/finish line only a car-length ahead of the race leader.

He was still on the lead lap!

"Way to beat the leader back to the line!" Will called into the hastily retrieved radio headset as he watched Rob chase off after the rear of the field.

"Thanks for reminding me to get the thing in gear and drive on. It took me a minute to figure out where I was, and if you hadn't reminded me that the leader was coming so fast, I might still be sitting back there counting my fingers and toes," Rob radioed back once he had caught the tail end of the field.

"What?" Will asked, and he saw the puzzled look on Bubba's face as well. Rob had gotten the car moving before Will could get to his radio. Maybe Harry Stone had made the call.

"I'm glad you got going, too, Robbie," Stone was saying just then. "I couldn't see you for the dust and smoke and it sure was a relief to see you drive out of that mess okay."

Will's eyes widened, but he didn't have time to wonder. He had a pit stop to run.

"We are doing four tires and gas. No change on the chassis. Got that, cowboy?"

"Sounds good."

Now that the adrenaline rush from the crash was over,

the kid's voice sounded even more tired than ever.

The field rolled down onto pit road for what would certainly be the last stop if the race stayed under green to the finish. The Ensoft crew scrambled to crank off the best stop of the day and it did help. They actually picked up one position with the good stop. That left Rob in eighth spot with only nine cars left on the lead lap. With only sixty-six laps left to go, they would need a miracle to still get the win. That, or another caution period at just the right time.

"What happened back there?" Will finally asked Rob as they rolled slowly around behind the pace car, waiting for the safety crews to finish their cleanup.

"That sucker just ran over me! He's either blind as a bat or mean as a snake."

"Now, calm down. We still got us a race to run."

"I don't like to complain, but it's still about a thousand degrees in this car."

"You're fine. We only got about sixty laps left. It'll be over in no time. We still got to win this thing then I'll let you sleep in the refrigerator tonight."

There was a pause then before Rob spoke again. "Will, I don't know if I have it in me to win this race. It's so hot I'm hallucinating."

"What are you talking about? Suck it up. We didn't come all the way over here to throw in the towel if it gets a tad uncomfortable."

"I'm not . . . throwing in the towel. I'm cooked! And I mean . . . well done. I don't know . . . I don't know if I can . . . make it sixty more laps, much less . . . pass seven cars."

The kid seemed to be struggling for breath as he spoke, his voice hollow and distant. For a moment Will actually considered bringing him in, trying to cool him down and let him go back out and settle for whatever they could get. Lord knows he didn't want the kid to get heat stroke.

"Look, tough guy. We don't have time to argue. They're saying you're gonna get the green next time by. Now, you wanna quit or do you wanna get a cold shower in Victory Lane?"

There was another pause.

"Just tell everybody . . . that Rocket Rob . . . died trying to win a race."

"Ten-four."

Will switched over to the alternate channel and ordered everyone but Harry to stay off the radio. No talking. They needed to allow Rob to think only of bringing the car home.

Rob circled slowly behind the pace cars, eyeing the seven cars he needed to pass. With that many slower lapped cars lined up on his inside, he would have to work twice as hard. At least the car's brakes still felt good and strong.

He wished he could say the same for its driver.

As the field rolled under the flagstand the flagman gave them the "one to go" signal. Rob tried to marshal his strength to make this one last run. It would be easier if the spin had never happened. Now, there was almost a sense that they were merely hanging on, angling for a top five instead of an outright victory. That made the misery of the superheated cockpit all the harder to ignore.

"You can do it, youngster. Time to take it to the front. Run 'em hard and smooth, and you can still get this thing."

The heavy drawl of the voice in his earpiece was eerily familiar. But Rob wasn't quite sure who was talking.

"Come again, Will."

"I didn't say anything?" Will called back. "We may have somebody bleeding over onto our channel."

"Ten-four."

It was the voices. The ones that sometimes rode with him.

I just hope you fellows aren't as blamed hot as I am, he thought.

Will turned to Bubba with a worried look on his face. The kid was struggling even more than they had thought.

"I'm thinking about bringing him in. Reckon Rex would drive the rest of it for him?"

Lawford had been caught up in the wreck at Rob's spin and was out of the race.

"He would. But think about it. You bring that kid in now, even if it might save his life, he's never going to forgive you after it's all over. He'll make it 'cause he's tough and determined. He's about to learn for himself what he's made of. When a man has a shot at winning, and when he craves winning as bad as that kid does, he can do a lot of things he never thought he could."

Will took his finger off the microphone switch before he went ahead and ordered the kid to come in anyway.

The green flag fell on the restart with the field charging off yet again into the first turn. With the laps winding down and the race on the line, the fans were on their feet for the duration of the contest. And those following the red 52 Ford were seeing a show.

Rob Wilder drove as if he was possessed, trying to clear all the lapped cars while still making up ground on the leaders. Slowly, maddeningly slowly, a car at a time, he started working his way to the front. It was clear that when he wasn't being held up in traffic he had the fastest car on the track.

But would there be enough laps to make it all the way to the point? Would the tires and the brakes hold, or would they fade at the end and leave him punchless? Would he make it? Or would the searing heat claim his faculties, his judgment, ultimately his desire?

The kid tried to shove those thoughts out of his head. Somehow, the harder he concentrated on piloting this race car to the front of the field, the more he felt as if he had found a second wind.

First, he eased by the sixth-place car, then the fifth. Car by car, he advanced on the leader, who was now in sight once again, twenty or so car-lengths ahead of him. The leader himself was already skirmishing with the second-place car, trying to hold on to his spot up front.

Time was running out on Rob Wilder. But he told himself to drive as he would if they had a full race to go, to be smart but aggressive as the laps rapidly wound off.

"Twenty to go," Will called, keeping his voice even. He resisted the urge to try to push his driver harder, or to cheerlead. Rob was giving it everything he had already. The times on the stopwatch showed that. Either it would be good enough or it wouldn't. The next twenty trips around this place would tell.

Before he knew it, Rob was closing in on the third-place car. The veteran driver was smart, protecting the low line around the track as he fought to hold the position. This close to the front and at this point in the race, those cars who had survived were closely matched in both speed and handling. There would be no outside passes. It would be an inside pass or nothing.

Rob tried desperately to get a fender beneath the Ford that was holding third place. But the other driver rebuffed every attempt he made. The wily veteran had been in this spot plenty of times before. He seemed to be psychic, able to foresee every move before Rob even started to make it.

But even as they scrambled for the position, they managed to close the gap on the two cars up front. It had become a four-car race.

Rob knew he had the fastest car still running. If he could only make the pass and claim third, there was no doubt he had something for the leaders. He pushed the car even harder, craving the chance to get up there and mix it up for the win.

It was within his reach. He had to find a way to get it in his grasp.

But the ferocious battle with the third-place Ford was eating up the laps he had left. He had to get by now or he was going to run out of time. He would have to settle for third. And he was too hot and tired to do that.

Nope. Winning. That's what would make all this torture worthwhile.

Once more out of the corner, Rob managed to get a fender alongside the veteran. The two of them charged off down into the next turn almost side by side, neither car nor driver giving anything to the other. Somewhere in the back of his feverish mind, Rob knew this would likely be his last shot. In the next instant he would have to decide to let it all hang out, risk it all for the pass and a shot at the lead, or back off and settle for a top-five finish.

He made up his mind right then and there.

He drove the car deep into the corner, deeper than he had driven it all day. The car running on the outside was helpless now as they raced into the corner. He fought to stay even, to keep his car on the track at all.

Rob prayed the car would stick, that he could keep control of the bucking steering wheel that threatened to tear itself loose from his exhausted arms. He jumped hard on the brakes at the last instant before he sensed he would lose the car. He could only hope there was still pressure in the pedal. If not, he and his fellow combatant were bound ignobly for the outside wall and the rookie would have plenty of explaining to do.

If so . . .

He jammed the pedal with his left foot, sensing more than feeling the calipers tighten, and the car began to slow. Would she hold? Was he demanding too much from this hunk of machinery? No! No more than he was demanding of himself.

The car careened through the corner, inches away from the door of the other Ford, her tires squealing, brakes grinding. And she held. Impossibly, incredibly, she held her line while her exhausted driver steered her, and she sailed right on through. The other Ford couldn't maintain its position.

Rob pulled ahead as they came off the corner and he guided her on down the backstretch, looking now to the two other cars, separated from his own hood by fifteen car-lengths.

Now, could he actually catch them? With this car, yes. Yes, he could. But could he get by them once he ran them down? That was the question nearly everybody in the grandstands was asking. So were the commentators on the television broadcast and the radio team and countless millions out there listening and watching. This was promising to be some kind of finish!

Billy still stood silently next to Jodell. Michelle was beside herself. She couldn't remember breathing since the near-tragic spinout. Christy had called her a half dozen times on her cell phone and they had tried to calm each other down without much success.

Christy had seen everything on television, heard the announcers talking about how Rob was getting over-heated, saw the spin replayed over and over and over and still had trouble believing he had driven away from it. But he was still out there, still making his way to the lead. Surely, he was okay. She had to think he was.

"What do you think?" Billy Winton asked the old driver.

"He'll catch them. That's for sure, Bill."

"Can he get by them?"

"I don't know. If they had another twenty laps, I'd bet the farm on the kid. There's not really enough laps left.

But then the way those two are racing each other in front of him, anything can happen."

"I just hope he can hold on to what he's got. I'll take third and go home."

"Yeah, Billy, but your forgettin' one important thing."

"What's that?"

"Third ain't winning!" That said, Jodell turned back to the race.

Rob Wilder had almost forgotten how unbelievably miserable he was. Even the sweat in his eyes couldn't keep him from seeing the first two race cars up there in front of him. And they were not nearly so far away as they had been mere moments before. He was gaining on them. Lord, he was gaining.

"Five to go."

When Will made that call Rob was only a couple of car-lengths behind the second-place car who was, at that moment, still trying to get momentum for a good run on the inside of the leader.

Rob knew now that he would have to be smart, not overly aggressive. If the leaders wrecked themselves as they fought for position, the win would be his. That is, unless he got embroiled in their crash. Then he might finish twentieth if he was lucky. But there weren't enough laps for him to be too cautious.

No, he needed to make that inside pass right now. There was no time to waste. The decision made, he pulled in tight on the back of the second-place car. Not a fan was in his seat anywhere around the speedway as they all braced for the shoot-out that was coming.

The driver in the Pontiac up front was still doing all he could to try to make his car as wide as the track itself, to keep anyone from getting around him. He was especially conscious of the inside line, trying to make sure a pass would have to come to the outside, the hard way around.

"Two to go," Will called, trying to keep his voice calm so as not to rattle the kid behind the wheel of his car. He couldn't believe that they were actually racing for the win.

Rob was charging, trying to get a nose under the second-place Chevy as they dived into turn one. The cars touched slightly before Rob was forced to back off or risk spinning both cars. The Chevy didn't allow the touch to deter his own bid for the lead, though. He tried to get a run under the Pontiac as they exited the corner but the leader held his ground as the trio of roaring race cars ate up the pavement down the short straightaway.

As Rob pushed his car even harder, he realized that the two cars in front of him were actually holding him up. The Ensoft Ford was easily the fastest car on the track. It would be the driver who would make the difference now. And this particular driver had been doing this for only a few short months.

Now, a driver like Stacy Locklear would have bulled his way right on through. Rob resisted that urge, even as he pressed the other two cars hard.

He could see the white flag waving as they came out of the corner, racing down to the stripe on the pavement that marked the finish line. One more trip around the track and the day would be done.

Other drivers would have backed off, let the other two fight it out and either hope they wrecked or settle happily for third place. That would actually be the smart thing to do, especially for a youngster like Rob. He had proved his point already. Winner or not, he would be the story of this race.

Sweat soaked the inside of his driving uniform as he focused on the two cars in front of him. It would be so easy to lie back and take his hard-earned prize. His tired arms ached, his stomach and chest cramped, he could hardly see for the perspiration, he was so dizzy he could barely hold his head up, and he had lost most of the feeling in his feet and legs.

So easy. So easy to settle.

Somehow, though, settling wasn't in him. He fought the wheel as he dived down to the inside, trying to build speed going into the corner. Then he saw exactly what he had been waiting for. An opening so quick, so tiny, a blink would have curtained it.

But he did see it, and he still had reaction enough to rush to the inside and take a shot at hitting it. He nosed the Chevy out of the preferred groove and drove impossibly deep into the corner, way lower than any car should be able to hurtle at that speed. But the kid's inside pass on the two veteran drivers was there. He had seen it, and he was going to take it once it was offered.

Rob half prayed that he could hold the car down there as he pulled up side by side with the Chevy. He used the momentum he had gained by running deeper into the corner to try to ease on past him and get beside the leader, all in one smooth, implausible move.

The leader seemed surprised to suddenly see the red Ford next to him. He instinctively cut down on Rob, trying to block him, make him back off, but that opened the outside line to the Chevy. Its driver didn't miss his chance, either. He immediately tried to take advantage of his own opening that had been offered.

Now the leader seemed confused for an instant. There was the familiar car he had raced against for so many years, trying to take the point away from him on the high side. And there was the bright red Ford of that rookie— what was his name?—coming up on the inside.

The leader made his choice and moved up to try to block the devil he knew.

Rob never hesitated, never backed off, even in the face of the leader's initial block. Now, there was a minuscule hole there, so tiny but so welcome, and Rob moved to shove his car through it, even as the three of them raced hard down the backstretch for the final time this day.

Will saw what was happening as he craned his neck to watch the cars race for the final turn. The opening was there for Rob. But would it stay there long enough for him to make the pass? Did Rob have the strength? Did the car have the brakes to accomplish such a move?

They would soon know. Rob managed to get a fender to the inside of the leader as the three cars dived into turn three with unbelievable momentum. Fans all around the track sucked in their breath. No way could those three stay on the track. No way. Somebody would have to give quarter, back off.

The leader realized immediately that Rob had taken the opening he had left for him. Where had this kid come from? How dare he try to get around someone with more Cup wins than this kid has candles on a birthday cake!

He pinched down low, their race cars rubbing together hard, rattling both men's teeth. Smoke puffed up from the contact. Rob tussled with the wheel that was trying to jerk itself from his hold. He could feel the wheels beneath him losing traction, feel the car seem to skate as the impact with the other car, the speed into the corner, and the heavy hand of centrifugal force tried to seize control.

But he had to hold on, had to keep the car under him. There would be one last shot at the win, and that would come as the cars exited the corner. If he was still around to exit, that is.

Somehow, he managed. Somehow, he kept the car in line through the turn.

Then Rob felt a bump in the rear as he and the Pontiac raced out of turn four. The Chevy he had just passed wanted to remind him he was still back there and that he had not surrendered either.

With the touch, the Ensoft car skated again for an instant. But Rob couldn't panic now. He held on. No matter that it took everything he had to keep the car going forward instead of skittering right out to the wall.

But then he saw it. The checkered flag was down there, directly in front of him.

The Pontiac had the preferred line coming off the corner. That gave him a big advantage. But Rob begged the Ford for one more gallop, one more leap forward as he hammered the throttle so hard his foot might easily have shot through the firewall.

The two cars rocketed toward the line, crossing the line together, taking the checkered flag with the Chevy following so close he might just as well have been attached at their bumpers.

"Way to hang in there! Good job!" came the rapid fire Virginia drawl, the voice that was now so familiar to Rob.

And then, dark clouds rolled across Rob Wilder's vision, and he felt his chin fall involuntarily to his chest. There was blackness.

Dark, hot, foggy blackness.

As good as last

Rob Wilder would never be able to explain how he managed to steer the race car back around the track, down pit road, and to the gas pumps. Somebody told him later that he waved to the winner in the Pontiac, showing his congratulations, but he didn't remember it at all.

He dimly recalled trying to unsnap the safety belts once the car was stopped. And arms reaching in for him, helping him free, and dragging him outside where it was amazingly cooler. And someone unzipping the top of his racing suit and pouring cold water on him and pushing ice down the front of the suit.

Someone else wrapped cold towels around his neck while he gasped for breath, trying to get his vision and hearing back, trying to figure out where he was and how he got there. The first thing he heard was Will, shooing the growing crowd back so he could get some air. And he saw Michelle's beautiful face there through the fog as she wiped his forehead with another cold rag. And there were Donnie and the rest of the crew, all grinning as they talked, all at the same time, about what a great job he had done and what a wonderful race it had been and how he almost pulled it off at the end.

But he had lost. He had come in second. So close. Lord, so close. But he had lost the race.

The infield care center doctor had wanted to take him on to a hospital by ambulance, claiming he was likely a victim of mild heat stroke. But Rob was feeling much better by then and convinced the doc he would drink plenty of liquids and stay cool.

He did, too. Michelle stayed with him, keeping cold towels around his neck, even as he did the obligatory television and radio interviews while propped up against a nearby wall. Finally, finished with that, he tried to rise unsteadily to his feet. Jodell and Billy were coming their way.

Michelle helped him stand, and he turned to thank her for nursing him back to life. She wrapped him up in a big hug, told him how glad she was to see him feeling better and how worried she had been about him. Rob returned the hug, but as she started to release him from the embrace, she suddenly reached up, put her arms around his neck, and kissed him full on the lips.

"What was that for?" he asked, surprised.

"Just because."

Billy and Jodell were there then.

"I see Florence Nightingale finally got you revived," Billy said.

"You had us worried," Jodell added. "Your eyes were all rolled back in your head when they dragged you out of that car."

"I gotta tell you. I don't remember the last hundred laps or so. Or how I got the car off the track. First thing I knew was when somebody poured all that ice down the front of my suit. But whoever did it might've saved my life."

He gulped down a big swallow of the sports drink Michelle had just handed him.

"Trust me, Robbie. It'll all come back to you. You'll want to remember those last hundred laps for a long time," Jodell said with a gentle pat on the kid's back.

"Second place! A whale of a finish, kid," Billy said, beaming like a proud papa.

They were surrounded then by some of the other owners and their crews who wanted to congratulate Billy, Rob, and the others on the fine run. Even the driver he had almost beaten came by to check on him and tell him what a fine race he had run.

Rob accepted the praise humbly, smiled weakly, and finished the drink in a couple more gulps.

Jodell Lee eased down next to him when the last of the well-wishers had gone on. "Son, I've already seen you do some amazing things in a race car. Today takes the cake, though. That pass on the leader? Man! That was one fine run you made today, and especially considering the circumstances."

"Thank you, Jodell," Rob said. "Coming from you . . ."

But there was something in his voice that the old driver picked up on at once. "Still left you hungry for more, didn't it?"

Rob wiped his bloodshot eyes with the towel and looked over at his mentor. "If you'd have asked me this morning how I'd feel about finishing second, or how I'd like to have a chance at making an inside pass and winning it all coming off the final corner, I would have grinned and told you I'd settle for that. That it would be great to be in that position."

"But it wouldn't have been the total truth, would it?"

"No, sir. It wouldn't. Not if it meant finishing second instead of first."

"Second ain't winning is it, Robbie? It just makes you hungrier. Makes you wantto win all the more, don't it?"

It sounded as if Jodell Lee was singing a very familiar song, but that he had finally found someone who actually understood its true meaning.

"Absolutely. I would give anything to be able to go out there right now and run another twenty laps with that Pontiac and that Chevrolet. I could've took 'em, Jodell. I could have! I just ran out of race, that's all."

Jodell patted the youngster on the knee.

"You'll get 'em, kid. Don't you worry. They know you got their number now. They'll remember that old inside pass you made the next time, rest assured of that."

"But if . . ."

"No 'ifs'! I expect another stock car race is gonna break out somewhere next week, and you'll get your chance. Come on, and let's go get some supper. Besides, there's a mighty pretty woman waitin' for you over yonder."

Sure enough, Michelle Fagan had finished getting the dignitaries on their way and the crew busy taking down the Ensoft hospitality tent out in the parking area. Jodell hopped to his feet as deftly as a man half his age and helped the young driver to stand up. Maybe merely being around a promising young driver was making the old man feel renewed.

Michelle met Rob, slipped her arm around him, and steered him toward the hauler and a shower. Without even thinking, he put his own arm around her and pulled her close as they walked.

Yep, next week. Who knows what next week might bring?